THE PARABLES OF

ANCIENT EARTH

The First Scroll:

Rephidim, City of Reptiles

Rephidim

Banquet-Cross Publications of Mayer
hdanyone.com

ISBN: 978-1-61658-047-6

TO:
THE TEENAGERS OF THE FINAL MILLENNIUM

Note to the Reader:

These texts were translated from ancient Garble on scrolls discovered in a remote location of Antarctica. As a result, any inconsistencies in word choice or tone are a direct result of the fact that very few translators of ancient Garble exist.

ACKNOWLEDGMENT PAGE

My Heartfelt Gratitude To:

Denise DiPietro for editing
these translations of ancient garble.

Beverly Allisone for changing the layout
from prehistoric scrolls to book format.

Sharon Recker for her ability to see the vision and create
the cover painting of ancient earth.

June Finnegan for her art work in accurately depicting
the beautiful old world map of Pangea.

Raini Erwin for designing hdanyone.com
to connect with landkind in the final millennium.

PARCHMENT I

*"The world was once
a single Continent ..."*

The parable begins
with a bird and a boy.

"You're only a stupid songbird," said the boy.

"Warbler. I am an O-l-i-v-e W-a-r-b-l-e-r," spelled out the bird.

"Olive *Whatever*," said the boy with disrespect.

The warbler had perched on the sill of a barred earthen jail window some ten feet above the thirteen-year-old boy who sat cross-legged on the dirt floor of the cell. The boy wore a brown woven sack with holes ripped open for neck and hands. The garment hung on him like a dreary dress revealing pale, sickly, skinny legs and knobby knees.

"You are imprisoned," said the bird looking at the boy.

"Well, isn't that stating the obvious? For a talking songbird, you're not very bright, of course I'm imprisoned!" The boy glared. His purple, sunken eye sockets revealed years of malnutrition and poor rest.

"It is *not* so obvious. It is possible to be imprisoned and free, or free and imprisoned," said the bird. "Regardless, you should be grateful. Normally, only first-born nobles receive an Airborne Counselor on their thirteenth birthday, and you are far less than a Noble. You are an imprisoned commoner, a lowly slave."

"Counselor? What kind of Counselor are you? You are the tiniest bird on the Continent! What can you do for me besides harass me?" The boy shook his head and turned a vacant gaze toward the iron bars that kept him from a torch lit hall.

"Well. I assure you. I may be small, but I am eminently capable of setting you free."

The boy jerked his head up and raised a hand to brush light brown dreadlocks from his eyes to better study the bird. The moon shining through the cell window made it possible to discern the creature. He wondered if the bird were teasing him: *a stupid songbird landing to taunt me with false hope.* The bird appeared too feeble to accomplish anything meaningful. Counselors were supposed to be Airborne Reptiles. *Songbirds don't speak.*

This simple bird was not more than five inches long from beak to tail, and had a grayish body with black and white striped wings. His vivid burnt orange head gave the impression someone had dipped him head first into a vat of honey. The black color of his tiny beak reached up and encircled his eyes like a mask.

"Set me free? What are *you* going to do, peck out the eye of the guard?"

"As you are so ungrateful, I'm not going to do *anything*. A common landling being sent an Airborne Counselor like myself and you don't even appreciate it!"

"Appreciate it? I don't even believe you. You're not a Counselor. Only Airborne Reptiles have the gift of speech. You must be a mutation of some sort to have developed the spoken word. And you come here no bigger than my fist and tell me you are able to set me free, all the while wearing a mask. I'll bet you're hiding something!"

"Everyone has something to hide," said the bird.

"See!"

"The question is am I hiding something good or hiding something bad?"

"No one has to hide good things," said the boy.

"Wrong," said Bird.

"No, not wrong!"

"Why are you in this cell then?"

"What's it to you?" the boy snapped.

"I simply wish to make my point."

The boy hesitated. *Who is this pesky winged thing?* The boy hated to admit it, but it pleased him to have conversation, even if it was unpleasant and antagonistic. It was, after all, his thirteenth birthday. "I'm in here for stealing."

"What did you steal?" asked Bird.

"Food."

"Why?"

"To feed my sister."

"And did you try to hide the fact that you were stealing?"

"Yes, of course."

"But you were stealing for what you felt was a good reason, correct?"

"Yes, of course."

"So, you were hiding something good because you were doing something bad, but you were doing something bad, because you were doing something good. Bad and good, black and white have shades of gray." Bird

4

lifted his black and white wings and pointed his beak at his gray chest as if to drive home his point.

"Bird, you're giving me a headache. I'm already tired and strained from a day of scribing, so free me, or leave."

"I am not going to free you—"

"I knew it!"

"—yet."

"Why not *yet*? I've been in here for five years!"

"You're not ready."

"Not ready! I get only a fist of bread in the morning, a slice of cheese at midday, and a fist of bread for evening! And the only reason I get cheese is because they noticed the scribes die off less and get more done if given a piece of cheese every day! I'm whipped if I *don't* get enough work done, and I'm whipped if I *do* get enough work done! I almost died once from a beating, and I've not stepped outside this dungeon for five years! I never see the sunlight because I work during the day by candlelight in the scriber's cavern, and at night, I see only the giant orb that lights the night sky. I try to sleep, but am greeted by nightmares. What on earth would make me ready to escape if not these things?"

Bird looked at him, tilted his head right, and then tilted his head left. "Definitely not ready," he asserted. With a nod of his head, Bird flew off.

"Come back!" Boy screamed.

A passing night guard banged a club on the boy's cell door. "Silence in there!"

Boy rolled into a ball and began to cry quietly.

⤙　⤙　⤙　⤙
⤙　⤙　⤙　⤙

The next morning, the guard came to fetch Boy. This same guard had fetched him every day for the past five years. The guard was huge, some six and a half feet tall. He wore a leather vest and pleated skirt and sandals, and always held a very thick club with pointed iron spikes. An iron helmet that fastened in front of the mouth allowed only his dark eyes to peer from the cold metal. A large, dark raven's feather plumed the helmets crown.
The only words Guard ever spoke to Boy were, "Time to scribe." The words sounded muffled given the impersonal clasp that hid the man's mouth. The guard would then unlatch the iron door and lead Boy to the scriber's room, a clay walled area with a large wooden table and stools. Guard then attached Boy's ankle to the table with a chain. Torches and candlelight lit the dark table boards.

5

Day after day, Boy dipped his iron-tipped wooden pen into ink and copied the Sixteen Absolute Laws, referred to only as 'The Absolutes.' The High Ruler of the Iron Hall had authored 'The Absolutes' and had ordered copies posted on every commoner's door in each of the seven cities.

Boy glanced down at the master copy of 'The Absolutes' placed on the table before him. It was his duty to make copy after copy, day after day, week after week.

The Absolutes

The Teachings are to be administered by the Council of Twelve in each of the seven cities.

Three hundred first-born of nobility will elect each Council of Twelve. One of the twelve will be appointed Lord or Lordess as Proconsul, and these said elected officials would in turn elect two representatives of nobility to sit on the High Council of Twenty-four acting as pleators for their respective cities. All officials are elected for life.

The High Ruler of the Iron Hall must be of nobility and be elected for life by the Council of Twenty-four and will remain unwed.

Each of the Councils of Twelve will have supreme powers of government in interpreting the Teachings, or Six Sacred Scrolls, and the order of Law descends from the High Ruler of the Iron Hall to the seven councils of the Seven Cities.

Each Council of Twelve will hold trials to condemn or acquit an accused of civil matters and lesser offenses are punishable by imprisonment and the more serious by the severing of a finger and treason by death on a cross.

All trials will take place in the Judgment Hall for the City in which the offense took place. An unresolved trial will move an accused to the Fourth City where the High Ruler of the Iron Hall will determine judgment. The same applies for crimes against the Continent.

Commoners are not to discuss, read, write, interpret, or possess the Teachings.

The High Seraph is a myth and must not be spoken of.

Airborne Counselors will instruct only first-borns of nobility for it is an abomination for an Airborne to counsel a commoner, and each council member will pass judgment under guidance of her or his respective Airborne.

Each of the Seven Cities will erect and maintain the four mandated structures according to the prescribed structural design, which includes the Judgment Hall, Prison, Quarry, and Mind Sculpting Center or MSC.

Lords and Nobles will adhere to the covenant of the neck rings.

All Landlings on this great Continent of Pangea will tithe ten percent to the High Ruler of the Iron Hall on the biannual trek of the Feast of Adoration. Half of the nobility will send tithes at the summer feast and the remaining half at the winter feast as directed by the city Law-ers.

Give of the first fruits as prescribed in subsection 13 to the Council of Twelve in your respective cities on the twenty-fourth day of each month in order to subsidize both the Council and required structures.

All four-legged creatures are cursed to be Servants of Burden to the Landlings who care for the Continent.

Gunners are warriors of Noble descent trained to maintain the peace and as such are to be obeyed and permitted to enforce order and are trained for war. No commoner can participate in the trainings.

Honor the High Ruler of the Iron Hall.

Boy had watched many scribes die off from hunger or beatings until there were only a few scribes left. Sometimes there would be a new scribe or two also making copies, each one chained to a table leg like him. Boy thought these new scribes were new to the art as indicated by their unskilled scribbling.

The scribes were not permitted to speak to each other. For if one scribe so much as glanced in the eye of another, both scribes would be whipped by Guard.

Today, Boy sat at the table and thought about the strange visit from the songbird. It was the first conversation he'd had in five long years. It had been a cruel joke to promise to free him, and then just fly off. Boy tried not to let his tears run onto the cypress page. If he were to smear a word, the beating would be horrible.

Twelve hours later, after a two-minute break that permitted Boy to swallow a piece of cheese, Guard led him back to his cell and tossed a fist of bread onto the dirt floor.

Boy grabbed the bread and bit it ravenously.

"Hello again," said Bird.

Boy looked up gulping the bread down his dry throat. "What do you want, to make me more miserable?" His stomach churned from sadness, but Boy attributed this agitation to hunger.

"No. I have come to cheer you up."

"Then free me as you promised!"

"No. You must first share your bread with me."

Boy dropped his jaw. "You're a *sick* bird! I'm starving to death, and you have free range of the earth! You should share *your* food with *me!*"

"I will share food with you," replied Bird.

"Where is it then?"

"There are many types of food. I have food to eat that you know nothing about."[1]

"Where *is it*?" Boy demanded.

"You'll see."

"You're a liar!"

"To trust, or not to trust," Bird mused.

Boy took another hungry bite, noting he had only one bite left.

"I'm waiting," said the bird.

Boy chewed slowly as he thought about Bird's request. He looked up at Bird, down at his bread and glanced up warily again at Bird. *It is sad to admit,* he thought, *but if I don't give this bird a piece of bread, he might not come back.* Whether or not the ornery bird freed him, this cruel visitation was the only interaction with outsiders he could recall since his imprisonment.

"Fine." Boy pinched a small piece of bread from his last bite, and threw it up to the clay sill.

Bird took the piece of bread and flew off.

"I hate you!" screamed the boy. He curled into a ball trying not to cry, but cried himself to sleep anyway.

In the middle of the night, Boy was awoken by a sound. He sat up. The sound was the loveliest he had ever heard, and it was coming from the windowsill. The light from the moon showed the warbler sitting on the ledge, the bird's orange-gray breast heaving in and out, as he sang from low to high, chirp, chirping quick patterned sweet notes to long drawn out full tones. Boy stared in silence. Moisture rolled from the corners of his eyes. He scarcely breathed for fear the song would stop, but the singing continued on and on, finally lulling the boy back to sleep. It was his first sleep without nightmares in the five years of his imprisonment.

The next evening, Boy waited, bread in hand. He stared at the windowsill. His heart fluttered when the flap of wings arrived.

Boy pinched a piece of bread, threw it up onto the sill, and watched to see what would happen next.

"Why, thank you," said Bird.

"What are you going to do tonight?" Boy asked in a hushed voice.

"Last night, a song, tonight a story."

Boy was silent. The silence filled the air with expectation.

"Heh, hem," Bird cleared his throat. "Tonight, I will tell you of the High Seraph—"

"No! Shush! You must not!"

"No, really, I must."

"No, you mustn't!"

"Why mustn't I?"

"It's a crime to speak of such things!"

"I am an Airborne. They can't do anything to me."

"But they'll punish *me* if I listen!"

"What can they do? Throw you in prison?" Bird chuckled.

"They might cut off one of my fingers!"

"You'll have nine left then. Now let's see, where shall I begin."

9

Boy crept close to the wall beneath the sill, and then glanced wide-eyed at the bars to see if the night guard was approaching.

"The High Seraph, Eloam, is a giant white bird with a wingspan of forty feet. His eyes are crystal blue and his sharp beak, golden. He speaks things into being. He says a word, and it is so."

"The High Seraph is a *myth!* I write this each day in the High Ruler's law."

"Of what you write you know not. I myself have seen the Seraph at the top of the Scrimshaw Tower, and don't interrupt me, or I won't finish the story."

Boy half thought it might be better not to finish the story. He glanced again at the bars, but seeing no guard, remained silent.

"Now, where was I … ah, yes. The High Seraph speaks things into being. His greatest creation on the Continent was Lord Gargoyle, a most incredible creature, for he was an Airborne with a beautiful brown wingspan of some twenty feet, and he was given a face, legs, and a torso just like you Pangean Landlings.

"*But* the High Seraph made a mistake—a regrettable, unrepeatable mistake. He wanted Lord Gargoyle to be able to create and in wishing this gift for him he gave him hands. Seeing that this combination was very effective, High Seraph created thousands upon thousands of gargoyles.

"*But* giving Lord Gargoyle hands and the ability to fly turned out terrible. It made the gargoyles powerful—far more powerful than Airborne's with beaks and wings. And Lord Gargoyle led the gargoyles to do dreadful things. Eloam, the High Seraph, to this day, has never again allowed for this combination on the Continent. That is why Airbornes don't have hands, and Landlings don't have wings. Only in the After-sky is this permitted for it is the Land of Hands and Wings."

"I don't believe in the After-sky," said Boy. "But what did Lord Gargoyle do that was so dreadful?"

"Lord Gargoyle decided that if he could create like the Seraph, he should possess the Emerald Scepter to rule the Landlings, and a battle was waged in the air for control of the Continent.

"The High Seraph did not want war, and offered to appease Lord Gargoyle. He told him he could have dominion over all the Airbornes, that he could feast freely on the sea creatures, and coast on air currents through silver-lined clouds, and even assist the Landlings as the Seraph directed, but that Lord Gargoyle could not possess the Emerald Scepter, for the Landlings must learn to govern themselves."

"And Lord Gargoyle didn't agree?" asked the boy.

"No," said Bird. "Lord Gargoyle insisted upon receiving the scepter."

"But why *not* let him rule the Landlings? What difference could it make? If Lord Gargoyle was good enough to govern the Airbornes—if he was the Seraph's '*greatest creation*,' as you say—why *not* let him rule the Landlings?"

"A self-righteous rule is merciless," said Bird.

Boy squinted at him while trying to process this information. "So what happened? Did the battle end?"

"What do *you* think?"

"I think the gargoyles lost. The Emerald Scepter is in possession of the High Ruler of the Iron Hall."

Bird gave the boy a piercing stare. "I assure you, Lord Gargoyle still seeks the scepter."

"All of this is a fabled scroll," said Boy. "I don't believe in gargoyles. No one has ever seen one. Lord Gargoyle *must* have lost. The gargoyles— if they did exist—are extinct. And no one can access the scepter in the Iron Hall."

"Why would you care who controls the scepter?" asked Bird.

"Everyone cares who controls the scepter! It is the scepter that gives power to the High Ruler to counsel the Continent."

"The High Ruler and all council members, under the direction of their Airbornes are *supposed* to counsel Landlings to fight the Allure. But in their power they have become self-important and misinterpret The Teachings, therefore making nobility ignoble."

"You're foolish, Bird. Being in power is good. Nobility is the envy of all commoners. I'll be a Lord or a Noble someday when I get out of here. I'm going to become wealthy. I'll be a leader even without the neck rings of birth. You'll see. Commoners have married into wealth before. I've heard of it being done. And I know the daughter of a noble who fancies me."

"You? Fancies you? Why on earth would *anyone* fancy you?"

"You're cruel, Bird."

"And you're delirious."

It was as if the boy hadn't heard the insult. He gazed sideways and began to speak as if he could actually see the daughter of the noble. "She has auburn hair and green eyes, and every half-year on the Feast of Adoration, she walks the prison and selects one prisoner to set free."

"If she likes you so much why hasn't she freed you?"

Boy's eyes darted sharply at the bird. "She's tried! Every year she passes my cell." He paused and his eyes softened again. "I see her approaching in green flowing robes, and she slowly swings her head in my direction, her auburn hair cascades like the lava from Cauldron Crater concealing one of her emerald eyes, and she lifts her arm— it's silky white and she raises it so elegant, like the neck of a swan—and points to free me. But every year, the guard says, 'No, he's a master scribe' and they pass on." Boy looked down and slumped as if the mere thought hurt him.

"So you're in love with a swanlike arm and an emerald eye."

"Don't mock me, Bird."

"I'm not mocking you. I'm sure she has a very lovely arm and eye. She, however, cannot free you. But I can."

"Well, then *free* me!" exclaimed Boy.

"I will free you, but it's not that simple," said Bird. "I can't just free you, I have to teach you to be free."

"But how hard can that be—to teach me freedom? Simply let me out and we'll be done with it!"

"Oh dear …" Bird gazed downward and to the left, his eyes became unfocused as if thinking about something remote and far away, or deep and hard to fathom. "Oh, Boy." Bird shook his head. "My dear, dear boy. True freedom, is so much harder than one might think."

"But then I don't necessarily need *true* freedom, I'd be happy with just *some* freedom—so get me out of here!"

Bird looked directly at him. "The *only* freedom is *true* freedom or it's simply slavery in disguise."

Boy sighed and crossed his arms. "You know, you're too much of a perfectionist, you should let me decide how much freedom is enough freedom for my liking!"

Bird chuckled and shook his head. It wasn't necessarily a happy chuckle, but more of an, *I know better than you,* kind of chuckle. "Oh … in the end," said Bird, "you *will* decide."

Boy wasn't sure he liked the sound of Bird's tone, but it came as a concession of sorts and he took some solace in it.

"So, when will you free me?" asked Boy.

"When you're ready, of course."

"But when will I be ready?"

"That is up to you."

"But I don't know how to be ready!"

"Exactly my point."

"You make no sense! I *hate* you, Bird!"

"I know." Bird hunched and spread his wings. "It's good for you." With that, he flew off.

The third night brought a new twist. Bird arrived, and Boy fed him. But Bird insisted there would be no song or story tonight. "I want to know about you," he said. "Tell me, how did you become a scribe?"

Boy sat cross-legged, with elbows on knees, chin on thumbs. "How I became a scribe?" he repeated.

"Yes. How did you become a scribe?"

There were a few seconds of silence, and then Boy began. "I come from a family of wordsmiths. As you know, it is difficult and rare for a pale skin commoner to earn status as a tradesmon. But, my father attended the Mind Sculpting Center, or MSC, to learn an intellectual instead of a physical trade, which makes him an elite tradesmon to have gone four years. He then became a wordsmith to Noble Ganarats, who is on the governing board, the Council of Twelve, for this city.

"And I'm certain you have heard that wordsmiths are required to learn seven words for every one thing they wish to say. It is not enough to know 'pretty,' one must know 'beautiful,' 'lovely,' 'enchanting,' 'captivating,' 'breathtaking,' 'gorgeous,' 'stunning,' and so forth.

"Our power is in our vocabulary, for nobles love to have advisors who can capture a concept in a word. This enables nobles to write powerful laws, powerful scrolls, indisputable rules, and infallible guidelines to govern the people. Entire laws can be disputed over the meaning of a simple word, and so selecting the precise word to convey the precise meaning is essential for one to govern precisely.

"In a word, words are considered not only art forms, but weapons because of their power.

"Well, my father was also learning to be a pleator to plead cases of law because of his command of language. And so I was trained from the age of five onward, memorizing word after word, meaning after meaning. My father hoped that he would be promoted to pleator, and then I could take my father's place as wordsmith to Noble Ganarats, and, of course, all wordsmiths double as scribes in order to commit the laws to parchment paper. The minute Noble Ganarats approved a verbal presentation, my father would scribe it onto a scroll, and I assisted him."

"I see …" Bird mused. "That would explain your vocabulary and your diction. You speak almost as well as an Airborne. It's surprising to find this in a common pale prisoner of thirteen years of age. It may be the first redeeming quality I can think of about you ... yes, I'm quite certain that it is."

"Thanks a lot, Bird." Boy's voice was sarcastic, but the backhanded compliment made his heart feel softer. "But you know, when I get out of here, I'll never scribe again!"

"We'll see about that," said Bird. "So what happened to your father? As a son of a wordsmith employed by one of the twelve council members, you should never have needed to steal food to feed your sister."

Boy breathed in deeply and heaved out a sigh. "There is a quarterly forum in the quarry where different tradesmon are called to compete; the sword smiths for strength in battle, the wine pressers for the finest taste, the tailors for style, and so forth with competitions in every imaginable category from singing to dancing to wordsmithing.

"My father had never lost a competition. When a word was presented to both he and a challenger, my father could always name more words of similar meaning. But one day, he lost. It really shouldn't have mattered that he lost. The events are suppose to be for fun, a celebration of the arrival of the seasons, but Ganarats was furious and said it reflected poorly on him. He cast our family to the street with no warning.

"My father tried to find work, but all the other nobles had not only wordsmiths hired on, but also many in training. My father even begged Lord Ipthsum to have mercy on him saying he'd scribe anything, even if it were instructions for troops or guidelines for guards and handmaids. But Lord Ipthsum refused him as well. And my father hadn't any other skills.

"I think sometimes now, that there must have been something he could do. My mother took a job as a fuller, cleaning and whitening clothes for nobility. This made my father even more bereft because everyone knows the hazards of being a fuller and having to breathe the fumes for bleaching garbs.

"Then one night, we came back to our hut and found ..."

Boy wiped his tears in the triangle of his bent arm. "Well, Father made his decision. And I think it was the easy way out." Boy then buried his face in both hands. Very softly, he finally spoke with a tremble in his voice. "I had to cut him down."

Bird appeared to be—for the first time—at a loss for words.

Several silent minutes passed until Boy finally looked up. "But, so Bird ... you never told who won the battle in the Air."

"Suffice it to say, the gargoyles were given a second chance."

"How so?"

"The High Seraph gave them a new environment of forgetfulness. This brought the opportunity to make better choices."

"You mean they forgot the battle?"

"They forgot everything. They had a second chance to use their creativity for good instead of evil."

"I wish I could see a gargoyle. Are they as hideous as the statues on this prison?"

"Be careful what you wish for," said Bird.

"I'd like to *fight* one someday. I hear they are powerful!"

"You *will* fight a gargoyle. And they *are* powerful," said Bird.

"How do you know I will fight one?"

"I know things."

"I bet I would have to be out of this cell to fight a gargoyle!" said Boy with hope.

"Perhaps, but not necessarily."

Boy pondered this with eyes cast downward and to the right. "So. When will you free me?"

"I'm not sure you want to be freed," said Bird.

"Are you of unsound mind? Of course, I want to be freed! My life is excruciating!"

"But, there are terms to your deliverance." .

"Terms?" Boy squinted at Bird up on the windowsill.

"Yes. If I free you, you must do whatever I say, and if you break your promise, you will find yourself back in prison."

"Whatever you say?" Boy repeated.

"Yes, you must in essence obey me."

Boy plopped on the ground and placed his forehead on his palms and elbows on knees. He sat quiet for a minute and a half.

"Well?" asked Bird.

"I'm thinking," said Boy.

"I thought you said your life was excruciating?" prodded Bird.

"Well, yes, but to obey you—*that* would be excruciating as well." Silence for another minute. "For how long must I obey you?"

"Until you are ready to govern yourself," said Bird.

"So, I will be free of you at some point?"

"You can be free of me now, if you like. I'll simply leave." Bird hunched and spread his wings outward getting ready for takeoff.

"No! Wait! I'll do it—I'll obey you." Boy stood and lifted his face expectantly at Bird.

"Good."

Silence.

"Well?" asked Boy in anticipation.

"Well, what?"

"I'm ready to be freed."

"No. You're not ready yet. But at least we have an agreement." And with that, Bird flew off.

Boy kicked the dirt, stubbed his toe, and plopped back on the ground.

Bird returned before morning light, which was unusual. Previously he had come in the evenings. "Okay. Here's the plan—"

"An escape plan?" Boy spoke with hushed excitement.

"No, not an escape plan, but the *first* plan."

"How many plans do we need?"

"Are you going to do what I ask or are you going to keep asking what I'm doing?"

Boy was silent.

"Okay," said Bird. "You will steal a piece of parchment paper, pen, and ink."

"Steal! That won't get me out of here—that's how I got in here! If they catch me, they'll cut off a finger!"

"Then you'll have nine left."

"Stop saying I'll have *nine left*. I want all ten. Are you a counselor or a criminal? You know … I really question your authority. I can't believe a counselor would ask me to steal!"

"Just a few items. I'm only asking you to steal a few simple items. As I told you before, everything has shades of gray. You are stealing for a purpose. You'll need the items to begin your quest."

"Quest?" Boy's eyes widened. "Am I to go on a quest to be a Noble or a Lord?"

"A Noble or a Lord," repeated the bird. "A Noble or a Lord … hmmm … no, but you *are* to be a *scribe*."

"I'm *already* a scribe—I hate being a scribe!"

"A scribe is a noble trade—"

"No—a *Noble* is a noble trade!" Boy's lower lip protruded, his brow furrowed, and the corners of his mouth sagged.

"Look, it hasn't even been a day, and you already don't want to obey

16

me. I'm not sure if this relationship is going to work. You must be awfully fond of prison. I may have been accidentally sent to the wrong cell. You are self-centered and difficult. I'm going to double check my assignment parchment to see if my directions are wrong. I was probably meant to counsel the person two cells down." Bird spread his wings.

"Wait! Okay. I'll do it."

"Do what?" spoke a strange voice. "Who are you talking to?" *Bang, bang,* the guard hit the bars with his spiked club. "Silence! Time to scribe!"

Boy followed Guard down the hall. Boy's knees were weak knowing he had been commissioned to thieve. He tried to imagine how he would do this. *What if another scribe reports me?* He inadvertently wiggled each of his ten fingers.

Seated at the table, leg chained, he tried to eye the two other scribes without being seen. The two boys were as thin as he was. One kept coughing, a hacking sickly cough. The other shivered. But both, like him, immediately began to scribe, fearful of a beating.

Boy began to plan. Guard would speak with another guard at lunch hour. Though they both stood nearby, the communication might divert their attention enough for him to slide one of the pens from the middle of the table, under a scroll, and he could grab two scrolls instead of one and try to slide the bottom one, at some point, under his clothing and up beneath his waist string. The main problem was the inkwell. Though several wells sat in the middle of the table, where on his person could he conceal one?

Lunch came. Boy wondered if the others would tell on him. With a trembling hand, he grabbed two parchment papers instead of one. No one seemed to notice. He heard the two guards speaking and laughing. He reached for a second pen, coughed into his left hand, and slid the pen between his legs with his right. He then returned to scribing, trying to keep the letters from smearing while his hand trembled with fear.

He still had no idea how to hide the ink.

Boy knew the time to return to his cell was approaching. He knew this not from any sunlight as there was none. He knew this because he knew that in twelve hours he could scribe twenty-four scrolls, or two an hour. He was now halfway through his twenty-fourth scroll. The boy to his right started coughing and spittle flew accidentally onto the scroll. The guard pulled him up to smack him. This was Boy's opportunity. He grabbed the inkwell and quickly poured the liquid into his mouth. It tasted odd, but he was relieved the act went unnoticed.

Back at his cell, the guard latched the barred door and left.

Boy sat waiting. He wondered how much his saliva would weaken the ink. He had nowhere to put it.

Bird arrived shortly, but Boy couldn't explain his predicament.

"Did you get the items as I instructed?" asked Bird.

Boy nodded and pulled the paper and pen from his waist.

"Where's the ink?"

Boy pointed fervently at his mouth.

Bird tilted his head to the right and then straightened it. "Incredible. Doesn't that taste disgusting?"

Boy bugged his sunken eyes out as if to say, "Do something."

"Oh. Yes. Give me a minute," said Bird who flew off forcing Boy to wait without swallowing.

A few minutes passed and Bird returned but not alone. A raven arrived with a sphere in his widespread beak. The object was released and it rolled to Boy's feet.

Boy's eyes widened with a look of disbelief and reverence. It was an *orange*.

"Peel the fruit carefully," said Bird. "And leave the bottom portion intact like a cup. Then you can spit your ink into it. Be sure to hide it in the darkest corner."

Boy's hands trembled for the third time this day, only this time from anticipation. He carefully peeled the top off the orange and made sure to keep the lower portion intact. He emptied the contents of his mouth into the peel and spit several times to the side to rid his mouth of the taste of the ink. Then, ever so carefully, he picked and ate each piece of white membrane from the succulent fruit. He nibbled slowly and next gnawed the white part from the inside of the top half of the rind. He delicately broke the orange in half trying to prevent the tiniest drip from squirting away. He pulled an orange section loose, and placed a corner in his mouth and bit down gently. The flavor burst onto his tongue like nectar from the After-sky. He bit the piece and chewed it, and chewed it, and savored it, and savored it, and finally, when it was nothing more than a soggy piece of pulp, he swallowed it. He continued to do this unaware that Bird and Raven had left. He was so enraptured by the taste of the fruit that he delighted in each section and finished his meal by consuming the top peel and savoring every bit of the rind. The whole process continued on for an hour and a half, and Boy finished by licking his fingers and curling his body into a ball. Moisture slid from his eyes. *This was the best day of my life.*

The next night, Boy waited impatiently.

"Well?" he demanded as Bird landed.

"Well what?"

"I did what you said—so free me."

"You aren't ready yet," was Bird's quick reply.

Boy's shoulders sagged. "You've got to be joking. I risked my life to do as you said!"

"Hardly much of a life anyway. Not much to risk."

"I can't believe you! You're terrible! I can't trust you! I *hate* you!" Boy thought to throw the ink rind at the feathered fiend, but restrained himself, fearing he could not successfully pilfer a second time. "I suffer so much! How can you say I'm not ready? The best day of my life was *eating an orange*—I deserve freedom!"

"You must scribe."

"I scribe all day!"

"No, you must scribe what I tell you."

"I *hate* you!"

"Yes, I believe we covered that already. So are you going to scribe or snivel, write or whimper, move forward, or moan in misery?"

Boy shook his head. *This is unbelievable!* "You are too cruel for words you … you … you … *idiot!*"

"Very impressive vocabulary. You could have used *charlatan, fake, imposter, swindler, con, quack,* and *pretender*—was that seven? Yes, I believe it was, but you have come up with the pinnacle of all derogatory slander, and called me an idiot. I'm very impressed. Now … I want you to scribe: I was in prison and I was a lousy servant."

"I'm *not* going to write that!"

"I can only free you if you do what I say. Once you have scribed six lines for me, you will be truly free."

"Well, that's *stupid, inane, brainless, unintelligent, thick, dull,* and *dim-witted.* Who in their right mind would be anything *but* a lousy servant—nobody wants to be a servant—my life is *horrible!*"

"You've a terrible case of self-pity. You are trying my patience. You did, after all, eat an orange yesterday, and look at you. Most ungrateful." Bird shook his head back and forth.

"Why do you want me to scribe that anyway? What purpose could it

19

possibly serve? Are you going to make me read it aloud to be ridiculed?" Boy asked.

Bird continued shaking his head. "You aren't very trusting are you? Not a big picture person. Mr. I-know-seven-words-for-every-one-of-yours. Did it ever occur to you that a sentence might have two levels of meaning?"

Boy rubbed his eyebrows between his thumb and finger pushing his brows inward and outward as if this would somehow help him to think.

"Okay," said Boy. He stomped to the corner where his stolen goods were hidden. He plopped on the ground eyeing the hall, slapped the parchment paper in front of himself, and grabbed up the pen. He dunked the pen heavily into the ink jerking back at the last second so as to not penetrate the rind. He then heaved an exasperated sigh and began to write: **I was in prison** ... in beautiful calligraphy, perfect penmanship from years upon years, hours upon hours of scribing ... **and I was a** ... he paused and looked at Bird, "I hate you, you know" his tone seething. Then he returned to his assignment ... **lousy servant.** "There! Are you happy you Demented Demon?"

"The question is, are *you* happy?"

"No!" Boy jumped to his feet and spit at the object of his loathing. The spitball flew some four feet upward and then curved and landed on the dirt floor.

"Well, that will be all for this evening," said Bird, and he flew off.

Boy let out an "Aaarrrggghhh!" and hit the cell wall beneath the window with both fists.

"Silence!" Guard bellowed from down the hall.

✦ ✦ ✦ ✦
✦ ✦ ✦ ✦

Day after day came and went. Each night Bird visited, and each night Boy felt soaked in bitterness. Boy began to feel he would never be free. He didn't understand the creature that taunted him, made him promises, tested his patience, hurt his feelings. Bird had told him he'd be free upon scribing six lines, but then had only asked him to scribe one senseless line.

Over time, Boy stopped asking for freedom. He began to believe Bird's promises to have been the cruelest of all possible lies.

Boy was now half way through his thirteenth year, and no deliverance. He rarely spoke to Bird; he simply let Bird ramble on about whatever the lecture of the day might be. Boy would half listen and daydream of the noble girl in green robes pointing at him, asking the guard to free him.

On one night in particular, Bird especially angered him. So much so,

Boy thought it unforgivable.

Bird arrived as Boy was etching something into the clay walls with a twig.

"What are you doing?" demanded Bird.

Boy jerked, startled by the voice. "Nothing."

"No, I can see you are doing something. Are you trying to dig your way out?"

"Foolish bird. Behind the clay are iron bars. There's no escaping this prison."

"Interesting."

"What?"

"You mean to tell me, that inside the clay that crumbles there are iron bars?"

"Yes. That's exactly what I mean."

"So the unseen portion is stronger than the seen?"

"Yes. Why do you ask?"

"Because that is what I wish for you."

"What?"

"Inner strength."

"You want the walls to keep me in?"

"No. The world speaks to us in parables if we can but listen."

"You make no sense, Bird."

"That is because though hearing, you do not hear or understand."[2] Bird tilted his head. "So what are you doing?"

"Nothing."

"No, I can see you are clearly up to something. I'll come and have a look."

"No!"

But Bird flew down as Boy flailed his arms trying to keep the creature from drawing near. It was to no avail. Bird landed in front of the earthen bricks.

Boy thought to kick the bird, but instead heaved a heavy breath and closed his eyes with embarrassment.

"Hmm. Hmm. Yes ... I see," said Bird. "I believe you would call this poetry. At least *some* might refer to it as poetry. You are etching poetry into the walls. And I can see your emotions are completely off center. You're obsessed. Displaced feelings of deliverance. Quite definitely. Am I reading it right?"

"Leave off, Bird. It's none of your business!"

Bird began to read it anyway.

> **Autumnal hair like brown-red leaves,**
> **enfold her face like wind-swept trees;**
> **her green eyes oceans lit by day,**
> **her skin same ocean's foam white spray.**

"Are you smitten?"

"No." Boy looked at his feet.

"You are. You are definitely smitten."

Boy cleared his throat and looked up at the ceiling. "No." He pressed and rolled his lips inward.

Bird shook his head. "This will never do. You have better things to do than pine over a girl who's not for you."

"How do you know she's not for me?"

"I know things," said Bird.

"Like what?" Boy demanded.

"Just ... things," answered Bird.

"You know *nothing!*"

"I know that *girl* can't do anything for you. You have abnormal feelings of adoration because you think she can free you from what you perceive yourself to be lacking, namely, freedom and feelings of inadequacy. But she can do nothing for you. And I can."

"*You* have done nothing for me! I hate you!"

"Hate me? Why do you hate me? Hate yourself for not being ready. I can free you all right, but you've learned nothing these past six months, and I'm beginning to wonder if you will ever learn anything."

"I *have* learned something—I've learned *two* things!"

"What?"

"I've learned I don't trust you!"

"And?"

"I've learned I hate you!"

Bird looked up at him from the ground. His red-gray breast took a deep breath in and out. "I know." He flew to the sill, stooped, and looked back before lift-off. "It's good for you." With that he left.

✦ ✦ ✦ ✦
✦ ✦ ✦ ✦

After Bird had mocked the noble girl, Boy spoke even less, but one night, Boy felt so bored and lonely that he tried to amuse himself by engaging in cordial conversation with Bird, even though he now loathed him.

"Why do you call yourself a Warbler?" Boy asked.

"Because I sing," replied Bird. "It is my gift. Just as scribing is yours."

"Then you should talk less and sing more." Boy smirked at his insult. "But why Olive?"

"Because my kin are from the Olive Orchard outside the Citadel by the Sea."

"Well, what do you call yourself besides Olive Warbler? You have a name don't you? And why have you never asked me mine?"

"Someone took the time to name you?"

"Yes, Bird, my parents."

"Oh. Well, I don't really care what your name is. I will, at some point, I suspect, give you a new name."

"I don't want you to name me," said Boy. "I have a perfectly good name. And now I don't care to know yours." He crossed his arms and turned his back to the bird.

Boy heard a sigh.

"Hodos," said Bird. "My name is Hodos."

Boy turned to look up at him. "Well, I'm Archippus. And my sister is—"

"Apphia," finished Hodos.

Boy gawked at Bird. "How do you know her name?"

Hodos stared directly into Boy's eyes. In a slow, deep, round, low tone, Hodos narrowed his eyes and said, *"I know things."*

Bird left.

The tone deeply disturbed Archippus.

⤙ ⤙ ⤙ ⤙
⤙ ⤙ ⤙ ⤙

Archippus did not sleep well. His mind raced fitfully as he tried to analyze what Bird meant by that tone he had used. And how did he know his sister's name? And something else kept playing through his mind. He kept hearing Bird tell him that scribing was a gift. It was the only nice thing the Plumed Perturbance had ever said to him. Archippus had never thought of scribing as a gift, and yet, when he did manage to steal a glance at the others' scrolls, their handwriting was nowhere near as seemly as his own. He assumed the others, having only completed the required year of Mind Sculpting, lacked appropriate skills. All commoners were required to complete one year at a Mind Sculpting Center in order to be able to discern letters to read the edicts posted from the councils. Archippus realized he had learned much from his father by candlelight, *but I've never thought of it as a gift,* he kept repeating to himself.

⤙ ⤙ ⤙ ⤙
⤙ ⤙ ⤙ ⤙

The next day, as usual, Archippus woke before the sun. He thought he smelled a hint of rain in the air. He sucked the fresh air deep into his lungs. *I have a gift.* He watched Guard unlock the bars, struggling to pin the heavy club under his elbow and against his hip. *He's never used the club on me.* Archippus followed Guard to the scriber's room and the boy observed the candlelight flickering. The warm glow cast shadows that danced upon the wall. He sat and let Guard chain his leg. He realized that while Guard was bent over chaining, he could in fact glance at the other two scribes.

Archippus caught the eye of the first boy. His skin was pale, his nose sharp. Dark black disheveled hair hung in bone straight clumps across his face, partially covering his bright blue eyes. Archippus shot him a smile. The dark-haired boy smiled back. He was missing a tooth on top and to the left, but his smile was big, toothy, and happy nonetheless.

Archippus glanced at the other scriber, a tall and brown-skinned boy with short, glistening, frizzy brown curls packed tightly against his head. His eyes were dark above a rounded nose. His arms, though thin, were sinewy and muscular and his pinky finger was missing on his left hand. Archippus smiled and received an expressionless nod in return.

Archippus realized by his glancing that neither of his co-workers were trained scribes. Their basic letters indicated they had completed the required year at the MSC in order to discern symbols as letters in order to read. This year of training was required because the councils insisted that all Landlings read, for ignorance of the law was not an excuse to escape punishment. The rudimentary copies of the law these two boys were scribing would most likely be posted in the poor section of the city, but his own work would be fit for Nobles.

Archippus began to work. He concentrated on the parchment in front of him. He applied himself to etching the words as perfectly as possible. For twelve hours, he was so intent on his scribing, that he was shocked when Guard unchained his leg. He thought he had hardly worked a single hour.

Back in his cell, he lay on his back slipping his hands behind his head with his elbows pointed outward and staring up toward the window.

Bird arrived.

"Hello, Hodos," said Archippus initiating conversation.

"Hello," said Hodos. "How was your day?"

Archippus smiled. "I don't know. I ... I feel kind of funny."

"Funny how? Are you about to vomit?"

"No, not funny sick, funny good. I don't think I've felt like this before."

"Explain."

"Well, I was thinking today that maybe Guard isn't such a bad guard after all. I mean, he's punished me, no doubt, but he's always spared my life. Then I got to the scriber's table, and the other boys ... well, I smiled at them just to see what they would do. And then I decided, so what? So what if I have to do this? I am going to scribe these parchments in the most beautiful handwriting Lord Ipthsum has ever seen. And so, I did my very best, and ... well ... I think that maybe I feel kind of ..." Archippus thought to find the best word. "Grateful."

Bird plummeted from the windowsill and landed *pumpf* on the floor. A cloud of dust wafted upward.

Archippus jumped to his feet. "Are you all right?" He bent over at what looked like a carelessly discarded feathered banana peel. He'd never been this close to Hodos.

Hodos stood and shook the dust off alternating wings and then cleared his throat and whistled loudly, a single shrill whistle.

"Shhhh! What are you doing?" Archippus scolded.

A flap of wings, the scrape of something shoved across the sill, a thud that echoed with a ping. A raven had dropped a key.

"Thank you, Aro," said Bird to the raven. He then looked at Archippus. "You are ready," said Bird. "Don't forget your scroll." And with that, he and the raven took off.

Archippus ran and sat on the key. He feared Guard would come to check on him, see the key, and slaughter him. His heart pounded. He felt stunned. It was one thing to have a key, *but how do I get out of here?*

Archippus' mind raced. He then remembered the date. The Feast of Adoration was tomorrow night. He knew this from the tic marks he kept on one wall, counting off his days. *What if they will let her free me this time? Then I don't have to risk my life, and besides, I will get to see her one more time.*

Boy, deciding to wait, buried the key in the corner of his cell.

The next evening, Hodos arrived. "What are you *doing?*"

"Huh?"

"I said what *are you doing?* I told you to leave, and I had an eegwuhnuh snocked up, saddled and waiting for you! I convinced him to help!"

"Really?"

"Yes. Really. But now I *don't*. The owner noticed the reptile missing and retrieved it."

"Oh, sorry." And then, "Eegwuhnuhs listen to you?"

Hodos rolled his eyes. "Everything listens to me except for you."

"Well ... I was just thinking. It's still dangerous for me to leave. If they catch me I'll pay dearly for it ... maybe with my life!"

"If you *don't* do as I say, you'll lose your life," said Bird.

Archippus continued as if he hadn't heard. "And ... well ... maybe they'll let her free me this time."

"Who? Girl with hair like leaves?"

"The noble girl. Yes."

"Unbelievable."

"What?"

"You."

"Why?"

"Stubborn."

"Me?"

"Yes."

"Yes?"

"All right," said Hodos. "Go ahead. See for yourself. But *Branch Beauty* can't do anything for you. And when you *do* get out by use of the key *I* gave you, you are going by *foot*. Not by eegwuhnuh." Hodos flew off.

Boy waited.

Soon. Very soon she would be coming.

And soon he heard the echo of a door unlocking down the corridor.

Boy ran and wrapped his hands around the bars and peered up the hall to the left. He wanted to see her every second possible.

Shadows approached. Footsteps shuffled. The footsteps came around the corner with Guard in the lead. And there she was. Her long reddish-brown curls bounced off her shoulders, flickering wall torches reflected from her golden neck rings, the green folds of her gown played about her legs with each step. And as she had done each year, she tipped her head in his direction, and her shimmering hair slid to conceal her left emerald eye. She lifted her arm and pointed.

Archippus met her gaze.

Guard laughed. "You know better. You do this every year. He's *still* a master scribe, My Lady."

And as she passed, she turned her face, keeping eye contact until she disappeared down the lengthy hall. Archippus dropped his forehead onto the cold iron bar in front of him. His heart hurt. He hated Hodos for being right. Clearly, now would be the best time to leave. Now was his chance to be free.

He quickly dug up the key and tucked the scroll in his belt string. Gently he unlocked the bars, closed the cell door quietly, and hurried off. He rounded a corner and saw in a cell, the two scribes who had acknowledged him yesterday. They looked at him with eager disbelief.

The boy with the toothy grin grabbed hold of the bars. "Let us go with you!" he whispered.

Archippus hesitated. It would be more difficult for all three of them to slip out. His mind raced. *This could ruin everything.* With a nervous knot in his stomach and a reluctant hand, he unlocked their cell.

The toothy boy leapt forward fervently and hugged Archippus about the neck, half choking him in gratitude. Archippus pushed his arm away in order to breathe. The tall boy stepped out of the cell with a nod of appreciation.

The three hurried along the dark, narrow, twisting hall, only occasionally lit by torches. Finally, they ran up a staircase. At the top, they stopped and glanced around the corner. Across a clay-tiled room facing the moonlit street, a single guard, spear in hand, stood between them and freedom.

Archippus glanced at his newfound companions. The tall boy lifted his finger to his lips to shush the others, then slunk behind the guard on stealthy bare feet and cleared his throat. The guard spun to meet a punch between the eyes and fell backward unconscious. The tall boy unhooked the guard's belt and sword and buckled it about his own waist, and then grabbed the spear.

The three escapees ran up the moonlit street. Archippus glanced back toward the prison. The stone gargoyles that lined the rooftop seemed to sneer. Their hideous bodies hunched as if they were about to spring to life and come after them.

Archippus ran faster until the boys made their way into the woods. Once hidden beneath the trees, the toothy boy extended a hand. "Can't thank you enough. I'm Emoticas."

"I'm Archippus." He shook the hand in response. "And you are?" he asked the tall boy.

The boy said nothing.

"His name's Gershom. He took an oath of silence," said Emoticas.

"Interesting. Well, good luck. Have a nice life. Both of you." Archippus turned and burst into a run. He figured he needed to get as far away as possible before the guard noticed their absence. To his dismay, he heard two sets of footsteps pounding after him. Emoticas puffed and ran up alongside him. Archippus stopped.

"We've nowhere to go. We're coming with you."

"But the three of us are more likely to get caught—all dressed in prison garb—people will see us!"

"I can help with that. I'm a tailor. And Gershom—he's a hunter. You need us!"

Archippus thought about this. "You can make us clothes?"

"Yes! Gershom will hunt for skins and I can fashion them."

"Very well. We'll make as much headway as we can tonight."

Emoticas grinned.

The three pushed on running, panting, slowing to a fast walk and running again, pushing on and on refusing to stop, knowing at daybreak, they would find a hiding place and rest. Archippus' malnourished legs ached, and his unexercised lungs burned. Each step brought pain and cuts to his unshod feet. He placed a hand occasionally on the sharp pain in his side. His mouth was dry and thick with thirst. His head and heart pounded while his lungs screamed for air.

But the joy of freedom fueled his resolve.

Eventually, the sky began to lighten. The three spotted a clearing that had a grassy hill to one side. The hill was dotted with large boulders. It would make the perfect resting place.

Archippus lay on his back behind a boulder, resting on the soft grass. He heard the breeze rushing through nearby trees. He smelled the fresh dew and heard the morning songbirds. He looked up at the fading stars and wondered for a moment where Hodos was, and if he were now to be free of him, and then fell asleep the next instant.

⤎ ⤎ ⤎ ⤎
⤎ ⤎ ⤎ ⤎

Archippus awakened slowly from deep exhaustion. Without opening his eyes, he realized incredible warmth bathed his entire body. He realized this wonderful feeling came from the sun he had not seen for five and a half, long, dark, torturous years. He felt his eyes growing moist beneath his lids. *The sun, the beautiful, beautiful sun!* The corners of his mouth spread into a grin. He didn't want to open his eyes for fear he might be dreaming. He lay there soaking in the warmth, smiling.

"What are you smiling for?" came the familiar voice.

Drat! Archippus jerked his eyes open and saw Hodos staring at him from atop the boulder. *Not exactly the first thing I wanted to see.* Archippus sat up. His body ached. He felt famished. He closed and rubbed both eyes with his knuckles hoping that upon reopening, the sun would remain and the bird would be gone.

"I was smiling because I thought I'd be rid of you," said Archippus. "Where were you last night anyway?"

"I was above you, flying."

"Oh."

"I see you've already disobeyed me."

"Huh?"

Hodos tilted his head in the direction of the two sleeping companions. "I told you to take the scroll, not the entire prison population. What were you thinking of? They might not have searched for *one* prisoner, but for *three* they most definitely will."

"You're an awfully compassionate Counselor," said Archippus, his voice wrought with sarcasm.

"My job is to see that you finish your quest."

"And just exactly what is my quest anyway? To finish this silly little scroll?" Archippus pulled the document from his belt string and slapped it on the ground. "Tell me the remaining five lines and I'll be done with it."

"I can't just tell you the rest of it. I can instruct you once you are ready for the next statement and not before. You have to understand it."

"I still don't understand the *last* statement! Lousy servant! Why don't I compose a line I *do* understand: ***I was beaten down by a callous Counselor.***" Archippus shot a glance at his swollen bleeding feet. "And couldn't you have sent another eegwuhnuh?" He flicked his hand in the direction of his feet. "Where am I to go anyway? I need to eat, find clothes, and go back to the city of Ai to find my mother and my sister."

"Your mother is dead."

Archippus looked abruptly at the bird and squinted under a furrowed brow of distrust.

Hodos continued. "I didn't want to tell you this way, but you have to get returning out of your head. You cannot return to Ai."

"How would you know if my mother were dead?"

"I know things."

Archippus jumped to his feet and yelled directly at the bird on the boulder. "You're wrong! You're mean and spiteful! You're making it up to get me to not go back!"

The yelling woke his companions.

"Fine, don't believe me," said Hodos. "But, if I were making it up and really didn't know things, wouldn't it make more sense to tell you that your twin is dead also? That's the only way I could clearly prevent you from wanting to go at all. Then you would have no reason to return to the city."

Archippus looked warily at Hodos. "How did you know she's my twin? I told you only that she was my sister."

"I know things. And if this relationship is going to work at all, you are going to have to trust me."

Archippus clutched his hair in both hands. "My mother is dead?" He plopped to the ground on his knees. He looked back up at Hodos. "How? When?" His eyes turned glossy with moisture.

"She became sick. Her lungs filled with The Fluid. She died in her sleep. Four and a half years ago."

Archippus placed both palms over his eyes, and silently rocked ever so slightly back and forth.

By now, both companions were standing ten feet away, staring.

"Are you talking to a songbird?" asked Emoticas.

Archippus kept rocking silently.

"Allow me to introduce myself," said the bird toward Archippus' travel companions. "I'm Hodos."

"Fine!" Archippus yelled. "Tell them your name right away, but don't tell me for months. I hate you!"

Hodos shrugged and looked away from Archippus and at the other two boys. He tilted his head toward Archippus. "He hates me. But it's good for him."

The boys looked at Hodos and back to Archippus. Finally, Emoticas addressed Hodos.

"Who *are* you?"

"I'm his Counselor."

"But Counselors are only sent to first-borns of nobility. He's obviously not nobility. He hasn't the neck rings of birth. And ... well ... Counselors are airborne reptiles ... you're more like a regular songbird."

"I am also a songbird. I am an Olive Warbler." Hodos puffed his breast out at the announcement. This made him look a quarter of an inch taller.

Emoticas nodded with the corners of his mouth turned down. Gershom looked intently at the bird.

"I overheard you talking last night," said Hodos. "Gershom, you are a hunter. I wager the search has begun for the three of you. You'll need to down a caribou so that Emoticas can fashion some clothing. I'll scout for a herd, but first, I'll find you some water. Let me locate a brook, and I will return to guide you."

Emoticas continued to nod and Gershom lifted the spear in the air in agreement.

Hodos flew off.

Emoticas walked up to Archippus. "Handy friend of yours. Sorry about your mother."

"He's no friend of mine!"

"Right. Okay. I can see this is a very trying time for you, but a Counselor is a Counselor. Wish I had one."

"You can have *mine!*"

Emoticas took in a deep breath and released it. "Okay. Well, why don't we just give you some time alone." He glanced at Gershom and muttered, "Someone seems a little *moody* today, doesn't he?"

Emoticas and Gershom walked away from Archippus and sat in the grass. They conversed awhile, Emoticas speaking and Gershom nodding and shaking his head and pointing and signaling with his hands.

In a short time, Hodos returned, circling overhead.

"I have found a brook nearby. I can direct you." He flew over and landed on Archippus' right shoulder.

Archippus brushed him off. "Get away from me."

"Then how can I direct you?" asked Hodos.

"You can sit on *my* shoulder," said Emoticas excitedly. "I've never been up close to a Counselor!"

"Very well. You're less smelly anyway." Hodos flew over and perched on the shoulder of Emoticas. "Walk straight ahead to the tree line."

The three boys proceeded into the woods, winding here and there at Hodos' direction until they came to a small brook. The three boys fell to their knees, dropped their faces into the water and gulped insatiably, lifting their mouths only to breath.

After several minutes, Hodos spoke. "I saw a herd of caribou a stone's throw from that ridge over there."

Gershom leaned on his spear and pushed himself upright. He made hand signals to Emoticas and then took off toward the ridge with Hodos flying after him.

"Says he'll send Hodos for us after he hunts," Emoticas said to Archippus.

"How do you understand his hand signals?"

"Well, we were in prison together over a year. He would make hand signals, and I would guess and keep guessing until I guessed right. I learned the 'Unspoken' language. Good way to pass the time. Made it all kind of fun, actually."

"You have a strange idea of fun. Why the oath of silence? Sounds like a senseless resolution. What's the purpose? How long is he supposed to not say anything?" The dimples in the upper corners of Archippus' cheeks deepened as he scrunched his cheeks, trying to understand Emoticas' remarks.

"He said, well actually he *said* nothing, he signaled. And I would guess and guess until it became apparent that he had decided to take an oath of silence until the Airborne Monarch, spoken of in the prophetic book of Ezdra, takes control of the Continent bringing justice to the oppressed." Emoticas smiled, as if pleased that he had eventually understood all this from only a few hand signals.

"Airborne Monarch?" asked Archippus.

"Yes. There must be a go-between. We Landlings look to the councils for justice and find none. But one day, a ruler will bridge the gap to judge the Continent in fairness. A ruler who understands both land and sky."

"That's insane. The Airborne Monarch is probably a myth, and if it refers to the Seraph, it is most definitely a myth. Who's oppressed, anyway? What's wrong with the Continent?"

"What's wrong?" Emoticas' eyelids widened causing his blue orbs to seem twice as large. "The oppression of pale-skinned commoners like ourselves, that's what's wrong! Prison, the prison you and I were in, is better than being a free commoner these days."

"I don't believe that. And if it is true, why did you ask me to free you?"

"Because you can't *do anything* about oppression while you are in prison. Allurian sentiments have infiltrated the councils causing them to look to their own well being above those they are entrusted to rule. With the scepter and the Sacred Scrolls, they hold the keys to knowledge, but they themselves have not entered into wisdom and thereby prevent all Landkind from entering.

"Gershom and I want to gather the commoners in a movement to be heard," Emoticas finished with intensity in his eyes.

Archippus forced a laugh. "Then as soon as we have our clothing and a good meal in our bellies we can part ways. The last thing I want to do is create a fuss, draw attention to myself, and return to prison. I am only concerned about finding my sister."

"Well, I can assure you, your sister is far better off than you."

"What do you mean?"

"How long were you in prison?"

"Five and a half years," said Archippus.

"Well, you obviously don't know about Title IX, Section Vc, because three years ago a mandate came down from the Fourth City deeming female commoners more valuable than males. Females receive preference for not only jobs with nobility, but can also purchase property, and, this is unbelievable, can even own male commoners as slaves. We are now the lowest ranking Landlings on the Continent. We have become Servants of Burden—no better off than the four-leggeds."

Archippus was silent, his mind raced. He had sought freedom only to emerge in a world of oppression, most specifically, his own. Somehow, he blamed Hodos.

"He should have told me," said Archippus.

"Who?"

"That stupid songbird."

"Hodos?"

"Yes. I'd have been better to remain in prison. I hate him."

"Can *I* have him?"

Archippus made a *'ch'* sound through touching teeth. "I wish you could. He says I am to be free of him at some point. But until then, I have to obey him."

"Why do you have to obey him?"

"It was the deal. He said if I agreed to obey him, he would get me out of prison. And in the end—it wasn't him at all. He sent a *raven* to drop the key. I've been given the smallest Counselor on the Continent. He's useless. I doubt he could lift a twig."

"He seems wise."

Another *'ch'* sound came from Archippus. "My life keeps getting worse."

At that very second, Hodos landed on Emoticas' shoulder.

"And worse," Archippus repeated.

"Worse what?" asked Hodos.

"Never mind," said Archippus.

"Good news!" said Hodos. "Gershom has downed a caribou. Food and clothing for all!"

It soon became apparent to Archippus that Gershom was adept at not only hunting, but also skinning, fire starting, and cooking. And Emoticas, being a tailor, knew how to help tan the hides by use of the animal brains.

Emoticas worked on transforming the skins into wearable clothing while Archippus gathered wood and Gershom cooked. The aroma that wafted from the fire was the finest fragrance Archippus had ever smelled in his life. All he could think about was the impending first genuine meal in five long years. They sat by the fire and Gershom handed them each a portion of meat on a stick.

Archippus looked at it, smelled it, and bit into it. The flavor rolled on his tongue and he grew angry with himself. He couldn't explain it, but the fact that he was eating an actual meal made him feel choked up, though he forced an expression of indifference and managed to finish the meat.

All three boys became quickly full, for their stomachs were unaccustomed to meat. Archippus tossed his finished stick into the fire. He eyed his two travel companions. He'd never thought to ask why they were in prison. What if they were dangerous? They didn't look dangerous. Not Emoticas, anyway. Archippus had to know. "So why were you two in prison?" he asked.

"Well, I lost my job to a *girl*," said Emoticas. "Can you imagine? A female tailor! But my old clients still loved me. They were giving me work on the side to design important clothing—not everyday wear. Clothing for the biannual treks, feasts, ceremonies of matrimony, Council robes. But the head tailor I had worked for found out. He reported me as working outside the guild. I was brought before the Council of Twelve, and fortunately, they spared my fingers since I need them for my trade. I was sentenced to two years and commanded to scribe. Though I knew nothing of scribing, I had completed the required year at the MSC, but that is all." Emoticas tossed his stick into the fire.

"What about him?" Archippus nodded in the direction of Gershom.

"Gershom's offense was far more serious than mine. The rumor spread of his oath of silence and the reason for it. It is treason, as you know, to criticize the councils. They accused him of having Fervian sympathies, which could cause him to support the Barbarian uprising. They cut off his pinky and sentenced him to fifteen years."

Archippus glanced at Gershom across the fire. Gershom eyed him back.

"I still remember my trial," Emoticas added. "The council members were seated on their thrones. They looked wealthy and aloof in their long, orange, bell-hemmed robes. I'd designed a couple of the robes myself! I had the tiny ringing bells imported by eegwuhnuhs from the Fourth City! Ingratitude if you ask me, and Council Member Ingle was one of the clients who came to me outside the guild! Hypocrisy. But I dared not say anything. They say if you *say* anything, it only makes it worse."

Silence settled over the group for several seconds.

Archippus broke the silence. "I was only eight," he said slowly while staring at the fire. "All I remember were the steps in front of me and the looming row of twelve thrones. The overhead roof openings allowed the light to shine on the hot rocks next to each throne where the Airborne reptilian Counselors were perched or lounging to heat themselves.

"I could hear two council members whispering. And they know sound carries in the hall of vaulted stone. But they did not care that I could hear them.

"The moisture pool to the left was giving off steam. I didn't know if I would collapse from heat or dread. One said, 'Give him life, we can use his skills.' The other, 'His offense is minor.' The Airborne's clucked and chided and put in their opinions as well. 'Don't forget the cause,' they said, and 'We must deliver and post the laws.'

"They returned to their seats. I held my breath. And one after the other, their gold-clawed gavels fell, resounding on armrests as each in turn announced my sentence. 'Life.' Not one said otherwise. They each said *life* in prison."

Emoticas shook his head. "They wanted free labor. What'd you do to get in court anyway?"

"Stole."

"That's a two-year, one-finger sentence."

"I know. I'd have gladly given a finger."

"So you see, my friend, there is no justice," Emoticas began to speak heatedly. "The councils have become corrupt. They blindly succumb to Airborne Council, and follow Allurian principles of looking out for themselves above the common good. They are like their ancestors who followed Lord Gargoyle, who taught the gargoyles and a third of the Airborne to follow the heart's desire regardless of consequence. This corruption was passed down through generations of Airborne's, and their philosophy has poisoned the councils and undermined The Teachings to fight the allure. The nobility rule at our expense, but they were intended to

35

instruct and protect."

"To follow the heart's desire is a good thing," Archippus interjected.

"Not if you desire wrong," said Emoticas.

"If being Allurian means to look out for yourself, then that's me," insisted Archippus.

Emoticas shook his head. "You're blind! Allurian sentiments put you in prison! They used you with no regard for justice!" Emoticas stared fiercely at Archippus and continued. "You freed us. And for that, Gershom and I owe you food and clothing. But beyond that, we must part ways."

"That would please me just fine," Archippus fired back.

Hodos had perched on a shrub near the fire. "So, you've alienated your first set of companions, Archippus. I'm really not surprised by this."

"Shut your beak, Bird," said Archippus.

"You're so congenial," said Hodos.

"Leave off!" said Archippus.

"I don't know how someone as affable as yourself could offend somebody," continued Hodos.

Archippus picked up a rock and heaved it at Hodos, who flitted upward and fluttered downward, landing wholly unharmed.

"I admire your self-control the most," the bird persisted.

"Aaarrrggghhh! Be silent!" Archippus jumped to his feet with a second rock poised in air.

"Leave off!" Emoticas jumped to his feet.

"You take him then! When we part ways, keep the Winged Mutation for yourself!" Archippus lowered the rock and twisted to face Emoticas, who charged at him with face thrust forward. Gershom leapt up, got between them, and shoved them apart.

"And your peacemaking abilities. I admire that also, Archippus," Hodos prodded.

Archippus spun back toward the bird, screamed, "I hate you!" and stomped off to a spot to sleep a stone's throw away. He was so angry at Hodos he began to fantasize about ditching him or plucking him, or plucking him and *then* ditching him. Regardless of the plucking, he would definitely do the ditching. Toward morning, he was convinced. Yes, he would definitely ditch the bird.

The next morning, Archippus was silent. He did as he was told to assist with making the clothing, but said nothing. He grunted every now and then when Emoticas spoke to him.

"The bird is right. You're not pleasant. You need to work on your attitude," said Emoticas.

Grunt.

"Here. Hold that end while I make the cuts. I'm fashioning these so that we will look like tradesmon. They won't suspect us as being prison escapees."

Grunt.

"I'm only doing this because you freed us. I feel I owe it to you. But I won't shed a tear when you leave."

Grunt.

"And that's an understatement," Emoticas added.

Emoticas used the waist strings from their prison garb as a measuring tape. He then used pieces of the same strings for laces in the V-necked tunics. Next, he designed the half-thigh skirts and under garb. Finally, to make sandals, he scratched outlines of their feet while each of them stood on a skin. Then he cut out the soles and used the remaining string for straps by punching upward through the base of the sandal, threading the string through the large and second toe, and tying the straps around their ankles.

Archippus was impressed at how well the vests, skirts, and sandals fit. He felt like a well bred, but said nothing as he tied the V-string at his neck.

Emoticas also made three water bags with a drawstring around the top that allowed the containers to hang from the waist.

Gershom dried meat for travel food, and they used remnants from the worn feed sack garb to create a bag apiece to carry the dried meat.

When handed his meat-filled pouch Archippus had a sinking feeling. He didn't know anything about hunting game. When he ran out of meat, he'd better have a plan. Maybe he should put up with the boys after all, but convince them to ditch the bird. But, of course, Hodos would be able to find all three of them no matter where they went. He was quite suddenly filled with uncertainty. *Why does Hodos insist on being my Counselor?* It would make more sense if Hodos were to counsel Emoticas. *At least Emoticas wants him. All I want is my freedom.*

"Good morning!" Hodos alighted from a nearby tree onto the shoulder of Emoticas.

Grunt.

"Good morning, Hodos!" said Emoticas. "It's a beautiful day, don't you think?"

"Most definitely," replied Hodos.

Grunt.

"Especially since *Mr. Seven-Words* seems to have forgotten how to speak," continued Hodos.

"I agree," said Emoticas. "And I hope he knows seven ways to say good-bye, because now is the time. We've finished the clothing and supplies. We owe you nothing now, Archippus." He placed a hand on each of Archippus' shoulders and tilted his head forward in the customary good-bye. Archippus did not return the formality. He backed away, turned, and headed off with a grunt.

"You are forgetting something," hollered Hodos.

"No, I'm not!" Archippus yelled.

"Yes, you are."

"Carry it yourself!"

"You know I'm too small to carry the scroll," said Hodos.

Archippus kept marching away.

"You promised to obey or return to prison," continued Hodos in a loud voice.

"You can't even carry a scroll! How can you return me to prison?"

"I can notify the guards of your location," Hodos answered.

Archippus stopped marching. He stood with his back still facing them for several seconds. Then, very slowly, he turned. He kept his eyes to the ground and reluctantly walked back as if his feet were heavy. He stooped and grabbed the scroll and shoved it in his belt string refusing to make eye contact with any of them. He then turned and stomped heavily and quickly away hoping to look confident, but he had absolutely no idea where he was going.

Archippus looked up at the reddish sky and tried to gauge the angle of the sun in order to figure the way to the next city. He had seen it on a mural in the Judgment Hall. Every Judgment Hall in every city was mandated to have the same design with a row of twelve thrones and a golden table on which to rest the Sacred Scrolls. A heated pool was to the left facing the thrones, and a mural to the right of the thrones depicted the layout of the Continent with the oceans in green, the land light brown, and a map of the seven cities in black.

Archippus heard that the Barbirians had once marred the mural in his home city of Ai. At the tip of the Continent, where the Trail of Tears wound upward through the frozen waters to the ice cap at the top of the world, someone had painted a tower depicting the legendary location of the High

Seraph. This defacing was a crime and a reward was posted, but the culprit was never discovered. The mural was scraped off completely. Holy water was then transported hundreds of miles from the Iron Hall to clean the wall of its desecration before re-painting the mural.

Archippus remembered staring at the huge mural that dwarfed him before his trial. The workmanship of the painter was unbelievable. The famed artisan, Malchiel Merari, painted all murals. And as nervous as Archippus was about the trial, for a few moments, his mind was lost in the mural.

He'd never been outside the seventh city, but the mural had shown him that the ocean was brilliant green with white waves crashing on the shore. This reminded him of his prison poem, and his heart ached in remembrance of the noble girl's green eyes. The ache increased as he realized that the present location of the sun and his short glance at a mural five and a half years ago would not get him to the next city. But he kept marching anyway.

PARCHMENT II

"... and what we perceive
to be the top of the world,
was actually the bottom..."

Across the Continent, the young High Ruler stood at an arched iron window and gazed through a cold iron helmet at the top of a tall iron tower. Her thoughts turned to her brother.

She had that recurring dream last night. Only this time, it ended differently. It played out each time just as she had lived it, peering from behind a white stone column on the Judgment Hall steps; her brother led up the steps in iron cuffs and chains. He spied her watching and mouthed the words, "Don't worry."

Next in her dream she had seen him in an earthen cell, skinny with sunken eyes, always in the dark, always hungry, always hurting. He would mouth the words, "Free me," and she would wake with moist eyes.

But last night, she saw him with sunlight on his face and she awoke with a start.

He's been freed!

She stared across the Continent, wondering where he might be, and if she might be able to find him. Every waking day she had hoped to free him, and as of six months ago, she now had the power to do so. It was for *her* sake that he had suffered. It had been an unexpected, unorthodox path to her election as High Ruler of the Iron Hall, and her mind drifted in remembrance.

She was only eight-years-old when a Judgment Hall Gunner had grabbed her from behind the pillar.

"No commoners on the steps!" he told her while tightly clamping her wrist.

She spat on him, causing him to release her. She tried to run.

He got hold of her long, brown locks and yanked her backward, forcing her to cry out.

"Stop!" cried a second gunner on the steps. *"What on the way to the grave* are you *doing,* Entimus? A gunner of the Fourth Field, assaulting a child?"

"She spit on me!"

The second gunner laughed. "Yes, I can see it is corroding your armor. Run quickly and wash it off or it may bore its way through your heart."

"Very funny," mumbled Entimus letting go of her hair.

Apphia stared with tear-filled eyes at the second gunner. "It will be a unanimous vote," she said softly to the gunner. "My brother will be given life."

"Oh, no. Don't do that. Don't get all watery eyed on me. It won't be a harsh sentence for your brother. It was only a petty theft. No one gets life for that. And I'll tell you one thing more," he smiled kindly at her. "The council members never agree on anything, not completely anyway. They've never voted unanimously since the hall was built." He winked thinking this would console her.

"But I saw the life sentence in a dream." Apphia wiped the corner of her eyes and spun to leave. This caused her to miss the wide-eyed glance the second gunner gave Entimus.

"Wait!" yelled Entimus as Apphia hurried away. "I'm sorry to have hurt you. Where are you going?"

She paused and hollered back over a shoulder. "To my mother."

"Let us help you," he persisted. "Come back. They are about to make the ruling."

Apphia thought his change in behavior sudden, but she wanted to hear the ruling. She returned slowly, eyeing the guards and Judgment Hall in turn.

Shortly, echoing from beneath the arches came her brother's sentencing. She and the guards could hear the mallets drop on the bird claw arms of the thrones one by one. "'Life,' *bang*. 'Life,' *bang*. 'Life,' *bang*. 'Life,' *bang*. 'Life,' *bang*. 'Life,' *bang*. 'Life,' *bang*. 'Life,' *bang*. 'Life,' *bang*. 'Life,' *bang*. 'Life,' *bang*. 'Life,' *bang*."

The second gunner raised his brow at Entimus.

Apphia's prediction of her brother's misfortune began several surprising events. She was lavished with food and clothing, visited by council members, questioned about sleeping patterns, and asked to describe visions and incidences of dreams come true. Apphia's mother, Mahna, kept telling her, "I am so proud of you, and your father would be so proud. He knew you had the gift of prophecy."

Apphia learned the second gunner was named, Shear-Jashub. He was average in height, but thick in stature with dark skin and muscled arms. His black eyes had a sparkle to them and sat above rounded cheeks. His hair rolled upward extending a hand-width above the crown of his head in small tight curls. A bristly beard with patches of gray dropped from sideburns to chin after circling around his mouth. His teeth flashed when he smiled, his thick gold neck rings indicated his nobility and the right to have received gunner training. Apphia surmised Shear-Jashub must have been into his third decade. He and Entimus befriended her and her mother, and they stood nightly guard outside the door. Entimus looked the complete opposite of Shear-Jashub—thin with no hair anywhere on his face or scalp—just a snippet of beard in the middle of his chin.

Five and a half months later, the council members announced that Entimus and Shear-Jashub would escort her and her mother to the fourth city: the City of the High Ruler of the Iron Hall.

Apphia sensed something would not go well for her mother and pleaded the Commoner's Right to remain in her birth city, but Mahna, wanting a new life, insisted upon going if the council would agree to release her son. Apphia tried to negotiate for her brother, but the council refused to release Archippus.

One seemingly kind council member explained in apologetic tones that it was at the direction of the Airbornes. "We cannot release him," she said. "Sometimes the Counselors know things we do not. Take heart. We must trust them."

"Take it up with the High Ruler," encouraged Shear-Jashub. "*She* has the power to override *any* city council."

This suggestion swayed Apphia to agree to go to the fourth city of the Iron Hall. If there were hope for her brother's freedom, she felt she must go and plead his case. But, having never been outside the seventh city, Apphia had no idea what they were about to embark on or what she was about to suffer. Even with her gift.

↞ ↞ ↞ ↞
↞ ↞ ↞ ↞

Shear-Jashub and Entimus showed up the morning after Apphia consented to make the trip, with not one, but two eegwuhnuhs. The expensive reptiles were amazing creatures. They had heads like snakes, only the crowns of their heads rounded upward. Their scaly lips blended into hundreds of raised leathery bumps that covered the cheeks and grew smaller as the bumps dotted down the thick neck in loose layers of skin. Their hide resembled the chain mail that gathered on a gunner's shoulders.

They were varying shades of green, their large, thick front legs were like elbows pointing backward, and their large, thick back legs had knees pointing frontward. At the end of each leg were five long leathery 'fingers.' The backs of the eegwuhnuhs were higher than the tallest soldier that Apphia had ever seen, and ridged with plates like rounded spikes jutting upward atop the spine. There was enough room to sit between the plates. In fact, each creature carried two padded saddles cradled between the several spinal plates and secured to the plates as well. Apphia eyed the creatures from their nostrils to the end of their long, scaly tails, a distance of about twenty arm lengths.

"I've never ridden an eegwuhnuh!" cried Apphia with delight.

Shear-Jashub smiled at her enthusiasm. "This one is named Muppim," he nodded toward the closest one. "And that one, Huppim. All packed?" he asked Apphia.

She nodded. Her wide, brown, eyes sparkled. Other than the onslaught of food and unusual attention they had been receiving these past few months, this was the most exciting thing that had ever happened to her. She felt happy, but when she recalled the dreams of her brother in his cell, her mood turned suddenly sad.

"What? Don't worry," said Shear-Jashub, misreading her quick change in demeanor. "They don't bite. They eat only snock leaves!" He hoisted her into the second saddle, placing her deerskin-clad feet in the iron stirrups. Shear-Jashub had given a pair of the furry boots to Apphia and her mother explaining that their journey would be very cold.

Shear-Jashub climbed into the front saddle and grasped the reins to the iron bit. With Mahna and Entimus on the second eegwuhnuh, and packs of food and clothing, tents, and bedding all tied to the reptiles' remaining spinal plates, the gunners pulled their reins to the right, and the reptiles turned and headed toward the mountains.

Shear-Jashub turned his head to speak over his shoulder to Apphia.

"We'll have to scale one of the upper ranges of the middle mountains. It is a trail through the outskirts of the Sixth City of Shambala, which is known for its shepherding and wool, and is a twin city for the Fifth City of Fallow. It is not a direct course to the Fourth City, but it is the quickest route that can be traveled without risking a Barbirian attack."

Apphia's cheeks were bright red from the crisp wind. She smiled and nodded. Somehow, she felt she was safe and she trusted Shear-Jashub.

The large lizards had been lurching left and right as they walked. She saw Shear-Jashub release his tight hold on the reins, and the eegwuhnuh sprang forward into a fast run. The lizard's choppy gate actually became smoother with the quickened right to left swinging movements, but Apphia still clung tightly to the plate in front of her for fear of falling. She glanced at her mother, who likewise was clutching tightly to a plate. Her mother managed a slight smile and a nod. Reassured by the acknowledgement, Apphia looked forward again, and in spite of the fast pace, tried to take in the scenery.

They traveled down wooded roads that occasionally opened into grassy clearings. All the while, Apphia realized that hour after hour, the mountain range grew closer. It amazed her that the eegwuhnuhs could travel so fast and far without lessening their pace. Finally, Shear-Jashub raised his right hand while pulling back on the reins with his left. This signaled Entimus to pull back as well and the four-leggeds came to a stop.

Shear-Jashub hopped down and helped Apphia to the ground. "Stretch your legs," he said. He then unfastened a feed sack from around a rear plate and pulled out several snock leaves. "These potent plants keep their blood warm," he explained. Entimus and Shear-Jashub fed the giant lizards while Apphia and her mother snacked on dried deer meat and drank water from a pouch.

It was in this manner that the journey continued for two days, stopping only at midday to eat. Each night, they pitched two leather tents, one for Apphia and Mahna, and the other for Entimus and Shear-Jashub. A fire was built, and they ate dried meat while listening to the gunners speak of Hieropolis the Fourth City, and of their travels, fights, and battles, all the while warning of the Barbirians, inhabitants of the Middle Mountains.

"They want the scepter," said Entimus.

"Well, yes, that, but they've also stolen a set of the Six Sacred Scrolls. They say the scrolls are theirs to interpret, that the councils interpret them loosely, and that this will cause the corruption of the Continent. They want control of the Iron Hall to have power over the councils—all seven of them," said Shear-Jashub as he stared into the fire. "They would take Hieropolis by force if they could."

The talk of war frightened Apphia. "How many of them are there? And could they ever take over the Continent?" she asked.

"No one knows how many," said Entimus. "They are scattered all over the middle mountains in the coldest of areas where snow often falls and where eegwuhnuhs cannot live for extended periods of time. It is said, however, that they ride on the backs of well-trained behemoths and that they have formed an alliance with the Cyclops of the desert craters—mutated

47

creatures with super-Landling strength. They will be a formidable foe if their numbers continue to increase, and if they can obtain plans for the fire propulsion system weapon."

Apphia shuddered.

"That's enough talk," said Shear-Jashub. "You're scaring her."

"She asked!" snapped Entimus with indignation. "Why do you always act like I don't mean well?"

"Don't be defensive," said Shear-Jashub.

"Someone has to defend me! We've been all this time together, through gunner training up to the Fourth Field, mission after mission, and you never give me the benefit of a doubt!" Entimus' voice was full of resentment.

"You're in such a mood, have a jigger of snock," said Shear-Jashub trying to sound lighthearted.

"Maybe I will!" Entimus stomped off toward the tents.

"Sorry about that," said Shear-Jashub. "He's temperamental, but as good a gunner as one could ever hope to serve with."

Apphia nodded, but wasn't certain she agreed.

✦ ✦ ✦ ✦
✦ ✦ ✦ ✦

After weeks of travel in this fashion, they finally came to the base of the jagged, northern mountain range.

"Is there no way around?" asked Mahna. Her face was pale except for wind-burned cheeks and bloodshot eyes, and she coughed repeatedly.

"We have to take the quickest route because the eegwuhnuhs have a limited supply of snock leaves, and we must get out of the cold country before we run out. This is the range with the shortest peaks; furthermore, there's no getting around these mountains. They continue up the peninsula to the Trail of Tears that winds through the ice ocean to the snow-capped country of the Legendary Tower and the *Seraph*," said Shear-Jashub.

"Oh, you had to add those words," said Entimus with annoyance. "It wasn't enough to say the 'Legendary Tower,' you had to add what you are not to speak of. I could turn you in for treason."

Shear-Jashub laughed. "But you won't, my friend, because you realize that we would not have the Airborne Counselors, Sacred Scrolls, and Emerald Scepter if there were no *Seraph*."

"Stop saying that forbidden name!" insisted Entimus.

"What name?" teased Shear-Jashub.

"You know!"

"*Seraph?*"

"Stop it!"

"Stop saying *Seraph*?"

"Yes, stop!"

"You don't want me to mention the High *Seraph* of the Scrimshaw Tower?" Shear-Jashub jested, innocence in his voice, as if he were naïve about the law. "How can a *word* be illegal?" he continued. "It's a *foolish* law because it simply makes it all the more tempting to say it."

"*You are foolish!*" Entimus abruptly yanked Huppim's head toward the mountain.

Shear-Jashub twisted his torso in the saddle and winked at Apphia over his shoulder, and she giggled.

There was a hint of a narrow road heading up the mountain. They began to climb. On the left side of the road, jutting rocks threatened to cut into the eegwuhnuh's leathery sides. The higher they climbed, the deeper the drop-off on the right. The eegwuhnuhs wide bodies occasionally wedged Apphia's left knee against the sharp rocks. She stifled any complaints, but could see blood oozing through her leather leg coverings. Behind her she occasionally heard her mother give a muffled cry. At one point, the road had fallen away entirely. Their only choice was to detour upward along a rugged and steep slope to avoid the gaping hole.

"What now?" Apphia questioned loudly against the howling wind.

"We let the eegwuhnuhs scale the cliff," said Shear-Jashub, as if it were no big deal.

Apphia's knees went weak.

Shear-Jashub pulled Muppim's reins to the left, guiding him face first up the cliff spurring him with an iron heal clamp fastened around his rabbit hide boots, and simultaneously relaxing the reins and leaning forward. Apphia leaned forward and clutched the spiked plate in front of her. She couldn't decide if she were more afraid with her eyes open or closed. Both options were terrifying. She chose to leave them open. *If Muppim falls, I may be able to leap and grab hold of something.*

The huge reptile placed one front claw in front of the other and pulled himself up the steep rock face. She watched the claws grip and dig into the minute uneven pieces of the cliff as if they were tiny ledges. With amazing dexterity, the huge lizard shoved his body forward with his hind legs, one leg at a time, grasping here and there, maneuvering along the mountainside. Because of the near vertical position of the lizard, Apphia realized she could now shift her body to sit on the padded portion of saddle that had supported her back. *So that's what those cushions are for.* She could see Shear-

Jashub's hands lightly pulling the reins in the direction of the next section of road. She made the mistake of glancing downward. Her arms and legs went immediately weak. *I won't do that again,* she counseled herself.

In less than a minute, Muppim had dropped himself back onto the road. Apphia slid back onto the seat portion of her saddle and glanced behind. Huppim dropped down just behind them. She saw her mother smile and nod in relief.

Apphia turned back in excitement toward Shear-Jashub. "How do they do that?"

"These are highly trained eegwuhnuhs from Rephidim, City of Reptiles. They don't do it naturally, but neither do they do well in cold. The training from the cliff races and a good supply of snock leaves permit these creatures to go virtually anywhere on the Continent."

Apphia began to imagine what a cliff race would be like and to envision herself as the rider. This entertained her for a good portion of the remainder of the day, which took them over the summit, down the other side, and part way across a large field. In the waning light, she saw distant campfires.

"Sheepherders," announced Entimus.

"They'll be friendly then," said Shear-Jashub.

"How can you tell they are sheepherders?" asked Apphia.

Shear-Jashub pointed ahead. "See all those fuzzy, round grazing things?"

"Oh." Apphia felt foolish for asking the obvious. This almost made her not ask the next question. But she had noticed that as they rode the enormous reptiles through the field dotted with what, by comparison, were very tiny helpless looking sheep, the sheep merely lifted their heads and continued chomping. "Why are they not afraid?"

"They know the eegwuhnuhs don't eat meat," answered Shear-Jashub.

"How do they know?" she persisted.

"Because eegwuhnuhs have the odor of plant eaters."

"Oh."

Shear-Jashub laughed. "You, on the other hand, smell like a meat-eater, and a very smelly one at that."

"Well, it's *your* fault, you gave me the meat and we've had no baths." Apphia tried to sound angry, but it made her happy to be teased by Shear-Jashub, because her father used to tease her.

Several silhouetted figures walked toward them from the fires. They were garbed in long, heavy mantles striped in different colors. They stopped at a distance.

"Your purpose?" hollered one with uncertainty in his voice.

Shear-Jashub nudged Muppim forward. As he did so, Apphia noticed the shepherd who had called out had fiery red hair, a rare hair color on the Continent.

"We ask only to stay the night. We are gunners of the Fourth Field transporting a mother and child to the High Ruler of the Iron Hall," Shear-Jashub called out. He nudged the big lizard forward and produced the scroll with the High Ruler's seal: a scepter's outline stamped in red, round wax.

"You are welcome then," said the shepherd. "You may chain the eegwuhnuhs near our largest fire. This will help lessen their snock consumption."

"Thank you. We are most grateful," said Shear-Jashub.

They rode to the largest campfire, and as had been the custom each night, the gunners pounded stakes in the ground chaining one of each lizard's legs to prevent them from wandering. The reptiles scooted as close to the fire as possible. It appeared to Apphia that they did not intend to wander from the fire's warmth.

The shepherds were friendly, offering stew and conversation.

"Before you were close enough, in the fading light, we weren't certain if you were riding eegwuhnuhs or behemoths," explained the shepherd with the red hair.

"That *would* raise concern. I apologize to have given cause for alert," said Shear-Jashub. "Only Barbirians ride behemoths." He turned to Apphia. "Behemoths are large, hairy creatures—have you ever seen one?"

"No."

"Well, the large, hairy creatures have amazingly long snake-like noses." Shear-Jashub stuck his arm out alongside his nose to demonstrate, waving it up and down. "And they have huge, white horns on either side." He pointed a finger from either side of his nose. "And legs like tree trunks." He held his arms in a wide circle. "They can withstand cold without snock leaves, which means they are perfectly acclimated to the freezing temperatures of the middle mountains. And it's been rumored that the Barbirians are training them as battle mounts." He raised an eyebrow and tipped his head at her to emphasize the implication.

Apphia's mother began to cough. Her coughing ended in a crescendo of raspy phlegm. "Excuse me." She trembled and stood.

Apphia ran to her and helped her into the tent.

"I'll be fine," her mother insisted.

But the voice in Apphia's mind warned: *no, she won't.* A vision of her

51

mother flashed in Apphia's mind. *Her mother's face pale, lips blue, her lifeless eyes open, and from the left corner of her mouth, a trickle of blood.*

Frantic, Apphia attended her mother all night with warm cloths and water. Shear-Jashub came by the tent and checked on them occasionally throughout the night.

"You've done all you can, you need your rest, I can watch her," he told Apphia.

"No, I have to watch her. I have to make sure it doesn't happen." Tears slid down her cheeks. She feverishly wrung another cloth from the clay container.

Shear-Jashub looked at her with compassion. "Give her another snock jigger." He produced a flask and poured the liquid into an acorn shell jigger. "I'll sit by just outside."

Apphia nodded. "Thank you." Her soft voice cracked as she choked back a sob.

At early morning light, Apphia, exhausted, lay on her side next to her mother. Despite her resistance to sleep, she had dozed off. She woke in a panic, rolled over, and discovered her mother with face pale, lips blue, her lifeless eyes open, and from the left corner of her mouth, a trickle of blood.

"It did me no good!" she screamed, dropping her cheek to her mother's breast and sobbing.

Shear-Jashub flung back the tent drape and hurried inside. He dropped to his knees and cradled Apphia in his harms.

"It did me no good!" she cried.

"You did all you could, child."

"No, you don't understand. My vision, it came too late! It is *not* a gift—it's a *curse!*" She sobbed and shook in his arms.

Shear-Jashub stroked the back of her hair. When she finally stopped sobbing, he gently lifted her chin and looked directly into her swollen eyes.

"I lost my child," he told her. "I will tell you of it someday. I lost both her and her mother. But, the important thing now is to remember that all events, both good and bad, have a purpose. The terrible unveils itself with reason in time, although we do not always see it, and rarely understand it. You must trust the Seraph. And so I must ask you, because I think it is meant to be, will you be my trust-child?"

Apphia's chin quivered, tears rolled from the corner of each eye, and she nodded producing a faint smile.

Shear-Jashub hugged her and kissed her forehead. "Good then. Get some rest. We will stay another day to allow you to gather strength. Tomorrow a Sheole can be prepared for your mother. The shepherds will provide the burial cloth. I must take her from you now."

Apphia closed her mother's eyelids and whispered, "To the Land of Hands and Wings." She crawled under a blanket and cried until exhaustion overtook her.

The next morning, several female shepherds woke her. "We must dig the hole," they told her.

According to custom, the women went a distance, selected the site, and used iron spades and hands to dig the second womb, the Sheole, that some believed to be the end, and some the birth to a second journey.

Apphia dug with her hands, she thought the iron instruments too impersonal for the task. She clawed and dug, clawed and dug and the women helped. The shepherdesses sang songs of hope as they dug, as if they believed this Sheole were in fact a second womb. As they lowered the shrouded body into the ground, Apphia saw a momentary vision: *her mother, rosy cheeked, with vibrant eyes, surrounded by pearl colored wings.*

The women filled the Sheole with dirt, and covered the top with a mound of rocks. When finished, Shear-Jashub came forward. He lifted his arms and hands behind his neck, unclasped his highest neck ring, and fastened it around Apphia's neck. It was a sign that she was now his trust-child since the act signified both a sacrifice and a risk: the sacrifice being each gold neck ring was worth a year's wages, and the risk, one less ring weakened Shear-Jashub's neck. If all or even too many rings were removed from a Noble, the vulnerable neck could snap.

Apphia's hand touched the neck ring. The tears that had slid down her cheeks from sadness, now slid for a moment in gratitude.

The final day's trip did not matter. In a daze she clung to the eegwuhnuh's spinal plate lamenting the loss of everything she had ever held dear: her father, her brother, and her mother. She again touched her neck ring and then pulled her new shawl tighter across her shoulders. Shear-Jashub had presented her with a white wool shawl to console her. He explained that the shepherds had made it, and that it was called a Shawl of

Reassurance. For while a shawl such as this is being spun, the shepherds continually speak phrases of hope from the Scroll of Affirmations. These shawls, he told her, were reputed to soothe the soul, and were the only ones on the entire Continent made in such a manner. The shawl was beautiful and soft—so soft that she continued to clasp the front of it in her left hand and the eegwuhnuh's spike with her right. She would not let go of the gift from her trust-father. Shear-Jashub was now her only family.

She rode in a daze until they finally reached their destination.

"Look!" cried Shear-Jashub. "Look!" He pointed animatedly.

Apphia looked and saw up ahead, on the mountainside, way in the distance, past fields dotted with tents and weapons, an enormous dark edifice set on a green lush mountainside. It was so dark in color that it screamed out from the landscape. The Seventh City from where she had come was white. Everything white. Columns and buildings, sculptures, and fountains—all white. But this looming structure up ahead was like nothing she had never seen. Black arches, black spirals, and black walls. Apphia counted seven spirals. The castle looked ominous. It looked frightening. It looked beautiful. It looked magnificent.

"Yes, it's all iron," explained Shear-Jashub. "The only city of its kind. It won't burn under attack." He smiled over his shoulder. "I'm taking you to the safest place on the Continent."

Apphia forgot herself as they rode across the seemingly unending flatland. And as they rode, what had seemed tiny tents were finally confirmed to be actual tents.

"The First Field," Shear-Jashub announced to her.

"Why do they call it the *First*?" she asked.

"When gunners train," he explained, "there are four levels of training. The entry-level gunners keep camp at the First Field to complete the basic battle tactics training. They camp at the outskirts because, should an attack occur, they are the first line of defense. Though lesser in skill, they would weaken the onslaught and lessen the strength of any foe that should happen to make way past them and on to the Second, Third, and then Fourth fields. As a gunner receives higher training, he advances from Second to Third field. And those who have actually engaged in battle advance to the Fourth."

"So you have done battle?" asked Apphia.

"Yes," he answered. "And so has Entimus."

Entimus grunted an acknowledgement.

"But he fights like a girl," added Shear-Jashub.

54

Entimus flicked his thumbnail outward across his teeth in the direction of Shear-Jashub.

Shear-Jashub laughed and so did Apphia. It was an inappropriate gesture for an inappropriate insult.

They continued to ride toward the first field. Crimson stained crosses met them on either side of the road.

"For traitors," explained Shear-Jashub.

Apphia shuddered.

Mile after mile they rode past tents. Heads would occasionally nod upward to acknowledge them. They observed gunners sparring with swords, and gunners tossing spears. Gunners heating food and gunners drinking snock. Gunners taking orders and gunners telling jokes. Gunners sharpening weapons and gunners stitching cloth. Many first-born gunners had Airbornes nearby perched on tents or on leather strapped to forearms. But somehow, beneath the din of random activity, there was a sense that *if*, at any moment, order was required, order *would* immediately occur, and military might would be forthcoming. This feeling made Apphia feel safe.

As they drew close to the Iron City, it looked large, dark, impenetrable, and intimidating. They followed a winding dusty road upward, and finally reached THE GATE.

Apphia realized THE GATE to the Fourth City of the Iron Hall governed by the highest council on the Continent was no ordinary gate. She noted that the bars were iron, but swirled with inlaid gold and jewels set in the swirls. The jewels were rubies and diamonds, and the most precious stones of all, pearls.

She noted THE GATE was by no means of average size. It was arched and wide and fitted into a massive iron wall. It was *possible* to see through THE GATE; it had squares upon squares to peer through, but Apphia could only stare *at* THE GATE and not really see past it. The stones sparkled and were so numerous that she was mesmerized. Apphia found herself gazing, counting stones, noting the reflections, and glancing upward at the incredible arch. If two eegwuhnuhs were set on top of each other, head to tail, she doubted they would reach the top.

Sparkling in the setting sun, the city was truly amazing. The group stopped in front of THE GATE and Shear-Jashub handed the scroll with the High Ruler's seal through one of the dazzling squares. A receiving gunner took it, unrolled it, examined the seal, and then signaled to his left. A clicking noise began and THE GATE rose just high enough for the riders and eegwuhnuhs to enter the central square.

At the center of the square, a tall iron fountain with level upon level of spouts shot water onto level upon level of basins that in turn trickled down into a large pond. There were beautiful, carefully trimmed plants, flowers, and trees. Trellises of ivy covered walkways, and shrubs were clipped in the shapes of circles and squares. The sound of the splashing fountain mingled with the conversation and laughter of hundreds of citizens. Shops of thatched huts faced the center of the square offering every imaginable goods or services such as pottery, ironwork, dried meats and fruits, tailor work, airborne forearm wraps, fuller services, candles, oil lamps, tapestries, hand mirrors, cosmetics, perfumes, hem bells, and bells of matrimony. Perfume wafted through the market, as did the scent of a hog roasting on a spike from a tradesmon selling hot meals. The sounds of blacksmithing, crackling fire pits, bartering, bells, and trickling water, echoed off the massive iron walls of the city.

They dismounted and Shear-Jashub handed the reins to a gunner who offered to watch over the eegwuhnuhs. Apphia patted Muppim's shoulder and ran her finger over the brand on his shoulder. She had noticed this brand—a circle with an Ei in the center—many times during the course of the trip. Today, however, as she watched the large lizard slowly lumber off led by a gunner, the marking made her think of her brother yet she didn't know why.

Shear-Jashub led her toward a merchant and exchanged a coin for three pieces of hog meat on a stick, handing one to her and one to Entimus.

Apphia nibbled the tasty meat as they navigated through a grassy landscape along a winding path toward a huge arch. As they passed beneath the arch, they entered an iron tunnel lit by endless torches along the walls. Between each torch was a portrait depicting a woman of dark skin, and behind each woman, an iron, heart-shaped throne. Apphia surmised this to be the Historic Tunnel where High Rulers of the past were recorded and honored, their images preserved long after their legacies. She examined each portrait as they passed. All the rulers appeared strong and all were beautiful.

Their footsteps echoed off the walls as they made their way toward the light at the far end of the tunnel. Apphia wished she could take more time to study the portraits, but Shear-Jashub hurried them along until they stepped out of the tunnel and into an enormous open square. Straight ahead was the Judgment Hall.

Each city was mandated to have a prison, a quarry, an MSC, and a judgment hall—all of similar design. Six of the cities built these structures entirely in stone, but this was the Iron City, and the Judgment Hall was of iron steps and iron columns. It had the exact layout as that of her home city of Ai, but twice the size, and the iron made it look dark and foreboding.

Apphia looked up at one of the four corners of the Iron Hall noting that a mound of ivy covered each corner.

Shear-Jashub noticed her squinting and explained. "When the High Ruler mandated that the figure of the Seraph be removed from the corners of all judgment halls, they tried to remove the iron shapes, but could not. So they just grew ivy to hide the figures."

They climbed the iron steps and entered the hall. Apphia's eyes tried to adjust to the dim light in the dark chamber. The roof openings filtered light onto the iron hot rocks next to each throne. This helped her regain her focus. She heard a female voice speak with a slight echo.

"I've been expecting you."

Two guards pulled back a crimson curtain and hooked it to the sidewall with a gold braided rope. Ahead, on an Iron Throne with a heart-shaped back inlaid with jewels, was the High Ruler. No one else, except the guards, was present in the hall.

To the left of the throne, shining brightly within arm's reach was the celebrated Emerald Scepter. Its pointed shaft was set in a small, shallow hole built into the floor. At the top of the scepter was a round, green sphere, the size of a large hailstone, and several inches below the sphere, a hand-shaped iron glove gripped the shaft. The glove looked like part of a suit of armor meant to cover a hand, but it just hung there, clasping the scepter and leading sideways to nothing. Apphia thought it very odd and wondered if someone had tried to steal the scepter, but the hand was lobbed off in the process. She then wondered why no one would have removed the hand. Wouldn't it have begun to stink? She squinted at the scepter. The green light emanating from it was bright enough to make it difficult to stare at the stone, and yet, she couldn't help but stare.

"Look at me," demanded the High Ruler.

Apphia's eyes shifted to the High Ruler and she realized her mistake. She had been so distracted by the scepter she had forgotten to pay respect. Shear-Jashub and Entimus had already taken to one knee on either side of her. She immediately dropped to one knee also.

The High Ruler looked directly at Apphia. "You must be tired from your journey, and you must be wondering why you are here."

The High Ruler was stunning. Awestruck, Apphia could only nod. The High Ruler's flawless skin was the color of rich brown river silt. Her dark eyes gleamed and her neck was elongated by rows of golden rings. Her slender arms moved like graceful snakes as she adjusted her peach-colored robe with a crimson floral pattern. Tiny bells dangled from the hem of her robe and tinkled softly each time she moved.

"You are here because of your gift," said the High Ruler. "Your only responsibility is a very simple responsibility, and yet it is of the utmost importance. I will provide you with a noblemon's chambers in the sixth tower, and will endow you with a noblemon's rights. In fact, you will be permitted all the privileges of nobility. The only thing that I ask of you," the High Ruler paused, "is that you notify me immediately...." The Ruler narrowed her eyes. "Wait," she said. She pulled her right sleeve downward, stretched her bared arm toward the scepter, and slipped her hand into the Iron Fist. The scepter immediately brightened.

The High Ruler gestured to Apphia. "Step forward."

Apphia rose and walked to the scepter.

"Look directly into my eyes," commanded the High Ruler of the Iron Hall.

Apphia obeyed.

"You must promise that you will notify me *immediately* if you have *any* visions pertaining to the scepter. Do you promise?"

Apphia nodded.

"Answer me out loud, child!" The High Ruler's raised voice echoed throughout the Iron Hall.

"I promise!" Apphia shouted out of fear.

The High Ruler looked intently at Apphia as if reading her face. The top of the scepter brightened even more and the High Ruler nodded as if satisfied and removed her hand from the iron glove.

"Good," she affirmed. "I see you are trust-bound to Shear-Jashub. And Entimus knows of your origins. They will both be your guardians for the duration of your stay."

"How long will I stay, Your Eminence?" Apphia asked, though uncertain if she should.

The High Ruler smiled. "Why my dear, logically, and in the interest of the Continent in order to ensure the safety of the scepter," she lowered one arm in the direction of the scepter. "Surely you realize that you *must* stay in the Iron City for the remainder of your life." Both hands came back and settled on the throne's claw-shaped armrests.

Apphia stared at her.

"You have nothing to go back to," continued the High Ruler. "I am informed of your mother's death and truly sorry for your loss."

"My brother," mumbled Apphia.

"What?" The High Ruler raised an eyebrow.

"Can you release my brother?" Apphia's question came out clear and hopeful.

"I rarely interfere with rulings from the individual councils," the High Ruler said flatly. She shifted her focus to Shear-Jashub.

"Your trust-child is overly bold, Shear-Jashub."

She leaned forward, narrowed her eyes, and stared at Apphia for several seconds. "Escort her to her chambers!" the High Ruler shouted. Her words echoed off the walls of the dark vaulted hall for several seconds.

Apphia felt horrible. Her stomach churned as Shear-Jashub led her gently by the arm through another iron hallway lit by torches. She had come all this way and lost her mother in order to free her brother, only to be refused, and now she pondered if she had not lost her freedom also.

"Why?" she asked aloud.

"Hmm?" responded Shear-Jashub. He appeared preoccupied as they passed open arches for other tunnels leading this way and that. "It's been a while since I've been back here," he explained. "Entimus, which is the arch to the sixth tower?"

"The second up ahead on the left."

Apphia asked again. "Why didn't she agree to free my brother?"

"Oh. Well, I wasn't quite certain what would happen, but don't take it too hard. Overriding an independent counsel rarely happens. In fact, no living person remembers exactly how long ago it was that the High Ruler last overrode an independent council on matters concerning commoners. It's viewed as inconsequential."

"Then *why* did you tell me to try?" Apphia was angry. "I *lost* my *mother* coming here!"

Shear-Jashub stopped and placed a hand on each of her shoulders. "Because, how could I have possibly known for certain? She *might* have granted your request because you are of value to her. And how could I have possibly known your mother would die? And, most of all, I *know* you possess the gift to protect the scepter. It is for the good of the Continent that we brought you here. To what higher honor could one aspire?"

Apphia looked up at him. She could see in his eyes he meant well. "But *why* is it so rarely done? *Why* can't she just grant my brother his freedom?"

Shear-Jashub heaved a sigh. "Because. In order to override an independent counsel at the request of a commoner, the High Ruler must invoke the guidance of the scepter."

"So?" Apphia persisted.

"So, in order to do so, she must point the scepter at the petitioner."

"So?"

"So, the problem is, if the individual has selfless motives, the scepter will brighten as an indicator that the petition is to be approved—"

"But my motive *is* selfless!" Apphia insisted.

"I'm not finished. As I was saying, the problem is that, if in *any way* the petition is self-centered in nature, the scepter will brighten intensely and a ray will shoot from the scepter's end, and the violence from the heated beam will zap the heart from the chest of the petitioner resulting in, of course, sudden death."

"Oh." Apphia immediately began a self-analysis. A small element of selfishness was involved she supposed, in that she *missed* her brother. She began to wonder what would have happened.

"I'm sure your motive *is* selfless, my dear, but I'm also certain that the High Ruler is figuring we can't afford to lose you."

"Oh."

They passed through the second archway on the left, and a spiral staircase greeted them. It wound upward, round and round as far as Apphia could see. As they climbed the stairway, each step echoed against the walls of the iron cylinder. Round and round they hiked, passing an occasional landing barred by iron doors with peepholes. Finally, they came to what she counted as the twentieth landing. She was winded and her calves ached from the climb.

Shear-Jashub banged on the door. An eyeball assessed them through the peephole, a latch lifted, and the door swung open. The guard that opened the door had been seated in a foyer. He nodded and left.

Apphia stepped into the foyer, a small square entrance lined entirely by drapes. This permitted privacy to the resident of the chamber while a guard stood nearby. Shear-Jashub whisked back the drapes revealing her new residence. An oil lamp chandelier hung from the high ceiling. The floor of the dark chamber looked like polished glass. Straight ahead through an arch was an outside balcony with an iron handrail. The room was furnished with an iron bed, an iron armchair, and an iron vanity and stool. Apphia walked over to the bed knowing that only nobility possessed furniture. She had always slept inside a dirt-floored hut on leaves stuffed in a large feed sack. She reached out and touched the spread. It was rich red in color and embroidered with a black and gold design. The edge of the spread was lined with gold tassels. She pressed down on the spread. Her hand sunk into it. She flung the cover back and gawked at white linens. She pulled back the linens and pressed both hands into a feather-stuffed mattress. She squealed in delight and plopped in a sitting position onto the mattress, bouncing up and down, smacking the softness on either side.

"Look at this! A mattress! An embroidered bedspread and feather-stuffed mattress!" She bounced again.

Shear-Jashub chuckled.

Apphia jumped up and ran through the archway and outside onto the balcony. She was so high above the castle that she could see for miles. Below her off to the right was the clearing with the Iron Hall and quarry, and in front of that the busy entrance to the square, and beyond that the fields dotted with gunner tents, and beyond that the vast, green grasslands, a river to the south, and black snow-capped mountain ranges with watch towers. Never in her life had she imagined such luxury would be hers.

She breathed deeply and almost squealed in delight. Her mind raced to take it all in, and she wondered why a verse from the Scroll of Cautionary Writings came to mind. She had learned to copy the verse during her year at the MSC. "All luxury comes with a price," the scroll had cautioned.

Her smile faded. She turned and walked back inside her chamber.

During the next five years, Apphia was never permitted to leave the sixth tower. She could only stare at the beautiful square below. She was permitted to go to the dining room, the sparring court, and the heated pool in the Iron Hall, but that was it. She had no one her age to befriend her.

If it weren't for Shear-Jashub, she might have jumped from the tower. But he had convinced her that she mattered to the Continent and to him. He would bring her games and tell her stories, and say, "I cannot bear to lose another child."

When Entimus stood guard, he remained aloof behind the foyer curtain. But Shear-Jashub would stride to the center of her quarters and lower his bulky body to sit cross-legged on the floor and play the games with her. One of the games was called Conquer the Continent. It was played on a flat papyrus map of the Continent. The coastline and cities were painted on the yellow parchment. Little iron-hewn figurines traveled about the parchment, moving according to cast lots. The goal was to overtake the seven cities. Whoever gained control of the most cities could then cast lots for the Iron

Hall to win the game. The two of them would play on into the night by lowering the oil lamp chandelier to hover close and illuminate the map.

Apphia felt that Shear-Jashub was happiest when she beat him even though he would moan and groan, and complain and carry on each time he lost. She knew it was all for show for she knew he wanted her happy. He was proud and pleased of her in many ways, and acted especially so on her thirteenth birthday.

Having been granted a first-born noblemon's rights, she received an Airborne Counselor that evening, after which a rapid, bizarre series of events unfolded. The High Ruler took ill and perished, the stuffy council members voted, and Apphia was elected High Ruler of the Iron Hall—an outcome that utterly astounded her. Who was *she* to rule the Continent? And why not elect someone else? Someone older? Someone with the neck rings of birth? Someone wiser? Someone dark of skin? She knew her Airborne Counselor had pushed for the approval before the High Council, but as to why she could not say. All she knew was Shear-Jashub told her of a prophecy whereby a prophetic twin was to take the throne and perhaps the Council believed her to be the one. But Apphia had an uneasy sense that the reason was sinister for the untimely death of the last High Ruler was inexplicable and unnerving.

The day of her inauguration, Shear-Jashub came to her with an iron helmet and apologetic tone. "Your subjects will not understand if you are light of skin. They will not accept you. The council wishes to present the new High Ruler to the people. But you must remain clad in armor with your face behind this helmet. Your subjects will be easy to convince that this is in the best interest of your safety, for times are growing treacherous, and a traitor's spear could pierce you."

Since her inauguration six months ago, she had lived with a gnawing sadness knowing that she had the power to free her brother, but her Airborne Counselor, Pterodactyl Eri, had warned that Archippus was a threat. This made her fearful least Eri learn of her vision for she felt Eri would have Archippus hunted down. She suspected Lord Ipthsum would not report his escape. Twice she had flown to the Seventh City on Eri's back, at Eri's bidding. It had pained her greatly to be in the city of Ai and not be permitted to see her brother. And Eri insisted she tell Lord Ipthsum he would be killed if Archippus escaped. Based on this threat, she calculated Lord Ipthsum would hide the mishap of her brother's escape and imprison more unsuspecting scribes to continue to copy The Sixteen Absolutes.

Maybe Eri was right. Maybe Archippus' heart had turned dark in the darkness of his cell. Counselors are supposed to be right, always shedding light on The Teachings and the Truth. So many times, she felt she was going against her gut, but the more she went against it, the more natural it felt. She was young, as Eri often said, and had much to learn in order to see clearly to rule the Continent. Eri seemed harsh, but often reminded her, "You can't fashion iron with feathers."

Regardless, she decided not to tell him about the dream of her brother's escape.

A loud whoosh of wings and the big dark gray, almost black, pterodactyl approached from the right of her balcony. Lizard-like tongue flapping in the wind, Eri landed on the nearby rail and hunched his shoulders, black eyes glinting. Rows of sharp, jagged teeth lined both upper and lower portions of his elongated, slightly yellow beak. The crown of his head was narrow and the membrane above his beak continued upward; the gray skin forming a long, narrow crown to his skull. His shoulders jutted outward in long leathery wings, the length of which was remarkable. Not many pterodactyls were large enough to transport Landlings since most had wingspans of only two to four feet. But Eri had a wingspan of thirty feet. He had hints of long arms covered with wing skin and sharp claws that appeared at what would have been the end of his arms, but were really the mid-tip of his wings. He had claws for feet, and his backbone continued in a long narrow tail cropped with three feathers—the only plumes on the leathery reptile.

"Are you ready for gunner class?" Eri asked.

Apphia slumped. "I hate gunner class. Why do I have to take it?"

"You know you must take it. You must do everything you can to protect the scepter. It is not enough, the armies, the weaponry, the Iron Hall. What if you were to become the last line of defense? You must be bold enough and strong enough to fight for the scepter by evacuating to the Echoless Pit to toss down the scepter. Better for the scepter to be gone, than in the hands of an infidel."

"But it is difficult to train wearing armor! Why can't I remove my helmet, at least during training with Isui?"

"You know we can't have anyone seeing you are light of skin, can we?" Eri said with soft persuasion in his voice.

Apphia's sigh echoed from inside the helmet. "But can't I trust Isui? He's been sworn to protect me as head gunner!"

The reptile rolled his eyes. "I'm not going to argue with you. You have Shear-Jashub as your trust-father. That should be enough for you. He and Entimus guard you with their lives. You are sounding ungrateful. I was assigned to you because of your gift, but you have risen to authority because of *my* counsel. You have to obey me or the scepter could be in jeopardy. You've not had any recent visions in regards to the scepter, have you?"

"No!"

"And I trust you would tell me instantly?"

"Yes … of course. We've discussed this many times. Don't you trust me?"

The reptile smiled, as much as Apphia thought a reptile *could* smile, showing little wrinkled creases curving around the base of his beak. "Of course I trust you, my dear, but it pains me when you question me, and so I find that I have to question you back. Leave off the questions and be obedient, won't you now?"

A sigh again echoed from within the helmet.

"It's a lovely helmet anyway," said Eri. "Especially with my tail feather for a plume. You know it hurt me *terribly* when you yanked away my feather."

Apphia laughed. She had *enjoyed* yanking the feather and hearing him holler.

"Follow Shear-Jashub along to gunner class now," Eri insisted.

Another sigh came from within the helmet.

"Go on!" he repeated.

Apphia glanced over the handrail at the distant mountains and wondered of her brother's welfare and whereabouts. *What could he possibly be doing?*

PARCHMENT III

"... for everyone knew, naturally,
to fight the magnetic allure
that pulls downward."

Archippus hated to admit it, but he was half-glad that Hodos showed up to interrupt his thoughts. He would use Hodos to get to the next city and then *ditch* the bird. Hodos hovered and dipped in keeping with Archippus' stride.

"What do you want?" asked Archippus of the bird. "Why didn't you stay with Emoticas? He thinks you're an *asset, benefit, advantage, assist, quality, value, aid.*" Archippus spoke disdainfully so that Hodos would not spot his relief that Hodos had followed him.

"I'll have you know, *Mr. Seven-Words,* that I am all those things," replied Hodos.

"*Mr. Seven-Words,* is it? Is that my new name? The one you promised to give me when I'm ready?" More disdain in his voice.

"No. You are not ready. I will call you many things until you are truly ready. Only then will you earn your name. And it will never change again."

"Anything *you* call me, I'll not go by."

"We'll see about that. Head a little to the left."

Archippus felt stupid obeying the bird, but having no other choice, veered left.

"Where are we going anyway?" Archippus asked.

"Rephidim, City of Reptiles. And if you'd let me perch on your shoulder, it would be easier to direct you," said Hodos.

"Easier on whom? Me or you?" asked Archippus.

"I suggest it only as a *practicality, sensibleness, expediency, realism, reasonableness, sagacity, prudence,*" replied Hodos.

"Are you mocking me, Bird?"

"Perhaps."

"Well then, no, I don't want you on my shoulder. I'd rather grow a tumor."

"I'll let you get lost then." Hodos hovered and dipped and hovered and dipped.

Silence settled for several seconds.

"If you perch on my shoulder will you only speak when giving directions?" asked Archippus.

"If you insist. It will be boring and I will miss the banter. What will I do without your caustic verbiage?" he said as he landed on Archippus' right shoulder.

Archippus cringed by sinking his right shoulder downward and sliding his neck left. He glanced at the bird, scrunched his dimpled cheeks, looked forward, and trudged onward with a sigh.

Day after day, Archippus hiked with Hodos on his shoulder. The tall trees turned to shrubs, the shrubs to yellow grass, and soon the grass began to disappear. Archippus stopped at the last patch of grass and stared ahead at the sprawling desert in front of him. Nothing but sand for miles ahead.

"You got me *lost!*" exclaimed Archippus.

"No I didn't," answered Hodos.

"Yes, you *did!*" repeated Archippus. "I don't see any city!"

"That is because to get to the City of Rephidim, we must first cross this desert."

"How can I trust you?"

"Did I or did I not free you as promised?"

Archippus sighed. "The raven you call Aro freed me. *He* dropped the key."

"At *my* direction."

Archippus sighed again and squeezed his water flask. It was still two-thirds full. Fortunately he had filled it at the last spring.

"All right, but the sun is hot. I'm dying from the heat. *Curse* the sun! We will travel at night."

"It matters not to me. Travel at night then," answered Hodos. "But don't curse the sun. It was not long ago that you were enraptured by it."

"That was after *five years* in prison. I'd not seen it in five long years!"

Hodos shook his head and said to himself, "Landlings. How quickly they forget to be grateful."

✦ ✦ ✦ ✦
✦ ✦ ✦ ✦

For three days, Archippus trudged through deep moonlit sand until the horizon finally switched from flat to rocky. A final night's travel brought him to the rock formations. The solid ground felt good after days of straining his calves in the deep sand.

He scaled an outcrop of boulders, crested the top, and suddenly dropped to his belly and slithered backward forcing Hodos to jump to the ground. Archippus had spotted a campfire below. He crawled to the top of the crest and eyed the enormous figures around the fire. The beings were two-legged with thick legs and arms, and clothed in leather skirts and fur sashes from shoulder to hip. Their massive muscles bulged and their baldheads held wrinkled brows. Curiosity caused Archippus to creep even closer.

"What are you doing?" whispered Hodos.

Archippus ignored him and hopped quietly down behind a boulder hoping to get a better look. A small rock rolled loose. One of the figures turned to look. A single large eye located directly in the middle of one of the massive foreheads, stared up toward the rock where Archippus was hiding. Archippus stifled a gasp. He quickly realized he had happened upon a group of The Cyclops of the Desert Craters. He had heard they'd been rumored to eat Pangeans. He felt horrified. He glanced up looking for Hodos. With a sinking feeling in his stomach, he wondered why he even bothered; the little bird was one of the smallest creatures on the Continent. Still, he looked for him.

He heard a guttural grunt. The one-eyed figure still stared upward.

All of a sudden, Hodos barreled downward, flapping, chirping, and swooping at the Cyclops, who waved his large arms to ward the bird away.

Deep chuckles and belches came from the other Cyclopes. *They must have figured the noise in the boulders had come from the tiny bird,* thought Archippus. They resumed their activities around the fire.

Archippus kept watching and saw a few smaller caped figures approach the campfire. The figures gestured as if trying to convince the Cyclopes of something. One of the Cyclopes kept shaking his head as the figure continued to try to persuade. Archippus wondered who the cloaked figures might be, and why the Cyclopes did not grab them and eat them. Finally, a nod and a grunt came from the Cyclopes' negotiator. The cloaked figure produced a pouch that clinked. Abruptly, two rows of the cloaked ones came from out of the darkness toward the fire pulling something large with ropes. Archippus heard the squeaking sound of iron wheels and saw an iron cage large enough to contain a Cyclops roll into the firelight. Since Archippus did not want to end up in the cage, and the Cyclopes were busy inspecting their new contraption, he took the opportunity to flee.

When he had retreated a safe distance from the camp, Hodos flew down and landed on his shoulder.

"I suppose you'll want to thank me," said Hodos.

Archippus grunted.

"You sound like a Cyclops," said Hodos. "One grunt means 'thanks,' two means you are an ungrateful wretch."

Grunt.

"I think your attitude is improving," said Hodos.

Archippus said nothing more. He continued his night of travel until something new greeted his senses. Moisture, he smelled moisture in the air. After two more nights of travel and a fortuitous encounter with a spring, he replenished his water. Another couple of nights and foreign-looking plant life appeared. The short foliage had wide flat, dark green leaves. Not long after, he walked past tall naked trees, save for handfuls of fanned leaves at the top. The terrain soon became dense with vegetation and bamboo shoots. He heard sounds from unseen creatures he had never heard before. He made his way through the dense terrain in the dawning sunlight, doubting as always, his Guide, and smacking at bugs on his skin.

"You've definitely messed things up this time," complained Archippus.

Hodos did not reply.

"Seriously, what kind of a place is this? No one could live in this landscape. There can't possibly be a city near here. And, I haven't seen any reptiles either."

"ROOOAAARRHHGGGAAAHHH" came a sound from a large reptile that suddenly stepped into view shaking the ground in front of them. The creature was enormous and stood upright on two colossal legs. His arms were tiny, but his head was massive with teeth the size of Landlings lining upper and lower jaw. He was greenish-gray in color and saliva dripped from his jaws.

"Aaahhh!" screamed Archippus, wide-eyed and frozen in fear.

Hodos, once again, flew directly at the creature to repel the danger. The reptile, waving his tiny useless arms, snapped at the little bird. Archippus seized the opportunity to run away, shoving aside plant leaves, hopping roots and fallen trunks, and glancing backward on occasion until finally he burst forth into a clearing.

To the left was a mountain of boulders, to the right a huge cliff wall jutted upward, and more importantly, just ahead, a Judgment Hall of the same design as the one in his home city of Ai. Archippus realized he had reached Rephidim, City of Reptiles.

He ran across the clearing to the Judgment Hall steps. He did not care that he was an uninvited Commoner committing a trespass. He hurried upward two steps at a time and ran into the edifice. There was no one inside. The hall was completely vacant.

Archippus began to wonder if over-sized, ill-tempered reptiles had eaten all the inhabitants, when Hodos arrived landing on a hot rock and began to speak.

"I suppose you'll want to thank—"

Grunt.

"You're welcome," said Hodos.

"Where *is* everyone?" Archippus asked. His voice echoed in the empty hall.

"It's daytime," answered Hodos. "Everyone lives underground in Rephidim. The Judgment Hall, quarry, and MSC are the only above ground structures, and the city life takes place at night."

"Why?"

"Because creatures, like your friend back there, are asleep at night."

Archippus heard voices and footsteps. Still shaken from his near-death experience, he dodged behind one of the Judgment Hall thrones.

"Hello!" came an overly cheerful and familiar voice.

Archippus stood up.

Emoticas and Gershom! Emoticas waved.

Archippus slumped. "Were you following me?"

"Yep." The 'p' on 'yep' came out pronounced and echoed twice in the Hall. Emoticas gave his big, toothy grin. "We saw you saved not once, but *twice* by your songbird." He laughed.

Gershom smirked.

Archippus groaned and slumped onto a throne.

"Don't be embarrassed," said Hodos.

"But it *is* embarrassing! You're a tiny, tiny … did I mention *tiny,* little songbird!" snapped Archippus.

"It's only embarrassing if you *allow* it to be," replied Hodos. "You must remember it is not the size of one's stature, but the size of one's intent that makes the difference."

A huge sigh escaped Archippus. He slid deep into the throne, draping a leg on one claw-shaped armrest while placing the back of his head on the other armrest. He stared up at the ceiling. He noticed no roof openings for the hot rocks.

"Why no roof openings?" he asked.

"Because, the trials are held at night. The sun cannot heat the hot rocks for the Airbornes to perch on for warmth during the trials. The rocks are

71

heated from beneath the floor with fires," explained Hodos.

Silence settled over the room.

"So what now?" Archippus finally asked. "That creature can't get in here, can he?" He sat up and eyed the entrance warily.

"You'll need to meet the townspeople and beg to learn a trade," said Hodos.

"But I already know a trade."

"But you need to learn a new one," said Hodos.

"What for?"

"What for?" answered Hodos. "What for he asks me?"

The bird looked in turn at Emoticas and then Gershom, and then turned to Archippus. "To learn something *new*," he said.

"But why learn something new?" asked Archippus.

"You see?" said Hodos to the two onlookers. "You see what I have to put up with? He doesn't want to learn anything new!"

Emoticas and Gershom shook their heads.

"You promised to obey me," insisted Hodos, "and I have now saved your life *twice*. That should count for something."

"I suppose," mumbled Archippus. "But *I* get to pick the new trade."

"No," said Hodos.

"No?"

"No," affirmed Hodos. "*I* will pick your next trade."

"But why? I just agreed to learn something new and now *you* want to pick what it is." Archippus jumped from the throne. "You are downright domineering!" he yelled at the bird perched on the hot rock.

"*I* will pick the trade, because *I* know what *you* need to learn."

"How would *you* know what *I* need to learn?" yelled Archippus.

"I know things," said Hodos, and he flew out the archway of the Judgment Hall into daylight.

"Aaarrrggghhh!" Archippus hollered and pulled at his hair. "You see what I have to put up with?" he demanded from the onlookers, gesturing in the direction of Hodos' departure.

Emoticas laughed. Gershom smirked.

Fearful to go outside during daylight, the three remained in the Judgment Hall.

Archippus announced, "I could get used to this," and draped his legs over the throne arm and reclined.

Emoticas and Gershom busied themselves reading from the Six Sacred Scrolls. Archippus occasionally glanced at them and realized they were having difficulty discerning some of the scrolls for Emoticas was reading aloud and mispronouncing words. All tradesmon learned basic reading skills during the required year at the MSC. The reason a year of schooling was required was that the councils wanted commoners to be able to read. Ignorance of the written word was to be no excuse for not obeying the law.

Each Judgment Hall possessed a set of Six Sacred Scrolls. In times long past, the scrolls were made available for commoners to read. The scrolls were stored on a stone table lined with a golden lip to prevent rolling off. In each Judgment Hall, the table was to the left of the thrones behind a curtain. But as laws became more numerous, the halls became too busy to provide access to commoners.

"This is fantastic," said Emoticas, "having an opportunity to view the scrolls." He reverently read each scroll's title aloud. "The Scroll of History, The Record of High Rulers, The Cautionary Writings, The Affirmations, The Prophetic Words of Ezdra, and The Book of Wisdom."

Emoticas unrolled a portion of The Affirmations. "Hey, Archippus, listen to this, 'A witless man can no more become wise, than a wild donkey's colt can be born a man.'"[3]

"Why are you reading me *that* one?" asked Archippus with suspicion.

"No reason." Emoticas glanced sideways at Gershom who gave a slight smirk with one corner of his mouth.

Gershom carefully unrolled and fervently perused The Prophetic Words of Ezdra.

-← -← -← -←
-← -← -← -←

As the sun was setting, Hodos returned.

"I have a new trade for all three of you!" he announced circling overhead.

"Terrific," responded Emoticas.

"*Terrific,*" mimicked Archippus. "What is our new trade?"

"Come with me," said Hodos.

He flew outside with the others following. Busy citizens moved about as if morning light had just arrived, but instead it was the onset of night. Many pedestrians carried lit torches on poles.

Hodos flitted ahead along a pathway leading up a mountain of light brown boulders. He disappeared for a moment up the pathway and returned with a heavyset, dark-skinned man with thick, long hair, shaggy eyebrows,

73

and a gray beard.

"Allow me to introduce Ezbon-Ishuah," said Hodos. "Your new trade master."

Ezbon-Ishuah walked directly up to each of the boys in turn saying nothing, but squeezed a bicep of each of the young men as if assessing the flesh on a four-legged. He then peered in each eye and ear and even stuck a finger in each mouth to examine the teeth.

"They look healthy enough," said Ezbon-Ishuah to Hodos.

"I told you they were sturdy," replied Hodos, pleased with himself.

"All right," said Ezbon-Ishuah. "I'll put you to work right away. Several moles quit last week, and we're behind on the upkeep." He turned and waddled slowly up the path and the boys followed.

The path wound through a field of enormous torch-lit boulders that cast large shadows one upon another. The boulders were too tall to see over, and the entire 'mountain' was comprised of these large rocks.

"This boulder mountain is known as the Dells," said Ezbon-Ishuah.

They came to a circular dirt clearing nestled among the giant boulders. A fire blazed near a tall, pale-skinned girl with long blonde hair and a single trust-ring about her neck, hammering on iron. She would heat the iron, pound it, return the iron to the fire, and pound some more. Her waist-long hair hung in two braids. Her eyes were dark brown and her nose prominent. She wore a tunic, skirt, and sandals—all of leather. Her arms flexed as she hammered, revealing pronounced biceps.

"That's Raimi," explained Ezbon-Ishuah. "She's second in command. You'll do as she says, or you'll not do well here."

Raimi nodded, but continued to work.

Ezbon-Ishuah walked over to a wall lined with what looked like farm implements. The iron handles cast shadows from the fire onto the rock behind. Ezbon-Ishuah grabbed one item at a time and tossed each in turn toward the new hires.

Archippus caught the handle of the item thrown to him and examined the heavy instrument. The iron handle was as long as he was tall. One end held a flattened square plate the width of his waist.

"Are we to defend the city from reptiles?" he asked Ezbon-Ishuah.

Ezbon-Ishuah let out a laugh that shook his midriff. He halted the laugh abruptly when he realized the question was in earnest. "Nothing *that* glamorous, Mole, although you *will* be assisting reptiles." He chuckled again. "And I will refer to you as 'moles' until you earn a promotion." He turned and strode from the circled clearing. *"If you ever do earn a promotion,"* he muttered.

The boys followed him up the path. Entrances into the mountain were spaced periodically between boulders along the pathway. Ezbon-Ishuah suddenly stopped and faced the trainees.

"Each entrance along the trail," explained Ezbon-Ishuah pointing to his left and right, "is the entrance to an eegwuhnuh lair. You have permission to access the lairs, *but do not go past the iron gate at the top of the trail.*" He tilted his head forward, his bushy brows raised, and he continued. "My commerce is known for *training* eegwuhnuhs to travel the Continent in the most expeditious manner possible, which includes, of course, scaling mountain walls, even if they be completely perpendicular to the ground. Raimi back there, fashions iron bits for the mouths of the reptiles. She is highly skilled and worked her way up from 'mole' to 'metalworker.' This gave her a higher burrow in the underground quarters, an extra denarius a week, and an extra meal a day. She understands your occupation completely, and can answer any questions you may have.

"Although these creatures are four-leggeds, they are considered to be the most elite reptiles on the Continent, save for, of course, the Airbornes. Were it not for the eegwuhnuhs, cross-continent travel would not be possible, as you well know.

"And so the important thing to remember is …" Ezbon-Ishuah paused for dramatic effect with the two fingers on his right hand raised high to garner their attention. *"Never argue with an eegwuhnuh. The eegwuhnuh is always right."*

"Do eegwuhnuhs speak?" asked Emoticas.

"Gracious grave, no. You are an ignorant bunch." He laughed and his midriff shook again. "The eegwuhnuhs do not speak with words, but they will tell you what they want, who they like, who they don't like, and they will let you know if you are caring for their lair in a manner they deem fitting. And if they become unhappy, well, I repeat, *never argue with an eegwuhnuh.*" He widened his eyes for emphasis.

The shovel felt heavy in Archippus' hands. He was not happy about anything he had been instructed about thus far. He was even unhappier as Ezbon-Ishuah led the group into the first lair on the right.

Archippus glanced around the dirt clearing encircled by boulders. The smell was overwhelming. Ahead in the torchlight stood an enormous eegwuhnuh with his leg chained to an iron stake. The reptile was thirty feet long. The eye—Archippus could only see *one* eye as it was set on the side of the head—was as large as an orange and set among circular wrinkles in the reptile's skin. The reptile's eye followed the boys as they entered without necessitating any movement of its head. The lone moving eye gave Archippus an eerie feeling, the creature zeroing in on him no matter where he walked in the lair. The tip of the reptile's very long tale flicked up and down slowly. Up against the boulders, splattered, piled, and heaped, was a mound of eegwuhnuh feces.

"They like to eliminate in the same place each time," explained Ezbon-Ishuah. "But as you can see, the lairs are out of control since the walk-out of my moles last week."

Archippus held his hand over his nose. "Is it always this smelly?"

"You get used to the odor," said Ezbon-Ishuah. "But this is definitely worse than usual.

"Now, the object is to shovel the feces into the cart, haul the cart down the path to the dumping circle, haul the cart back up, and refill it, etcetera. It requires no high level of thinking. Let me and Raimi do the thinking around here. The dumping circle is down the roadway to the right. You won't be able to miss it. You will each be assigned to ten eegwuhnuhs." He pointed at Archippus. "You are Dreadlock Mole, or DM. You will be assigned to the first ten lairs on the right of the path." He pointed at Emoticas. "You are Blue Mole or BM, take the ten on the left."

Archippus supposed this was in reference to Emoticas' eyes.

"And you," Ezbon-Ishuah looked upward at Gershom, "you are tall. You will be TM. Take the remaining lairs at the top of the trail."

"Don't you want to know our real names?" asked Emoticas.

"Not in the least." Ezbon-Ishuah shook his head and chuckled. "Moles," he said under his breath and waddled off.

The three young men looked at each other.

"This is *unacceptable*," said Archippus. "This isn't a *trade!* This is slavery!"

"He-hem." Hodos had apparently landed on a nearby boulder.

Archippus spun toward the bird. "You said I would learn a trade!" he yelled. "There's nothing to *learn* by doing *this! You* shovel eegwuhnuh dung!" He threw the shovel to the ground.

"Meals and living quarters sound good to me," said Emoticas. "I'm going to start on my lairs. Last one done is a smelly fool." He gave a toothy smile and left.

Gershom looked down his nose with disapproval at Archippus.

"What?" demanded Archippus.

Gershom just shook his head and left in the direction of the upper lairs.

"You're a cruel bird ... and I hate you!" said Archippus. "I was better off in prison, at least my trade required some *skill!*"

"Better off in prison, were you?" asked Hodos.

"Yes!"

"Very well then. I have another line for you to scribe. *I was freed,* but *longed foolishly for prison.*"

"I'll not scribe for you, and I'll certainly not do *this!*" yelled Archippus, his arms flailing.

"What part of *obey* are you having trouble with?" asked Hodos.

Raimi strode into the lair. "Why are you yelling? You'll upset the eegwuhnuh."

"Upset the eegwuhnuh?" Archippus repeated in disbelief. "Eegwuhnuhs don't have *feelings. Upset the eegwuhnuh? I'm* the one who should be *upset.* Look at this. There's feces *everywhere!*"

Raimi raised an eyebrow.

"I come from a line of master scribers," Archippus ranted. " My father was a wordsmith, a pleator, and a master scribe. I should be working for nobility. No, I should be *leading* the nobility because I can word-craft laws into finely tuned definitions. I should be *governing,* not shoveling eegwuhnuh dung!"

Raimi frowned and stared.

"What?" asked Archippus.

"You are upsetting the eegwuhnuh," she repeated.

"Who cares?" screamed Archippus.

The eegwuhnuh lashed him in the legs with his tail.

"Oouucchh!" screamed Archippus.

Raimi laughed.

"It's not funny!" he hollered and rubbed his legs. A red welt appeared. Archippus hustled to the far end of the circle pointing at the eegwuhnuh. "That's a *vile* creature!"

"No, this *creature* is Tandy. She's a gentle eegwuhnuh if handled properly." Raimi walked over and petted the eegwuhnuh's neck.

Archippus flattened up against the farthest rock. "You are crazy. I will not do this! What other work is to be had in this city?"

"None," she answered.

"What do you mean, none?" asked Archippus.

"Newcomers are only permitted to work as moles," said Raimi.

"You are saying there is actually a *conspiracy* against *newcomers?*" His

77

voice revealed disbelief. This explained the low number of citizens he had seen.

"Yep," she said.

"Whatever for?"

"Because, no citizen of Rephidim would ever shovel eegwuhnuh dung, but it has to be done. That last group of moles that quit had to leave town. No one would give them work."

Archippus stared at Raimi as she petted the eegwuhnuh. He ran through his options in his head.

"Will she hurt me again?" he mumbled.

"Here, give her a snock leaf." Raimi produced a large leaf from a pouch tied around her waist. She held it out toward Archippus.

Archippus walked slowly forward watching the lizard's eye follow him. He took the leaf and held it in the direction of the eegwuhnuh.

The reptile's tongue shot out and snatched the leaf, leaving a sticky substance on Archippus' hand.

"That's revolting," said Archippus. He rubbed his sticky hand on his tunic. "I'll not feed these things."

Raimi laughed. "You can feed them in a bin. I just wanted you to repair your offense."

Archippus slumped. "I'll work until I have enough coinage to leave." He shuffled over to the shovel, sighed, and tentatively approached the mound of eegwuhnuh dung. He sighed again, coughed, raised his tunic up over his nose, and began to shovel.

Raimi chuckled and left.

↞   ↞   ↞   ↞
↞   ↞   ↞   ↞

By the time Archippus had filled the first cartful of dung, his arms ached. He took hold of the cart's two protruding wooden arms attached to a hollowed out section of log with two wooden wheels, and pulled the cart toward the lair's exit. When he reached the threshold, he could see into the lair on the other side of the pathway. Emoticas was in there humming and scratching the eegwuhnuh's neck. The creature was thumping its left leg on the ground as if enjoying the attention.

Archippus rolled his eyes, sighed, and continued down the path.

He pushed the cart along the trail at the base of the boulders, and sure enough, the dump heap was easy to spot. He tipped the cart, shaking it by the handles to ensure all the contents fell onto the pile.

"Look, Mother, a new mole!" said a small child, pointing. The child's mother shot a superior glance at Archippus and took hold of the child's hand. "They stink," she told her child. "And that's why I want you attend the Mind Sculpting Center, so you'll never have to perform such duties." She pulled him off toward the MSC. The child held his nose, staring over his shoulder until his mother walked him through a white arch with a bell beneath that led into the learning center.

Archippus shook his head and sighed. He stomped back along the trail shoving the cart back to the lair and mumbling resentments at Hodos.

He began to fill the next cart.

"Shovel and heave, shovel and heave, shovel and heave," Hodos narrated while Archippus worked.

"Shut your beak, Bird!"

"I can't, it's part of your training for your quest."

"Shoveling and heaving is part of my training? That's ridiculous! My arms are burning. This is tiring. I ache all over. This is stupid. It's a *pointless, futile, senseless, meaningless, useless, inane, stupid* job!"

"No, I assure you it is not, Mr. Seven-Words. There are no small acts when in training. This lesson will become valuable to you at a later date."

"No, it won't!"

"Yes, it will."

"No!"

"Yes."

"This is meaningless!"

"On the contrary," countered Hodos. "Everything has meaning, or nothing has meaning. You can't have some things having meaning and others not, if you get my meaning."

"Why are you always talking like that? What you just said makes no sense. It means nothing to me!"

"Sure it does. Like shoveling, for instance. Shoveling has meaning if only you can see it. It will serve a purpose toward the final millennia, so do it well."

"That's ridiculous. This is a bunch of … *crap!*"

"That is such an unbecoming word. Better to call it *feces, manure, waste, dung, droppings, fertilizer, or poop.*"

Archippus heaved a shovel full of *poop* at Hodos.

The bird flitted upward and fluttered downward landing completely unscathed.

"I *hate* you, Bird," shouted Archippus.

The eegwuhnuh lashed at Archippus' legs. "Oouucchh!"

79

"I know you hate me," said Hodos. "But it's good for you." He spread his wings and flew away.

Archippus spent the remainder of the night cleaning two stalls.

Before first light, Raimi summoned the three of them, advising it was time to eat. They followed her back to the circular clearing with the campfire and were handed fresh roasted meat on a stick. They sat in a circle around the fire and ate. Despite Archippus' skepticism, the meat was delicious after the hard night's labor.

"So how do you train them?" asked Emoticas, nodding in the direction of the lairs.

"To teach them to rein is not so difficult. That can be done on flat ground. Teaching them to cliff train is another matter. The gunners practice on the low portion of the quarry cliff, and when the full moon appears, there is a competition. Two eegwuhnuhs race at a time. Whoever reaches the top first wins of course, and a lot of coinage is gained or lost on the betting."

Archippus looked up at the mention of 'coinage.'

"Who trains them?" asked Emoticas.

"I train them to rein," answered Raimi. "I fashion the bits and teach them to accept iron in their mouths. A handful of gunners then cliff train them. This requires strength and daring."

"Do the gunners race them?" Emoticas prodded.

"Sometimes," explained Raimi. "If the eegwuhnuh is well trained, a gunner will ride one up the higher portions of the cliff. Otherwise, they force slaves to do it because an untrained eegwuhnuh will try to rid itself of the rider. Climbing is not natural for them. They tire and become upset—"

"There you go again insisting they become 'upset.' They're just four-leggeds reacting on instinct. They don't have feelings," interrupted Archippus.

"Quiet Archippus," said Emoticas, "I want to hear what she has to say."

"Better to have her explain the betting," said Archippus. "That's at least useful information."

"I'm sure she'll explain everything if you let her," countered Emoticas. "Please," he said to Raimi, "continue."

Raimi shot an unhappy glance at Archippus. "So, when they become *upset*," she glared at him again, "they lower their backs and forearms and then shove rapidly upward with their hind legs. This often unseats the slave who, depending on how far up the cliff he is, and if the safety strap doesn't hold, has been known to unseat the slave. The fall often kills him."

Raimi received three sets of wide-eyed stares. Emoticas swallowed his mouthful of food with difficulty.

Silence fell upon them for a moment.

"Where are these slaves?" asked Emoticas.

"On the plain, south of the Dells. The slaves take care of the eegwuhnuh stockyard. You are caring for eegwuhnuhs in training, but over on the plain there are some seventy-five eegwuhnuhs. There are other trainers on the south side of the Dells and also breeders. The breeders raise them until they are old enough to train and then we buy them to bring to our camp for training. There is a shortage of slaves, however. It was good that you came along to help with the lairs." Raimi paused. "So, why doesn't TM speak?"

"He's taken an oath of silence until the Airborne Monarch takes the throne bringing justice to the oppressed," explained Emoticas.

"That's a noble cause for the Continent," said Raimi.

"No, it's not!" exclaimed Archippus. "How could one person swearing to be silent possibly benefit the Continent?"

"I can see an exception in *your* case," said Raimi.

"Very humorous. You are wrought with humor," responded Archippus. "I'll tell you what a noble cause is—no—I'll tell you *two* noble causes. The first would be to earn enough coinage to leave this city, and the second, for you to show us to our quarters so we can be rid of you for the evening."

"You mean for the morning," countered Raimi.

"Whatever you want to call it in this backward city that lives at night," said Archippus.

The light began to crest the horizon.

"I should stake you to a clearing and let the flesh eating reptiles have their way with you," said Raimi.

Archippus glared. "You *are* a gracious hostess."

"Tomorrow we will all get along better," Emoticas interjected. "You'll see, Raimi, he's really congenial after a good night's, I mean, day's rest."

"I can't imagine enough rest in the whole world to make him congenial," mumbled Raimi. She tossed an unfinished meat stick into the fire and stood. "Come this way."

As Raimi led them, Emoticas elbowed Archippus sharply in the side and whispered harshly. "You had better be nice to her. What if they decide to make us cliff race the eegwuhnuhs? We're newcomers here, we have no rights. Don't you remember the verdict in your birth city? If you couldn't

81

get a fair council there, what makes you think we have any rights here? You better get your wits about you." Emoticas stomped on ahead.

The trio followed Raimi to an opening in the ground on the east side of the boulders. The large round hole was approximately fifty feet across. The top of a wooden ladder protruded from the lip of the hole.

"This is The Pit," said Raimi. She stepped onto the top rung and began to climb down. The three moles followed.

They climbed downward to an earthen landing. A circular stairway carved into the clay walls spiraled down into darkness, though the stairs were well lit by torchlight. Here and there along the circular stairway were landings. At each landing, a *burrow* marked by an archway, entered the dirt wall. Archippus saw citizens walking up and down the stairs and sitting on landings visiting and going in and out of burrows.

They started down the stairway. Archippus felt weak at the knees. There was no railing along the edge of the stairs. He imagined it was a long drop to the pitch-black bottom. He ran his left hand along the clay wall for comfort as they descended.

"It's not safe to live above ground in the daylight," said Raimi. "And so the Rephidites sleep beneath the ground. We work, play, have our councils, quarry meetings, and cliff races all above ground at night, but sleep during the day in burrows. You will be assigned a burrow for sleeping." She continued to descend.

"So that's why he calls us moles?" asked Emoticas. "Because we sleep underground?"

Raimi laughed. "No. Then everyone would be a mole. You are moles because moles dig in darkness, and you shovel at night."

"Why don't they make slaves do our jobs?" demanded Archippus.

"I can make you a slave if you like," said Raimi.

"No, seriously, it's a repulsive job. Aren't there enough slaves?"

"Despite what you may think," said Raimi, "working with the eegwuhnuhs in training is an honor for a newcomer. Slaves are not fit for the position."

"How can you speak like that?" demanded Archippus at her back. "You defend four-leggeds and speak as if *lizards* are better than Pangeans."

Raimi stopped on the stairway and turned to look up at him. "*Some* lizards are better than *some* Pangeans." She glared.

"Let's not forget how nice he'll be tomorrow," muttered Emoticas through a strained smile.

Raimi shook her head and continued downward in silence.

Archippus peered into an occasional burrow. Most citizens had already retired onto leaf-stuffed feed sacks. Some snored, some tossed and turned, and some were sitting and visiting with burrow mates. The farther they descended, the stuffier the air became.

Finally, Raimi halted on a landing in front of a small burrow with two stuffed feed sacks. She pointed.

"TM and BM," she said.

"Thank you," said Emoticas, and he stepped into the burrow.

Gershom nodded at her and ducked in as well.

"Where am I to sleep?" Archippus tried to hide the concern in his voice.

"We aren't to your burrow yet," said Raimi.

He followed her down three more descending circles in The Pit wall. As they went down, they passed empty burrows.

"What's wrong with the burrows we're passing?" he asked her.

"Nothing," she said. "They are simply not yours." She removed a torch from the wall since no additional torches could be seen below, and still she descended. Finally, they came to the end of the stairs and the final burrow.

"Here you go," said Raimi.

Archippus stepped into the burrow. It was dank and musty and contained no mattress. Raimi stuck the torch in an iron ring mounted on the wall outside the burrow.

"Where's the bedding?" asked Archippus.

"You'll have to make or purchase a bed," said Raimi.

Archippus stood on the landing and slumped. Although the stairway had ended, The Pit had not. He peered over the lip of the landing. The sun was higher in the sky and daylight was beginning to filter downward. Still, the bottom of The Pit disappeared in blackness. This gave him an uneasy feeling. He hoped nothing lurked in the shadow of The Pit.

"How far down does it go?" he asked.

"No one knows. We have tossed objects down and no echo is ever heard. That's why it's called The Echoless Pit."

Archippus picked up a stone and tossed it into the precipice. No sound came up. He shuddered.

Raimi started the climb back to the top.

Having been up an entire day and night, Archippus was exhausted. He curled himself in a ball on the dirt floor of his burrow. It reminded him of prison. He didn't understand why Raimi disliked him so much. She had been much nicer to Gershom and Emoticas. He felt lonely. *I've been freed to live like this? Curse the bird wherever he may be.*

✦   ✦   ✦   ✦
✦   ✦   ✦   ✦

Archippus awoke to Bird's voice.

"Good evening," said Hodos. "Sounds funny to wake to 'good evening,' doesn't it?"

"Nothing you say ever sounds funny," mumbled Archippus, rubbing his eyes, "only annoying," he finished.

Oddly, he was glad to have company in his lonely, dank burrow suspended above The Echoless Pit—even if it was Hodos.

"I see you received the most personal of quarters. No noise to bother you here. You should get plenty of rest, that was very nice of her," said Hodos.

"I'm down here because nobody likes me," said Archippus sadly. "She didn't even give me a bed."

"I must ask you," said Hodos, "whose fault do you think that is?"

"Fault?" Archippus squinted at the bird. "I think she's simply mean spirited, and Emoticas and Gershom don't help any. They take her side continually."

"So, nobody likes you?"

"Nobody here."

"Has *anybody* ever liked you?"

"Of course!" snapped Archippus.

"Well, it can't always be everybody else's fault. Everybody else cannot always be wrong."

"Are you saying I'm unlikable?"

"*You* said it."

"But *you* implied it!"

"If you continue to blame everybody else, you are powerless," said Hodos. "But let's leave off bickering and have a better evening than last. What do you say?"

Archippus moaned and slumped.

"Come on, your friends have already headed to work."

"They're not my friends," mumbled Archippus.

"All right. Your enemies, who are forced to endure your company, have headed to work. Shall we go?"

"I suppose," mumbled Archippus. "But, Bird ..." Archippus paused because what he was about to say was very difficult for him.

"Yes?" asked Hodos.

"I don't know how to be likeable."

A pause hung in the air.

"Well …" said Hodos. "You could *try* thinking of yourself less often."

Archippus was quiet for a moment. "I suppose." He sighed, slumped, and began to hike up the stairs.

Archippus' calves began to ache as he climbed. "This is ridiculous. They should have dug several shallow pits with burrow holes instead of one gigantic and impossibly deep pit. I'll be ready to call it an evening by the time we reach the top!"

"But you see, *that* is part of your problem," said Hodos circling above Archippus' head. "I thought you had learned something in prison or I would not have freed you."

"*Aro* freed me!" retorted Archippus.

Hodos continued. "Don't look at a stair and see only a stair. Have some creativity about you."

"What do you mean? All I see is an endless number of steps above me in an ill-conceived pit!"

"You could learn from the world around you if you would but listen."

"I am listening!"

"No. You are not."

"Yes, I am! And all I hear is thud after thud of my aching feet falling on stair after stair!"

"I suppose that is what *you* would hear."

"Tell me then! What am I suppose to hear?"

"No. You tell me. The world speaks to us in parables if you would but listen, so tell me what you think you could possibly learn from this spiral stairway."

"Aaarrrggghhh!" screamed Archippus. "I hate you!"

"I know you hate me," answered Hodos, "and it's good for you." With that, the bird flew on up the staircase.

Archippus climbed and grumbled. He passed many people in burrows readying themselves for the evening. The closer he got to the top, the more people he saw doing the very same thing as he, climbing the stairs. The citizens would look at him, but no one said anything, and no one passed another for fear of falling into The Echoless Pit. This meant that if he got behind a slow climber, he would have to climb slowly, or if a fast climber were behind him, he was compelled to go faster. He thought to shove one unpleasant speeder huffing at his back into the pit, but thought better of it.

He reached the top and waited in line until he was finally able to climb the ladder and step onto open ground.

"So," said Hodos, perched on a nearby boulder. "Did you learn anything?"

"Yes," snapped Archippus. He placed his hands on his knees and leaned down, exhausted from the climb. "I learned that when you are at the *very* bottom it is a *very* long way to the top."

"Ho, ho!" exclaimed Hodos with excitement. "That is good! Profound really. There are no wrong answers, but I like that one very much. Let's see if you can learn something each day!"

Archippus squinted at him. He had meant his comment as a rude remark, but it pleased him to receive a compliment.

Archippus noticed three recently pitched tents in the clearing. Two of the tents had nobility standing in line. He knew them to be nobility from the neck rings as well as they were predominately dark of skin with an occasional pale female. The lines for the nobility were much shorter than the line for the commoners, since two tents served morning meals to nobility and only one tent served commoners. Archippus surmised that between the number of people in the pit and the number of people in line, only a few hundred citizens lived in Rephidim—a fact that did not surprise him given that everyone was forced to be awake at night.

He continued to view the torch-lit lines of meal patrons. An occasional first-born of nobility had their Airbornes with them, perched on a shoulder, or on a leather wrapped forearm. The Airbornes were all of similar physique: blackish-gray with narrow, elongated skulls that projected upward as far as their beaks jutted forward. They had sharp teeth, and wings that spanned from several inches up to a couple feet. Only a handful of the pterodactyls were rumored to have reached a size suitable for ridership. Archippus had never seen one of these larger Airbornes, but if they existed, he would give anything to ride one.

As he passed the back of the lines, he stared at a black Airborne with bright red eyes, perched on a noblemon's shoulder. He thought it a mockery that Hodos claimed to be an Airborne; even this smaller Airborne with not more than a two-foot wingspan looked incredibly fierce compared to Hodos.

The Airborne noticed Archippus' gaze. "What's on your shoulder, and what are you staring at?" asked the reptile with an ill-tempered tone.

Archippus shrugged defensively. "Nothing." He would have been embarrassed to claim Hodos was an Airborne. "I'm just looking for my co-workers."

"The new moles are over there," said the Airborne. He narrowed his eyes at Hodos.

Hodos chirped a few incoherent notes like an ordinary songbird.

Archippus spotted Emoticas, Gershom, and Raimi standing in the Commoner's line. They motioned him to come and stand with them. He cut in front of other Landlings who cast him disgruntled looks.

"He'll be late for mole work," explained Raimi to those nearby.

The unhappy commoners appeared to accept this, but took a couple steps back to distance themselves from Archippus.

"They act like I have a plague," muttered Archippus.

"No. You just smell." Raimi laughed.

Archippus sniffed himself. He did smell.

"Don't worry," said Emoticas. "We smell too, but Raimi says we need to finish early, bathe, and go to the quarry. The crier will be making announcements before dawn."

They reached the front of the line, Raimi paid coinage, and each was given a peeled banana on a stick drizzled with honey and an opportunity to fill their water flasks from clay jugs. Archippus surmised the honey to be from his home city of Ai.

The banana was delicious. Archippus had not had honey for a long, long while. The treat reminded him of how much he missed Ai, his sister, his mother, and especially the noble girl. He wondered if he would ever see the green-eyed girl or his sister again. And he wondered for the hundredth time if Hodos had lied about his mother. But the sinking feeling in his gut told him Hodos had not lied. He hated the bird, but for some reason believed him.

As they walked to the Dells, Raimi hung back to walk with Archippus.

"Your friends told me what happened to you, how you tried to get food for your sister but received a life sentence, and lost your mother."

Archippus walked on and said nothing.

"I'm sorry for you," said Raimi. "Let's try to get along better this evening, yes?"

Archippus nodded.

"Besides, the better your mood, the nicer the eegwuhnuhs will be to you."

Archippus nodded again.

"Why does the bird follow you everywhere, and why does it speak?"

Archippus shook his head. "I was in prison, and he arrived on my thirteenth birthday saying he was my Counselor."

87

"But Counselors—"

"I know. I don't understand. I'm not nobility, and I know songbirds are not supposed to speak. I don't know why he follows me. He sent a raven with a key to free me on the condition I have to obey him or I'll have to return to prison."

"That is the oddest thing I have ever heard. Are you going to obey him? Do you think they'll search for you, to return you to prison?"

Archippus shook his head again. "I don't know the answer to either question."

"I think I'd obey him," said Raimi. "He did free you and he seems wise. There must be a reason he accompanies you."

"He says I have a quest, but he won't tell me what it is. And you don't know him very well. He may be wise, but he's very harsh. Most of the time I hate him."

"Well, you can't fashion iron with feathers."

Archippus thought it an odd statement, but nodded and shrugged.

Archippus arrived at lair number three just in time to see Ezbon-Ishuah heading up the trail toward the gate. He thought it odd the burly man did not acknowledge him, but kept focused on his plan to complete two new lairs a day until all lairs were current and cleaned every day. As he worked, he thought about how this had been the nicest 'morning' he'd had since he could remember. He received a compliment from Bird, ate a delicious breakfast, and was treated with kindly conversation from Raimi. But as he shoveled and heaved, his arms became sore, and the nice 'morning' seemed a long time ago.

Eegwuhnuh poop was disgusting. No wonder he smelled after a day of such work. The feces were composed of two parts. The center part was a solid mass ranging from dark brown to black and for the most part held an oval shape. But around each center were clear liquid drippings that were sometimes more watery than others, but always gooey nonetheless. Archippus became lightheaded from trying not to breathe as he shoveled.

"Shovel and heave," announced Hodos as he lighted on a boulder.

Archippus spun toward him. "You find this amusing, don't you? You know I have a trade whereby I could assist nobility. Why did you bring me here? Is this the quest you called me to—the most disgusting work on the Continent? I was born to lead!"

"How can you lead if you cannot serve? You will remember this shoveling and heaving one day, and it will be just before you find your quest," answered Hodos.

"But what is my quest?" demanded Archippus.

"I will tell you when you are ready."

Archippus shoveled and then heaved the poop at Hodos, who again flitted upward and fluttered downward landing absolutely un-smudged.

"I'm not going to listen to you!" screamed Archippus. "I'm going to earn enough coinage to travel back to Ai. I'll find my sister and marry the noble girl. You'll see!"

"Your sister is not in the seventh city," said Hodos.

"How do you know *that?*"

"I know things."

Archippus tossed another shovel of poop at the bird and Hodos flew off.

Archippus had successfully worked himself into a silent sullenness, which continued even after Raimi summoned them to an early supper.

"I heard you hollering about a noble girl you are to marry," said Raimi as they sat around the fire eating meat.

Archippus said nothing and stared at the fire.

Raimi spoke again. "I won't marry until I see four-leggeds are protected from abuses."

Archippus shifted his eyes to look at her, but kept his head facing the fire.

"It's true," she said. "I bound it on my heart throne." She pulled a small leather pouch from beneath her tunic. The pouch hung around her neck on a leather strap. She opened the pouch and produced a tiny scroll, unrolled it and read, "...'to improve the fate of the four-leggeds.' The four-leggeds know how to seek shelter, food, and community, and they value life in that they flee danger. These truths make them akin to us and worthy of rights."

She smiled, re-rolled the tiny scroll, stuck it in the pouch, and tucked it back in her tunic. "That's my quest, like you were telling me of your bird having a quest for you."

"He's not my bird. He's my tormentor," said Archippus.

"I see your attitude has taken a turn for the worse," said Raimi.

"Where can I get one of those?" asked Emoticas, pointing to the tiny pouch scroll.

"They sell them at the tent square. They're the latest fashion," said Raimi. "They'll scribe on it whatever you like, but it should be what is most important to you, whatever reigns on your heart throne as your heart's desire. If you think on it each day, you will get your heart's desire."

"We should all get one!" said Emoticas. "If wearing the pouch and thinking the thought means we can achieve what we most desire, who *wouldn't* want to have a pouch scroll!" He was silent for a moment and then continued. "I can't wait to receive my coinage. Gershom and I decided that we first need to buy musical instruments to relax by and learn something in our burrow, but I must have one of these pouch scrolls." He pondered a moment, and then muttered to himself. "I don't know which one to purchase first, instruments or a pouch scroll."

"Gershom," said Raimi, "if you get a pouch scroll, you could have them write something like, *Silent until the Airborne Monarch reigns.*"

Gershom nodded and gave her a half-smile as if considering the suggestion.

They finished their meat and then followed Raimi down the road past the dump.

She addressed the boys over her shoulder. "I assume in your city you could not use the bath in the Judgment Hall." She said this as more of a statement than a question. "As commoners, neither can we use the bath in the hall." She pointed at a pond that glimmered under the light of the half-full moon.

The three boys grinned, eyed each other, and ran for the water. Their momentum carried them on into the chilly pond. They continued to run until they were waist deep, then dove and reemerged gasping from the cold.

The moonlight reflected on the ripples. In the distance, a small Airborne scooped something from the water and flew off. *Probably got a fish,* thought Archippus. The night sky was filled with the candle vigil.

Raimi laid three garments on the bank. "The last moles left them. They've been cleaned," she said, turning to leave. "Meet me in the tent square on the way to the quarry."

Emoticas tried to dunk Gershom. Archippus joined in to help, but Gershom held both their heads under for several seconds and then leapt from the pond.

Archippus was surprised by Gershom's strength and unhappily waded after him to the bank.

"That Gershom is part Cyclops," yelled Emoticas, rinsing his hair a final time and wading from the water. All three boys pulled on the clean, sleeveless tunics that dropped to the tops of the knees and laced partway down from their neck to their mid-torso. They spread their old garments on a boulder to dry, and then headed off toward the tent square located between the Judgment Hall and the quarry.

Raimi waved them over. Many citizens were going about the business of buying, selling, and trading goods such as pottery, candles, games, dried fruits, incense, honey, bells, musical instruments, and paintings, displayed on stands or little easels called l'easels. All of the tents were of similar design: square with a tall post in the middle of a draped roof. Door fabrics pulled back in the front of each tent displayed the merchant's goods on colorful rugs. Raimi pointed out the 'pouch scroll' tent then they continued through the square toward the quarry along with the other citizens.

Over a hundred torches lining the curved stone steps that faced the stage and the cliff lighted quarry. A fire on each end lighted the stage, and the front was lined with candles.

As was customary, the quarry faced something significant for the city. Archippus thought back to his home quarry that faced the woods. Ai was known for its large tiny-needled trees. The trees were celebrated as the Scented Trees of Ai for making aromatic incense. Ai was also known for producing honey from hives that hung in the famous trees. Here in Rephidim, the half circle of seats faced a cliff wall of a tall single mountain that towered over the surrounding humid terrain. In the half-moon, it was difficult to see to the top of the enormous peak. Archippus strained to see how high the mountain was and thought how horrible it would be to have to trust an eegwuhnuh to make it to the top.

The first fifteen rows of the semicircle seating was reserved for nobility, the middle seating area for tradesmon, and the top rows for commoners and slaves. The foursome climbed the side stairs to the top section, and side stepped past the jutting knees of other commoners to reach the center of the thirty-fifth row. Archippus craned his head to look behind him. The top row, which was the fortieth, held twenty pale-skinned males all seated approximately one foot apart, and dressed in tunics identical to his. A gunner stood at either end of the row.

Archippus nudged Raimi and jerked his head back toward the males. "Who are they?"

"Those are the slaves from the flat plain. They're chained together at the ankles."

"You gave us slave tunics to wear?" Archippus whispered indignantly. "What if we are mistaken for slaves?"

"This city is sparsely populated. Everyone knows you three are the new moles, and besides, you stunk. So you're welcome."

Ezbon-Ishuah arrived. He forced his rotund body past their knees with a nod and a "TM, BM, DM," and sat next to Raimi, which surprised Archippus, for Ezbon-Ishuah was a tradesmon and could have sat closer to the stage.

"I hope there's good news tonight," said Ezbon-Ishuah.

"There is usually something good," replied Raimi.

"Humph," was Ezbon-Ishuah's response.

The town crier took the stage. He was wearing a long brown robe tied with a golden belt from which hung bells the size of a handbreadth. The crier rang the bells now as a demand for silence and attention, and then reached for a cone-shaped voice enhancer known as a *megafone*, and pointed the wide end of the cylindrical horn toward the audience. An assistant unrolled a scroll and held it for him to read. The crier began.

"In this seventh month of our ten month agricultural year, this quarterly writ number DLVI, delivered by Airborne directly to Rephidim's Council of Twelve from Hieropolis, the city of the High Ruler of the Iron Hall, as drafted by the Council of Twenty-four, hereby states:

"Due to the Barbirian ambush of several eegwuhnuh transports containing the ten percent tithes en route to be delivered to the High Ruler during the biannual Feast of Adoration, and as a result of the loss of life and cargo, the Council of Twenty-four is prohibiting delivery of the biannual tithes via passage through the middle mountains. The tithes must be brought via the High Ruler's Way, or High-Way, which passes through the six cities at the outskirts of the middle mountain ranges. This High-Way will now be provided with periodic guard stations to assist in the protection of life and cargo.

"The Council of Twenty-four has also voted to approve an increase in law-ers to enforce the law of ten percent tithing. Whereas in the past, each city had a ratio of one law-er per hundred citizens, the council will now appoint one law-er per fifty citizens. These enforcers will have more time to monitor business and income and will therefore more accurately ensure that ten percent of all goods and earnings are transported to Hieropolis for the good of our government, the proper training of gunners, and the appropriate administration of the Continent.

"If at any point, you believe that a law-er has incorrectly calculated your tithes, all nobles and tradesmon have been granted the right to hire an independent law-er to act as a pleator to present your case to the local Council of Twelve."

"So far, nothing good," whispered Ezbon-Ishuah. "I hate law-ers."

The crier continued.

"You are to be made aware that all coinage that is tithed will go through a meltdown process and be re-minted to remove the outdated figure of the Sera—oops—excuse me—I mean *inscription* until all coinage eventually circulates and comes to bare the image of the Six Scrolls on one side, and the scepter on the other."

The crier stopped to take a sip of water from a goblet on a nearby stool and then resumed.

"The nature observationists have informed the Council of Twenty-four that ice has been discovered progressing toward the warm water regions outside the Citadel by the Sea, which is causing concern that the Continent may be cooling. This could have a negative effect on our snock crops and thereby harm our economy. As a result, the Council of Twenty-four is offering funding for snock commerce in order to increase our reserves for food to fuel our eegwuhnuhs. Anyone interested in obtaining special funds to go into the snock crop industry should get with a pleator and put forth a formal request before your Council of Twelve. Keep in mind you will have to convince the council that you can run the business successfully to produce not only the leaves for fuel, but the liquid snock from the plant's fruit, which is a potent medicine when prescribed by apothecaries—as opposed to your local tavern owner."

Chuckles came from the audience, especially the rowdy row drinking jiggers of snock.

"In addition, there is a reported increase in Barbirian ambushes across the Continent. It is therefore mandated that the age for gunner training be reduced from fifteen years of age to thirteen. This will immediately increase the number of trained fighters in each city, should defense of the city become necessary.

"It has also been reported that the Barbirians are working toward the development of their own Fire Propulsion System. This must be prevented at all cost, because the FPS is the deadliest weapon on the Continent. Anyone having knowledge of consultations with engineers or suspicious conduct relating toward development of such a weapon, must immediately report it to their respective councils, who in turn, will immediately send an Airborne to notify the Council of Twenty-four.

"It has been reported that Barbirians are living among us. They purport themselves as having come from neighboring cities, but are infiltrates and spies. Be on your guard against all outsiders, and again, report any suspicious conduct to your council members immediately."

Archippus couldn't help but notice that both Raimi and Ezbon-Ishuah glanced sideways at him.

"I'm not a Barbirian," he said defensively, meaning to whisper, but the whisper came out so loud that several heads turned to look at him.

93

Archippus rolled his eyes and shook his head.

"Oh yes," added the crier, "the Barbirians tend to be of pale skin and male gender. This is because they have been recruiting runaway slaves, the despots of our society, who having nowhere else to go for a sense of community and purpose, and are defecting to the Fervian interpretations of The Teachings."

Raimi and Ezbon-Ishuah glanced at Archippus again.

"Emoticas!" whispered Archippus again. "Tell them I'm not a Barbirian. You and Gershom could just as easily be Barbirians. Well, except for *he* is dark of skin. Tell them!"

"How do I know you were really in prison for stealing?" asked Emoticas.

"I hate you all!" Archippus stood up to leave.

"Wait," said Raimi. "I believe you."

"You do?" Archippus couldn't help but sound incredulous.

"Yes."

"Why do you believe him?" asked Ezbon-Ishuah.

"Because a Barbirian spy would want to blend in. This would force him to act agreeable even if he were not. Archippus is so ill-tempered he is not only immediately noticed, but immediately disliked," explained Raimi.

"Thank you!" said Archippus as if vindicated. "Thank you for sticking up for me since Emoticas and Gershom will not!"

Emoticas lifted his shoulders, widened his eyes below raised brows, and pulled his mouth sideways as if to insist, *How would I know Archippus' true origins?*

Gershom turned his head away to stay out of the matter.

Archippus continued. "So you see, *Emoticas* is more likely to be a Barbirian than I am." He flailed his hand at Emoticas. "Because everybody—"

"This concludes …" announced the crier.

"—likes him," finished Archippus.

"… the quarterly announcements," said the town crier. The audience stood and began to leave.

"No," said Raimi.

"No?" asked Archippus.

"No, Emoticas isn't a Barbirian either."

"Why not?"

"Because he knows a trade. He must be a tradesmon for he told me he is a tailor. And the crier said they are recruiting slaves, not tradesmon."

"But *I* know a trade!" insisted Archippus.

"What trade?" demanded Ezbon-Ishuah.

"He claims his father was a master scriber," said Raimi.

"No, I mean yes, but *I'm* also a scribe. I've been trained as a scribe and a wordsmith and could easily be a pleator if given the chance!"

"Prove you are a scribe then," interjected Ezbon-Ishuah. "I'll not have any Barbirians working for me."

"Fine," said Archippus. "I have a scroll in my burrow that the bird is forcing me to scribe. I'll show you. But I don't have a pen and ink."

"I'll procure the tools for you," said Ezbon-Ishuah. "We'll pick them up on our way back through the tent square. If you cannot scribe as you claim, there'll be no need for you to report to work tomorrow."

"What about Emoticas? Aren't you going to make him prove his trade?"

"*I'm* not worried about BM," said Ezbon-Ishuah.

"Why not?" Archippus whined.

"Because *he* is not *defensive*. Only those with something to hide have reason to be defensive."

"Fine," snapped Archippus. "I'll see you at my burrow." He stomped off ahead of the rest of them.

After much grumbling while descending stair after stair, Archippus arrived at his burrow. The sun had begun to rise, and this provided him enough light down through the gigantic hole to find his way, but the torch had gone out. He sat on the landing out front of his burrow. A small object barreled its way practically straight downward from the opening above. The darting entity pulled upward abruptly, flitted toward him, and perched on the landing.

"So. How was your day?" asked Hodos.

"Horrible," said Archippus.

"What makes you think it was horrible?"

"Everybody hates me."

"But that is how your day began. Did you do nothing to change it?" asked the bird.

"I was fine today. I thought of myself less. I held my tongue at evening meal, but they all sided against me. They want me to prove my trade to show I am not a Barbirian, and Emoticas does not have to prove anything because they already trust him. And Gershom does not have to prove anything either because of his dark skin. I am the most cursed of Pangeans. I'm either going to be mistaken as a slave or a Barbirian throughout the course of my life.

95

"I've lost everything dear to me, and you told me earlier that my sister is not in Ai. Well, if you know so much, tell me, where is she then?"

Hodos gave a long sigh. He looked up sideways at Archippus. "Your sister is the High Ruler of the Iron Hall."

"And *I'm* Lord Ipthsum!" exclaimed Archippus. "You know what? There's no sense talking to you! You are a cruel bird. Go counsel Emoticas." He turned his back to the bird, got up, and went into his burrow.

"All right then," called Hodos. "You will know where your sister is when you are ready."

Archippus said nothing. He thought about grabbing the bird and tossing him down the pit. But he would have to tie his wings first. He could use the string from his tunic ....

Archippus heard footsteps and turned around. The disbelievers entered the burrow with Hodos flitting above them. Raimi carried a torch followed by Ezbon-Ishuah, Gershom, and Emoticas. Ezbon-Ishuah handed Archippus a wooden pen with a metal tip and a clay container of ink with a grooved lip shut by a stopper. For a second, Archippus forgot the purpose behind the visit. He stared at the gifts feeling for a brief moment, touched. He had never possessed his own pen and ink in his life—always someone else's. But then he remembered he was to be tested. Gershom and Emoticas must have never noticed he was a scribe while in prison. After all, they were forbidden to glance. He grabbed up the scroll and unrolled it.

"Bird," he demanded flatly. "What was it you said I am to scribe next?"

Hodos landed on Gershom's shoulder and cleared his throat. "I believe it was, I *was freed, but longed foolishly for prison.*"

"I'm not going to scribe that, that's ridiculous! I don't long to go back to prison!"

"I told you he's not a scribe," said Ezbon-Ishuah to Raimi.

"No, I'll scribe *something,* just not that!"

"You are supposed to obey me," said Hodos.

"But I don't 'long foolishly for prison!'"

"It is not a physical prison that I speak of," said Hodos. "You always concern yourself with the physical. But the unseen is more real than the seen."

The group surrounding Archippus nodded.

Archippus rolled his eyes. "Fine, I'll write your nonsense. It has meaning to the fools around me."

Hodos flew out of the burrow and circled over the hole.

Archippus opened the inkwell. He flattened the scroll, kneeled on the bottom, and held the top flat against the dirt with his left hand. Raimi lifted the torch. Archippus dipped his pen in the ink and scribed in perfect calligraphy with no hesitation and beautiful strokes, **I was freed, but longed foolishly for prison.**

"That's amazing!" cried Ezbon-Ishuah. "Not only can you come to work tomorrow, but ... I wonder ... can you teach me to scribe?"

Archippus placed a rock on each end of the scroll to allow it to dry. He eyed the prime accuser. "I suppose, but you won't be proficient at it. It takes years of learning. It's not just the style, but the proper use and order of letters, which is called spelling."

Ezbon-Ishuah nodded. "Yes, I understand. I learned to read as do all of us during the required year at the MSC, but I still want to learn how to scribe." He turned toward the others. "Leave us be, will you please?" He motioned at them to be gone. "Leave the torch though, Raimi." She handed him the torch and the three of them walked out of the burrow.

"I will teach you," said Archippus. "But first, tell me, what is it that takes place beyond the gate at the top of the trail past the lairs?"

"Oh," said Ezbon-Ishuah. "It is not meant to be a secret. It's simply for the privacy and protection of the Airbornes."

"There are Airbornes up there?"

"Oh yes. They fly in from all across the Continent."

"For what reason?"

"To be cared for."

"But the Airbornes are the most intelligent life forms on the Continent. Why would they need to seek care from Landlings?"

"Well. I cannot explain it without breaking the law by mentioning the *High Serap—*"

"You believe there's a Seraph?"

"Most definitely. The High Seraph, as you may have heard, resides at the top of the Scrimshaw Tower in the coldest of climates on the upper most Frozen Peninsula. He has never been visited on foot. Many Landlings have tried and many failed. The leviathan that swims the waters surrounding the Trail of Tears, a narrow landmass leading from the Continent to the upper most Frozen Peninsula, killed all who tried to reach the High Seraph. They say there are sections of the trail where it becomes so narrow, that only stones can be stepped on to cross the ocean, and many Landlings have been swept from the rocks by water or the leviathan's tail." Ezbon-Ishuah gave a demonstrative swoop with one arm.

"Then, it has been rumored that the one or two Landlings in history that by some miracle traversed the trail, either froze in the cold or were burned by the red snow from Cauldron Crater, a volcano that spews scorching lava. In fact, it is doubtful that even if one were to make it to the base of the Scrimshaw Tower that one could ever actually climb it. It is rumored to be a millia passuum or one mile high."

"But then who built the tower, and what does it have to do with caring for the Airbornes?" asked Archippus.

"Ah, that is a very good question," said Ezbon-Ishuah. "The tower was erected from the bones of the leviathan's mate. No one knows how or why the gigantic sea creature died, but I'm certain it is the reason for his being so cross as to seek to kill any passersby. But to answer your first question, the only beings that could have possibly erected the tower in those temperatures at that height would be gargoyles. It couldn't have been Airbornes, for the skill to build the tower necessitated the use of hands."

"Gargoyles built it?" Archippus doubting the possibility, blinked several times.

"Yes. Gargoyles," insisted Ezbon-Ishuah.

"I don't believe in gargoyles, or the Seraph. Next you'll be saying there's an After-sky."

"Well, I certainly hope there is," said Ezbon-Ishuah. "I'm not getting any younger, you know." He tugged at his gray beard for proof. "But to answer your second question, the Airbornes used to fly to the top of the tower to visit the Seraph and receive counsel. They were supposed to go regularly in order to receive proper guidance so they could counsel the Pangeans on how to govern themselves."

"How do you know all this?"

"Because they speak to me," said Ezbon-Ishuah, "when I care for them. At least some of them do … others are very secretive."

"What do you do for them?"

"Well, when the Airbornes used to make the trip to the tower on a regular basis, the cold temperatures of the uppermost peninsula would kill their parasites and they would freeze and fall off. But over the years, the trips have ceased. The new ideology that the Seraph is a myth, combined with the allurian philosophy of total self-reliance, has caused even the best-intentioned Airbornes to cease making the flight. The Airbornes have come to believe that the Sacred Scrolls are sufficient, and that they have plenty of knowledge from which to offer advice.

"And the parasites have become a big problem. The Airbornes, not having hands, must come to my dells and I scrub a solution on them and the parasites die. It takes several treatments as well as a special mixture they must ingest."

Archippus' eyes widened. "How big was the largest Airborne that's come to you?"

"His wingspan," said Ezbon-Ishuah spreading his arms, "was thirty feet from wingtip to wingtip." He nodded for emphasis.

"Gracious grave ..." said Archippus. "That's large enough to ride."

"It was."

"Do you mean ..."

"Yes."

"No!"

"Yes. I have ridden an Airborne to the uppermost reaches of the Continent. I have seen the Trail of Tears and the top of the Scrimshaw Tower. We even soared so high that I grew faint. But before passing out, I saw and realized that the Continent and the waters it rests on are actually curved like the night orb that rules the night sky."

"*No ...*"

"*Yes!*"

"*No ...*"

They sat in silence for several seconds.

"*It seems so flat ...*" Archippus' voice trailed off as he tried to absorb the information.

"Yes, I know. The Airborne advised me to take a shrieking seedling with me to breathe through or I could never have ridden so high."

"What is a shrieking seedling?"

"A local plant. We use them when digging our burrows. If there is a cave-in, a worker could be trapped and the air will grow stale. When the air grows stale, the seedlings shriek. They have cone-shaped petals, and no one is quite certain how or why they shriek, but if you clasp the petals around your nose, you can continue to breathe for several hours."

"Really?" said Archippus.

Ezbon-Ishuah nodded.

"Do you think I could care for the Airbornes?" Archippus asked.

"Well ..."

"In exchange for my teaching you to scribe?" Archippus prodded.

"Well ... I suppose I could use some assistance, but you still have to do your day work. I haven't a replacement for you."

"Deal," said Archippus. He spit on his hand and extended it, palm up.

"Deal," said Ezbon-Ishuah in return. He smiled and spit on his hand smacking downward on Archippus' palm.

Ezbon-Ishuah stood. "We'll start tomorrow. After work, I'll come fetch you. When we are done tending to the Airbornes, you can begin to teach me the art of being a scriber."

"Why do you want to scribe so badly?" asked Archippus.

"I can't care for reptiles forever. It's physical labor as you know, and ..." he paused and smiled and tugged again at his gray beard, "I'm not getting any younger."

Ezbon-Ishuah left.

Archippus lay on his back in the bed of softened dirt he had loosened with a rock. He smiled. *Everyone may like Emoticas, he thought, but I earned myself a new position with our trade master. And I will ride an Airborne one day. A real Airborne—unlike the feathered annoyance trying to destroy my life. And I will make this real Airborne agree to be my new Counselor. And I will be a noble, I will marry the noble girl, and I will find my sister. And to make it all perfect, I'll invite my new Counselor to a morning meal and serve him roast warbler. I swear I will.*

Archippus woke and ascended the stairs. He knew Hodos was going to ask him if he learned anything when he arrived at the top. He didn't care what Hodos thought, but he did want to prove that he could come up with something new he had learned each day. He considered himself highly intelligent, and one day he would outsmart the bird and be free of him.

He reached the top of the ladder and stepped onto flat ground.

"So did you learn anything today?" asked Hodos.

"Yes. There are one thousand, five hundred and forty-six steps from bottom to top," said Archippus with anger in his voice.

"Oh. That's good, very good," said Hodos. "There are no wrong answers ..." Archippus stomped off toward the Dells completely ignoring the little bird.

Archippus arrived at his assigned fifth lair and went to work.

Hodos landed on a nearby boulder. "Shovel and heave."

Archippus spun around. "I hate you, Bird! My legs ache from climbing stairs, my back hurts from bending and scooping, my arms burn from shoveling and heaving. With every scoop, I hate you even more!"

"But you're getting stronger. Look, your arms are becoming quite muscular," said Hodos.

"I don't *need* to be *muscular,* Bird! I'm going to become wealthy through the use of my *brain*. And tonight I am going to start working with the Airbornes. The real Airbornes, not a pretending, lying, tiny, feathered one like you, if there are even any others like you on this grave ridden Continent!"

"Oh, you'll need to be muscular to finish your quest all right," said Hodos.

"Don't speak of my quest again!" screamed Archippus. "I'll tell you what my quest is! I'll earn enough coinage to go back to Ai. If you won't tell me where my sister is, I'll find her one day. But in the meantime, I will go back and marry the noble girl. I decided so last night. And I won't be needing any help from you, or advice, or orders. This is *my* life, Bird, and *I'll* choose my quest!"

"But the noble girl won't make you happy—"

"There is no one else to make me happy! My parents are *dead,* my sister is *missing,* and it certainly wouldn't be *you!*"

"Heh, hem," came a voice from the entrance of the lair.

Archippus spun around.

"Are you arguing with your bird again?" asked Raimi. A dark-skinned man clad in armor stood next to her.

"No! I mean … yes, I *am* arguing, but he's not *my* bird."

Hodos flipped his wings, jumped into the air and was gone.

"Well, he sure follows you around a lot not to be yours. And he does seem to care, but I know *I* wouldn't put up with you *yelling* all the time," said Raimi.

"What do you want?" snapped Archippus.

"The eegwuhnuh."

"Oh."

She gestured toward the man next to her. "This is Gunner Phicol. He works the eegwuhnuhs on the flatlands and the lower portions of cliff walls."

"Oh." Archippus felt humiliated in front of a gunner in gleaming armor and golden neck rings. He looked at his shovel full of poop and then back up at the gunner.

The gunner nodded, looked at the shovel of poop, and then back up at Archippus.

Raimi walked over to the eegwuhnuh, held the wide iron bit to its teeth, slid the bit in its mouth making sure the iron was over the tongue, and fastened the leather bridle behind the notch at the crown of the big lizard's head. She unchained the leg and led the eegwuhnuh over to the guard by the reins.

"Thank you, Raimi." The guard took the reins and led the eegwuhnuh out of the lair.

"I don't know why Ezbon-Ishuah doesn't have him do all the training," said Raimi to Archippus. "He's the only gunner who's not hard on the eegwuhnuhs."

Archippus felt angry all day. He shoveled and shoveled, pushing himself so he could finish early and go see Airbornes. It was the only positive thought in his mind. He wanted to be early for his meal so he could eat alone, which would also be pleasant. Then he would hurry to the airborne gate.

To his dismay, Emoticas and Gershom finished early as well. He took a seat, as did they, beside the fire in the circular clearing where Raimi did her metalwork.

"I had them finish early," said Raimi addressing Archippus. "I'm going to train Emoticas to work with the eegwuhnuhs on the flatland, and Gershom will help with the iron work, while I train Emoticas." She looked happy.

"Why did *you* finish early?" Emoticas asked Archippus.

"I'm going to work with Ezbon-Ishuah up past the airborne gate," responded Archippus.

"Really?" Emoticas eyes widened.

Archippus enjoyed the surprised looks from Raimi and Gershom as well.

"Yes, really," said Archippus. "He invited me to do so last night."

Silence fell on the four of them.

"So what did you all think of the announcements last night?" asked Emoticas.

"I think," said Ezbon-Ishuah as he entered the clearing, "that the requirement to use the High-Way will make it more difficult to deliver tithes to the Fourth City because it will take longer. This means that nobility will be able to afford to pay their caravans for the longer journey, but tradesmon and commoners will not. Likewise, I believe additional law-ers will be hard on tradesmon who already give what they can as tithes. Nobles can afford to hire law-ers as pleators, but most citizens cannot.

"And on the other matter, the idea that the Continent is cooling is absurd."

"It is cooling." Hodos landed on the handle of a shovel leaning against a boulder. "The Continent will heat and cool many times before the final millennia."

"How would you know?" asked Emoticas.

"I know things," said Hodos.

Archippus rolled his eyes and shook his head.

"Well, I think it's a bunch of gloom and doom," said Ezbon-Ishuah. "The criers never say anything good. It's almost as if the announcements are meant to instill fear to fetter us to those who govern." And then he added, "Or they tell us something sensational to keep our interest."

Gershom tapped Emoticas and made several motions.

"Gershom wants to know of the Fire Propulsion System," said Emoticas.

"Oh," said Ezbon-Ishuah. "The Airbornes tell me that the High Council of Twenty-four, *against* airborne advice, designed the weapon to protect Hieropolis, the High City of the Iron Hall. It is a large contraption extending some thirty arm-widths high with a long wooden launch that propels balls of fire a distance of hundreds of arm-widths. They figured it could be used to prevent an attack and that it could not be used on Hieropolis in turn since the iron city cannot burn. Launching burning balls against an oncoming army would cause a grass fire and kill approaching enemy forces. The problem is that should the Barbirians develop an FPS, they could use it to take the six remaining cities. The very weapon that was created to defend now stands to be the destruction of the Continent if successfully designed by Barbirians. That's our High Council in action for you. Whose brilliant idea was that?"

No one responded.

"Are you ready to go, DM?" asked Ezbon-Ishuah.

Archippus jumped up and threw his finished meat-stick in the fire, and followed Ezbon-Ishuah up the path past all the eegwuhnuh lairs. Ezbon-Ishuah used an iron key that hung from his waist to open the gate. They passed through and he locked it behind them.

It appeared that more lairs, much like the ones they had left behind, lined the trail ahead. Openings between the boulders served for entrances. They rounded the first entrance. A pterodactyl Airborne perched on a boulder next to a fire.

"They like the warmth," explained Ezbon-Ishuah. "Pterodactyl Dedan, allow me to introduce DM. He is the one I told you of. I'm finding I need assistance in my old age."

Pterodactyl Dedan narrowed black eyes in the direction of Archippus. "Couldn't you have picked anyone other than a pale-skin?" asked Dedan.

"I assure you, Counselor, he is a trained scriber. He is one of few people in this city who can not only engage in conversation, but actually understand it."

Dedan laughed. "I suppose you are right. I've observed the uneducated fools residing in this city. I suppose it is difficult to find quality personnel in a city that sleeps by day. So tell me, DM, I can see you to be a commoner so I suppose you have never had the privilege of airborne counsel, or am I to stand corrected?"

Hodos flashed in Archippus' mind for a brief second. "Never, Counselor."

"Well, you'll benefit from the interaction then. If you pay attention, speak little, and apply what you learn, you could progress in your occupation. Scribers have been known to become pleators to plead cases before councils. If eloquent enough, great pleators have persuaded entire councils," said Dedan, "even impacted laws."

Awe struck, Archippus could only nod. Dedan was small for an Airborne, but intimidating nonetheless. All Airbornes had similar build, with narrow foreheads, elongated beaks, jagged teeth, leathery wings, clawed feet, and sharp talons protruding from mid-wing. Archippus noted the long tail had only one feather at the end. Dedan must have caught him staring at it.

"I counsel a first-born gunner of the Second Field. I supply him with feathers for the front of his helmet. At times they fly off in a fight or get lobbed off with a sword. But it really is impolite to stare. The other Airbornes may not be as cordial as I," said Dedan. He stood and spread his dark wings.

Archippus swallowed hard and nodded again. He began to wonder if he were going to be too nervous to do this work, but then he envisioned flying through the night sky on the back of one of these creatures. He glanced at Ezbon-Ishuah for guidance as to how to proceed.

Ezbon-Ishuah lifted a bucket filled with watery solution. A bristled piece of round wood floated in the liquid.

"Are you ready for the treatment, Counselor?" asked Ezbon-Ishuah.

Dedan sighed. "Yes. It is humiliating, but yes."

"Why not fly to the Scrimshaw Tower?" asked Archippus. "Won't the parasites then fall off?"

Dedan tilted his head and eyed Archippus. "Why would I make an insufferably long trek to consult an archaic myth when with my own intellect I can interpret the scrolls as I see fit, and come once in a while to a warm climate for treatment and rest?" he said with annoyance.

Ezbon-Ishuah shot a sharp glance at Archippus.

"Yes, Counselor," said Archippus. "Forgive me."

The reptile hissed. Spittle flew onto Archippus' face.

"Forgive his impudence, if you are able, Counselor. I told him of the ancient treks in order to explain why the parasites became prevalent," said Ezbon-Ishuah. His hand shook as he dipped and lifted the bristled wood.

The reptile hissed and spit on Ezbon-Ishuah.

"I deserved that," said Ezbon-Ishuah.

Dedan glared at him. "You may proceed. But if I suspect you have been mentioning a certain alleged feathered resident of the Scrimshaw Tower, I will report it."

"Of course, Counselor," said Ezbon-Ishuah. His hand still shook as he lifted the brush. "I expect that you would."

Archippus was hardly breathing at this point. He envisioned the reptile latching onto his face and biting down with rows upon rows of razor-sharp teeth while clawing into his shoulders. He observed Ezbon-Ishuah as Dedan opened his mouth wide.

Ezbon-Ishuah stepped up to the reptile taking hold of the lower beak in his left hand. He scrubbed the solution on the bottom teeth first, and then Dedan lowered his head so the top teeth could be scrubbed. Ezbon-Ishuah picked up a second bucket and allowed the reptile to close and dip his beak into clean water to rinse off the solution. Ezbon-Ishuah then produced a snock leaf with a pasty substance rolled inside of it.

"Your medicine, Counselor," he said as he extended the bulging leaf.

Dedan snapped it from the open extended palm with his beak, flung his head backward, and swallowed the item whole. "Leave," he commanded.

"Yes, Counselor," said Ezbon-Ishuah, bowing and backing.

Archippus bowed and backed as well. He followed Ezbon-Ishuah down the trail and back through the gate.

Ezbon-Ishuah smacked him on the ear. "What are you trying to do? Get us killed?"

"No!" insisted Archippus, rubbing his ear.

Ezbon-Ishuah's face softened. "I'm sorry. But don't discuss any reference to the name I told you last night that I shouldn't be speaking of because you don't know when not to say what I said. Have you no judgment? Surely, you realize how serious this matter is. The councils have gone to great lengths to remove the images from all corners of the

Judgment Hall rooftops. And you heard last night they are removing his image from all coinage. The great artist, Malchiel Merari, has painted over the original depiction of that which you *know* not to say, but not *when not* to say it. I have heard he memorized the image, and has reproduced it so as to never forget the brilliance of the figure. They say some citizens even possess small recreations that he gives to Landlings who request a copy in secret."

Ezbon-Ishuah's eyes softened as he spoke. "Let's go back to the burrows. One Airborne is enough training for tonight seeing as you got us both gleeked with spittle. I doubt you could hold your tongue for a second treatment."

He paused for a brief smile. "You remind me of my son."

Archippus, still rubbing his ear, followed Ezbon-Ishuah down the trail. "You have a son?"

Ezbon-Ishuah kept walking and said nothing.

It surprised Archippus to find that Ezbon-Ishuah's burrow was a mere one and one half circle down the pit.

"I pay a high price to be near the top," Ezbon-Ishuah announced as they stepped onto his landing. They entered a narrow tunnel and walked the approximate length of an eegwuhnuh. The tunnel then opened into a large, round earthen room lit with candles and oil lamps. The room had a high round ceiling and two small burrows across from each other. Archippus saw stuffed mattress inside each of the small burrows, and in front of him, in the large round room was *furniture*.

In the center, on a decorative red rug, sat a couch facing a table. On the table was a l'easel with a boy's portrait, and behind the couch was a cupboard, and to each side of the couch was a chair. Archippus stopped and stared.

"You have *furniture*."

"Yes," said Ezbon-Ishuah. "I am one of the wealthiest tradesmon in the city." He walked over to the cupboard and opened a drawer and produced parchment, pen, and ink. He set them on the table in front of the couch. "Teach me," he said.

Archippus dipped the pen in the ink. "We will start with an 'a'..."

After Archippus etched the letter, Ezbon-Ishuah wrote it too. They worked into the 'evening' light, which everyone else on the Continent would have called morning.

As Archippus taught his craft, the two discussed many things.

"How did you become wealthy?" asked Archippus.

Ezbon-Ishuah stopped writing and sat back. He looked at Archippus' intent expression and smiled. "Now that is a question that could take us into the middle of next week. Suffice it to say, that commerce is an art form. And by that I mean, the most successful Pangeans of commerce, are creative."

Ezbon-Ishuah leaned forward and began to practice writing again.

Archippus could not let this go. "Explain," he said.

"Well, several years back, *everyone* was raising eegwuhnuhs. It requires no brain, merely brawn. And as you know, eegwuhnuhs are the most valuable and expeditious means of travel and transport across the Continent. A full-grown eegwuhnuh is worth several thousand aureus coins."

Ezbon-Ishuah sat back from his writing.

"But it wasn't always so," he continued. "When I began to raise eegwuhnuhs, they sold for a couple hundred aureus each. But my son and I began to devise how to produce the best, the finest, the most desirable eegwuhnuhs on the Continent. We realized that it wasn't merely the reptiles themselves. Breeding for temperament, speed, and size were all-important. However, the *real* value, the value that we discovered everyone would pay top coinage for was the *training*." His eyes widened under his bushy gray brows to emphasize his point.

"We realized that most eegwuhnuh breeders were selling the reptiles barely trained. This caused injuries and even deaths, so we developed the program we now have, which is gunners working them on the flatland and slaves on the cliff wall. If we lose a slave or two, so be it. It is better to lose a slave than a customer. *Buy and die* is never a good slogan."

Archippus wondered for a moment about the unfortunate slaves. He himself had been a prisoner, but it *did* make good business sense.

"Some of our best training tools have been Raimi's bits. She has designed several styles, and different eegwuhnuhs respond better or worse depending on the type of bit. One of her best designs is the 'V' bit. It connects in the middle by two round links, and the bit when pulled by the left or right rein, cues the eegwuhnuh more clearly in the intended direction of travel. This encourages sharper turns and is easier to perform when hanging from a cliff."

Raimi entered the room.

"Out late?" said Ezbon-Ishuah.

"She lives with you?" asked Archippus with surprise.

"I was playing Conquer the Continent with Gershom and Emoticas," said Raimi.

"Who won?" asked Ezbon-Ishuah.

"I did," said Raimi smiling.

"That's my girl!" said Ezbon-Ishuah. "Your friend here got us gleeked tonight."

"I'm not surprised," said Raimi who headed directly for the burrow on the left and plopped on the mattress.

"I let her move into my son's room after he left," said Ezbon-Ishuah in a hushed voice.

"Where did he go?" asked Archippus.

Ezbon-Ishuah looked down. The corners of his mouth turned down as well. "He moved to the Citadel by the Sea to sing and do theatrics. He's quite popular. But I never hear from him. The last time we spoke, we argued."

Archippus waited for an explanation.

Ezbon-Ishuah sighed. "He developed a snock habit."

"Oh," said Archippus.

An awkward silence followed until Archippus spoke again.

"Well, I think that's enough scribing for one night-day," he said to Ezbon-Ishuah, and then very loudly for Raimi to hear, "I'm off to that really *nice* burrow *at the very bottom of the stairwell.*"

Raimi giggled.

Archippus left.

At the beginning of the next two night-days, Archippus came up with something to say about the stairwell.

"I learned I am getting stronger because I stop less and breathe easier," he said.

"Good, good!" said Hodos. "So what you perceived as a problem is becoming an opportunity."

Archippus stomped on past the bird.

The next idea blossomed because Archippus was anxious to receive his first coinage. "I learned that if I skip every other stair, I get to the top twice as fast."

"Very good! There are no wrong answers," said Hodos to Archippus' back as he stomped off to the food line. Archippus was pleased to receive a mango on a stick in lieu of a banana this evening-morn.

Archippus shoveled quickly after arriving at work knowing he had to fit in the evening meal, the care of Pterodactyl Dedan, the scribe teaching to Ezbon-Ishuah, and a purchase with his first coinage. He shoveled fast, hardly noticing the burning in his arm muscles, and then hurried his cartload downhill to the dump. As he was dumping, he saw a cart drawn by two waist-high equines. A couple of slaves with metal neck clamps filled the cart with dung and began to lead the equines west, up the road that left the city. Archippus surmised this to be the High-Way referenced by the town crier.

As Archippus gazed in the direction of the departing dung cart, Emoticas came up next to him to dump his cartful of manure.

"Interesting creatures, those equines," said Emoticas.

"Huh?" Archippus turned to look at Emoticas.

"Raimi says they use the creatures to haul the eegwuhnuh manure to Calidron to fertilize the snock crops. But think of it. If the equines were only a bit bigger, we could actually ride them, and they could become the new four-leggeds of transport," said Emoticas.

"Do you think?" asked Archippus.

"Most definitely, and the great thing is, they subsist on grasslands. Think of it, they could travel and feast most anywhere, unlike the eegwuhnuhs who require snock leaves. It could revolutionize the Continent."

"That's an absurd idea," said Archippus. "Equines are waist high and will always remain as such."

Emoticas shrugged.

Archippus returned to the lair he had been cleaning. Raimi entered with a branding iron, stuck it in the fire until hot, walked over to the eegwuhnuh, and jammed the sizzling hot brand above its front left shoulder.

The eegwuhnuh flicked its tail, harshly smacking Archippus in the back of the legs.

"Ouch!"

Raimi laughed.

"What on earth did you do that for!" screamed Archippus.

"We have to brand them. Especially after we've invested training in them. If they should get lost or stolen, it is the only way to identify they are ours."

"That's not what I meant! You could have warned me! You take perverse pleasure in my torment!"

She laughed again.

Archippus rubbed his welts, cursing under his breath.

Raimi left without seeing Archippus bite his thumbnail and flick the nail at her backside.

Archippus eyed the eegwuhnuh. It appeared to have calmed down. He walked over to look at the brand—the letters *Ei* inside a circle—for what he inferred was *Ezbon-Ishuah's* initials. He returned to his work, angry with Raimi. His sullen thoughts lamented the loss of his mother, sister, father, and the noble girl. The hope of seeking the noble girl kept him from running down the path to smear eegwuhnuh dung on Raimi's face.

In his anger, he plotted his departure. If he could work until he saved coinage and earned the trust of a full-size pterodactyl, he could perhaps get the creature to take him back to Ai even if the creature would not agree to be his Counselor. Lost in his plans and thoughts, the evening-day passed quickly. After work, he marched to the main lair, extended his palm face up, and demanded his coinage from Raimi.

Raimi opened a pouch that hung from her waist and handed him three denarii.

"What are you going to do with your pay?" she asked.

"Save it so I can get out of here as far away as Landlingly possible from you, and Gershom, and Emoticas, and all the rest of this dung."

"That's nice," said Raimi, "lump us in with the dung. I wish you the Seraph's speed for your departure."

"Raimi!" snapped Ezbon-Ishuah entering the lair with Emoticas and Gershom at his heels. "I've already had a reprimand over saying *the name* from Pterodactyl Dedan, so weave your lips shut, will you?"

Raimi looked at her feet. "Sorry, sir."

The large man sighed. "Don't let it happen again. You are an integral part of the business. Dedan can snap your head off at the neck and you've no neck rings to prevent it. DM, are you ready?"

Archippus nervously licked his lower lip. "Well … actually … I wanted to get something from the tent square, and so I was hoping I could do that first and then hurry back to care for Dedan."

"How long will it take?" asked Ezbon-Ishuah.

"Not long," insisted Archippus.

"Well, hurry along then," demanded Ezbon-Ishuah.

Archippus darted for the lair's opening.

"We're headed that way too," said Emoticas.

But Archippus ignored him, and took off at a trot down the trail. He hurried to the square and ran up to the pouch scroll tent.

"I'd like to purchase a pouch scroll," said Archippus.

A tradesmon seated on a stool behind a rectangular wood table looked up at him. "All right," he said. He pulled a small, thin piece of papyrus parchment from a pile and positioned it in front of him. He dipped his metal tipped wooden pen in the ink and paused, waiting.

Archippus shifted his weight from one leg to the other and back. "Um ... could I scribe it myself?" he asked.

"Absolutely not," said the tradesmon. "No one touches my trade tools. Now what will it be?"

Archippus glanced left and right to make certain no one was listening. "Can you put, 'To marry the noble girl' on it?"

The tradesmon eyed him and laughed. "You?" He snickered. "Marry a noble?" He snickered again. "You look like a scrawny, unkempt slave with dreadlocks and pale skin! And you don't even know her name? Fat chance of you ever marrying a noble!" He shook his head but bent over the tiny parchment to scribe the request. "Now I've heard everything," he mumbled as he wrote.

Archippus felt his face flush. He thought about jabbing the tradesmon in the eye with the pen, but then thought the better of it.

The tradesmon finished and waved the inscription in the air to dry it, then rolled it up, stuck it in a pouch attached to a leather strap, and handed it to Archippus. "Here you go, Dreamer."

Archippus tossed denarii on the table, snatched up the pouch scroll, and trotted back toward the Dells. He passed Gershom, Emoticas, and Raimi but refused to look at them.

Back at the lairs, Archippus cautiously scrubbed Dedan's teeth. They were sharp as jagged rocks, and upon examination, Archippus felt certain they could snap a neck off. His hands trembled as he worked.

"You're doing well not to speak unless spoken to," said Dedan through the suds on his teeth.

"Yes, Counselor," said Archippus.

Dedan eyed him. "You're nervous. Why are you doing this?" he asked.

Archippus brought the dipping bucket over.

"Because I hate being at the bottom," answered Archippus.

"The bottom of what?" asked Dedan.

"Of everything," answered Archippus. "I'm at the bottom of the work force shoveling dung. I'm at the bottom of the social ladder, being pale and common. I'm at the bottom of the pay scale, the bottom of the pit, the bottom of the entire Continent."

"And how do you think scrubbing away parasites will help you?"

"I need a Counselor."

"It will never happen. You are not nobility."

"Then I at least need the opportunity to ride on pterodactyl wings."

"Ride an eegwuhnuh instead."

"No. You don't understand. I need to impress someone."

"Oh, I see. Well, there are only a handful of Airbornes large enough to carry Landlings. And even if and when one were to become available, they would only permit their wingmon, the Landling they counsel, to ride them. You would be hard pressed to negotiate a transit on an Airborne," said Dedan.

"But I think I could do it," said Archippus.

"On what grounds? What plea could you possibly make to convince a Counselor to do so?"

"On the grounds of love."

"Don't bother. Love is the most misunderstood emotion on the Continent. It is overstated and seldom pure."

"Then I shall appeal for mercy," said Archippus.

"Mercy is a weakness," said Dedan.

Archippus looked down. Perhaps it would be difficult to negotiate with an Airborne. Hodos never made sense—if Hodos were indeed a counselor as he proclaimed.

"Find out if there is a service you can perform," said Dedan.

"What?" Archippus was surprised to hear Dedan counseling him.

"Find out if you can negotiate a transit by discovering a want that the Counselor may have. There may be some infiltration, gathering of information, undercover work, you know, *spying,* that would be of value to the Counselor. In short, do not appeal to virtue, appeal to greed."

"Oh, thank you." This sounded odd to Archippus because Airbornes were suppose to be intrinsically good, not greedy. But, he thought, *the advice might prove helpful.* "Thank you," he repeated. He bowed and left.

Archippus arrived for evening meal at the circular area where the fire and branding equipment were kept and found his three co-workers had not only returned also, but were making a cacophony of unpleasant clamor. Gershom was blowing on a wing bone flute with seven holes, Emoticas was strumming a handheld psaltery, and Raimi was banging a tambourine with four pairs of metal cymbals spaced evenly around the circular handle.

"I thought you were getting pouch scrolls. Where did you get the coinage for this ruckus?" demanded Archippus holding his hands over his ears.

"We got both!" announced Emoticas with a huge grin.

"On three denarii?" asked Archippus.

"Raimi advanced us a month's pay to get started on our quest," answered Emoticas.

"I see," said Archippus. It bothered him to no end that the two received an advance. He could have taken an advance to skip town and be finished with this nonsense. "And what quest is that?"

"Well," said Emoticas, "when we sat up half the night-day playing Conquer the Continent, we began to discuss ideas on just exactly what would be the most effective means to actually conquer the Continent."

"And?" asked Archippus.

Emoticas smiled. "And we decided it would be *music*."

"I agree your lack of talent could slay people," said Archippus.

Emoticas laughed. "Well, not really. That's not the point. The point is to actually get *good* at playing and singing, and then we can go about performing music with themes that touch the hearts and souls of Landlings to bring about an inner change and motivate them to revolutionary action."

"That sounds like random idiocy," said Archippus. "I heard you speaking, but what you just said is the most incoherent string of irrational verbiage ever compiled into a sentence. I don't believe there was an ounce of reason to it."

"I think it's a noble cause," said Raimi. "And feasible too."

"So that's what you put on your pouch scrolls?" asked Archippus. "To play music that makes people promise to change if you promise to cease playing?'"

"No," said Emoticas. "As I told you, we will master these instruments. Look at my psaltery." He held forward a wooden string instrument with a square bottom and a hole in the center to allow the sound to resonate. Thirty-five metal strings ran from the bottom to top. At the top, the instrument had a concave half circle carved out of it that cascaded from a higher level on the left to a lower level on the right. This permitted the strings to be different lengths so that each produced a different sound. Emoticas plucked each one with enthusiasm to demonstrate the unique sound each string produced. During the demonstration, Gershom produced his pouch scroll and shoved the parchment in front of Archippus' face. It read, *To bring justice to the oppressed.*

"Mine says the same thing," said Emoticas.

"Fine," said Archippus. "You're three lunatic Landlings bent on changing the Continent. Well, I'm a *realist*. There's one thing I can change and plan on changing quickly, and that's my lot in life. If everyone took care of his or her *own* life, the Continent would be a better place. You act like we Pangeans can't help ourselves, and so you have to go about trying to fix everything for everybody. Good luck. Where's my evening meal?"

"We're eating oranges tonight," said Raimi.

"Oranges?"

"Yes. Oranges." She tossed him an orange.

"No meat?"

"No meat."

Hodos landed on a boulder. "Good morning-eve," he said cheerfully.

"Listen to this, Hodos." Emoticas strummed a few strings in an order that actually produced a simple coherent tune. Gershom then played a similar set of notes, and Raimi rattled her tambourine and hummed along.

"Very impressive," said Hodos.

"They think they can play music and change the fate of the Continent," said Archippus with mockery in his tone.

"Perhaps they can," said Hodos.

"Perhaps they can practice when I'm not around," said Archippus.

"Why are you so ill-tempered?" asked Hodos. "What difference is it to you?"

"You're right. It makes no difference to me. I have my own plans." Archippus inadvertently touched the pouch hanging from his neck.

"And what did you select for your pouch scroll saying?" asked Hodos. "I hope it has everything to do with discovering your quest, and nothing to do with Girl with skin like sea spray."

"So what if it does? There's nothing wrong with devoting one's life to love," snapped Archippus.

"What is lawful for one Landling may not be lawful for another," said Hodos.

"What's that suppose to mean?" asked Archippus.

"All things are lawful, but all things are not expedient. You must not be brought under the power of any,"[4] replied Hodos.

"You speak nonsense! Can anyone understand him?" exclaimed Archippus, glancing at the others around the fire.

"You adore something above all else and it controls you at the expense of your quest," said Hodos in an attempt to clarify. "This is an abomination of the heart throne."

Archippus seethed. "Are you calling the noble girl an abomination?"

"I am calling your excessive adoration an abomination, yes."

"Leave off!" yelled Archippus. He heaved the orange at the bird.

Hodos flitted upward and fluttered downward landing altogether untouched.

The orange, however, splattered on the boulder and slid sloppily to the ground.

Hodos looked down at the orange. His eyes were round and moist. "You've become worse since I freed you."

"No, I haven't. I hated you then and I hate you now."

"But I remember a prison boy who was grateful for an orange," Hodos replied.

"I'll be grateful for you to be gone," retorted Archippus.

"Very well, but you should be grateful for the food. Your eyes no longer look like olives forced through the small end of a funnel. In short, your sockets have filled in." He stooped, spread his wings, and took off.

"Did your bird seriously leave, like, permanently?" asked Emoticas.

"I can only hope," mumbled Archippus.

"Who's Girl with skin like sea spray?" asked Raimi.

"The bird mocks my love for the noble girl," said Archippus, feeling outnumbered and unpopular.

"Does she have a problem with her skin?" asked Raimi.

"No! He mocks my poem."

"Poem?" asked Raimi.

"Yes. Poem. I wrote a poem about her while I was in prison."

"Tell us the poem!" she exclaimed.

Archippus thought Raimi sounded excited to hear his poem, and it was the only interest anyone had shown him all night-day, so he took a deep inhalation and almost inaudibly, in very low, flat, reluctant, slow tones, he recited the poem.

> *"Autumnal hair like brown-red leaves,*
> *enfold her face like wind-swept trees;*
> *her green eyes oceans lit by day,*
> *her skin same ocean's foam white spray."*

Silence settled for several seconds.

"I think it's a beautiful poem," said Raimi. "Perhaps the bird is being a bit harsh on you. If your heart scroll is about the noble girl, then I wish you well with that."

Archippus was surprised to hear a kind word. He wasn't sure how to respond. But Gershom stood up abruptly, flicked his thumb at Archippus, and stomped off.

"What's the matter with him?" asked Archippus.

Emoticas sighed. "He was hoping you'd join us in our venture to improve the fate of the oppressed."

"What on Pangea would make him think I care about anything but myself?" asked Archippus.

"I'm not sure," said Emoticas. He wrinkled his brow, appearing to search for an answer.

"You *could* join us, you know," said Raimi. "You can write verse, and we need verses for our songs."

"I can't, I have other plans."

"Fair enough," said Raimi.

Ezbon-Ishuah rounded the corner. He was out of breath and his skin looked ashen.

Raimi jumped to her feet. "What's wrong?"

"Oh," Ezbon-Ishuah said between huffs. "Nothing, my dear." He leaned a hand on a boulder. "I'm fine, just a little winded." He huffed again. "Archippus, I need for you to finish the treatment on two additional Airbornes. I'm feeling a bit out of sorts. They are in the last two lairs on the right."

Archippus stood. "I'll see to it."

Raimi went to Ezbon-Ishuah and helped him walk in the direction of his burrow in the pit.

Archippus treated the two remaining Airbornes with the parasite solution. One of them was slightly smaller than Dedan, and the other only slightly larger. Neither was a candidate for transporting a Landling.

"I hope your master's health improves," said the second Airborne after Archippus filled the dipping bucket to remove the suds from the Airborne's teeth.

"Thank you, Counselor, I hope so too," said Archippus.

"It does not look hopeful, however," said the Airborne.

"What do you mean?" Archippus was concerned. Ezbon-Ishuah had become the only Landling remotely resembling a friend.

"You know what they say, 'Gray of skin, weak of heart,'" replied the Airborne.

This seemed callous and uncaring, and Archippus thought to dump the water bucket on the Airborne's head, but the thought of his sharp teeth stayed Archippus' hands, so he just bowed and left.

On his way down the pit, Archippus passed Ezbon-Ishuah's burrow. The opening was completely dark so Archippus thought it best to continue down to his own burrow.

He lay on his back on the soft earth bed for a long while wondering what would happen if Ezbon-Ishuah were to go to Sheole. These disturbing thoughts were interspersed with wonderings about Hodos, specifically if the feathered freak had in fact finally left him for good.

The next morning, however, Archippus was prepared to say something wise in the event the bird was waiting at the top of the hole. As he hiked upward, he thought of the aging Ezbon-Ishuah and his ill health and impending death. When he reached the top of the stairs, he was actually not shocked to find the Plumbed Perturbance waiting for him.

"So, did you learn anything from the stairwell today?" asked Hodos.

"Yes. I learned that the upward spiral, like aging, gives you an awareness of not only progress, but the existence of a top, a goal, a finality. The circles are like seasons. If you always experienced the same season in the exact same condition, or at the exact same level without the upward progression, you would not get anywhere or sense that you are getting anywhere. Therefore, as Landlings, we cannot simply be placed in containers that do not corrupt. We must have aging to sense that we are progressing through time, and we must be given a deadline, namely death, in order to be motivated to achieve. In short, you have to move upward in distance or time in order to leave the previous level, and perhaps to even find meaning."

Hodos blinked at him.

"Well, there are no wrong answers." He blinked again. "But, that was a bit too profound for me."

"Why are you still here?" demanded Archippus.

"Why would you ask that?"

"Because I asked you to leave."

"I did leave."

"I meant for good."

"I can't leave you."

"Why not?"

"Because I'm your Counselor. I chose you."

"Un-choose me then."

"I can't un-choose you."

"Why not? I hate you."

117

"You can hate me. *You* can even un-choose *me*. But having chosen you, I can't un-choose what I chose."

"This is insanity! *'Un-choose'* isn't even a word!"

"You said it first."

"You know what? You argue like a child!"

"I'm merely seeking common ground."

"Leave off! I *hate* you!" Archippus stomped off failing to notice the intense stare of a pitch-black, red-eyed pterodactyl.

For the next two weeks, Archippus' life was routine. He shoveled dung for the bulk of the night-day, and toward evening-morn, he treated pterodactyl teeth. Ezbon-Ishuah gave him more and more responsibility in an effort to exert himself as little as possible, for he was constantly winded and weak. The early sunrise became the hours Archippus valued most for he would return to Ezbon-Ishuah's burrow, and as he continued to teach him to scribe, Ezbon-Ishuah would continue to educate him on commerce.

Raimi was seldom in the adjoining burrow because she was practicing her budding career as a singer/musician. And despite Archippus' disdain, the music trio kept improving. He would hear them as he passed their burrow. They could now play two or three well-known songs, although they had not come up with any original verses. Raimi kept beseeching that he write verses for the new musical group, but Archippus always refused. He would go to his burrow, lie on his back, hope for the arrival of a transport-size pterodactyl, pine for the noble girl, and wonder of his sister's well-being.

PARCHMENT IV

"The lower oxygen levels of ancient earth
gave the sky a reddish hue, and the high iron content
made the ocean green."

On the twentieth floor of the iron tower, the young High Ruler stared into her handheld looking glass. Her head moved slightly as Shear-Jashub gently pulled back Apphia's hair to get at the roots with a bronze razor.

"It won't be as hot in your helmet without hair," said Shear-Jashub.

"But I'll look even uglier," said Apphia.

Shear-Jashub chuckled. "You aren't ugly."

"Well, I guess this gives new meaning to your name, *Shear*-Jashub, and I guess it doesn't matter if I'm ugly, since the High Ruler can never wed."

Shear-Jashub sighed. "The High Ruler must focus on ruling, not romance or matters of marriage. It's just the way it is. And you aren't ugly."

"Yes, I am," insisted Apphia. "I'm pale, and short, and small of nose." She looked in the mirror, but her only solace was in knowing her features resembled her brothers. This thought of her brother prodded her to tell Shear-Jashub of her dream last night and the secret she had been withholding.

"Shear-Jashub," she said.

"Yes?"

Apphia thought he seemed to be enjoying shearing off her locks. She noticed his wide smile as clumps of her brown hair cascaded to the floor.

"You are the only one I can ask for this trust-oath," she said.

"Yes?" He draped her hair over her forehead to make a cut. The hair tickled Apphia's nose and she sneezed.

"Can you stop for a minute?" she demanded. She stood abruptly. One side of her head was bald, but not the other. "I'm about to tell you something I've not mentioned to anyone, not even Eri. He will kill me if he finds out, so I need your trust-oath of secrecy."

"You dreamt of the scepter?" asked Shear-Jashub with widened eyes.

"No. My brother."

"Eri already knows you have a brother."

"But he does not know that six months back I dreamt he was freed from prison, and he does not know that just last night I dreamt Eri will go to Ai to check for my brother – which means he'll find out he's no longer there!"

"Oh," said Shear-Jashub, "but do your dreams *always* come true?"

Apphia crossed her arms, shifted her weight impatiently to one leg, and raised a single brow.

"Okay," said Shear-Jashub, "so what of it? Why could it possibly matter to Eri if your brother wanders the Continent?"

"He told me that my brother is a threat to the throne."

"A single, pale commoner threatens the throne?"

"It's not that *I* believe it, it only matters that *Eri* believes it," answered Apphia. "You know how uptight he is about the *throne threat* thing. Not a day has passed that he hasn't hounded me about my dreams and visions of the scepter. I'm beginning to visualize impaling him with that stupid green stick. Then I'd cast him and the scepter down the Echoless Pit along with my helmet."

"Don't talk like that."

"But you know Eri will kill my brother if he finds out," said Apphia.

Shear-Jashub frowned. "But you know the councils hate to kill commoners. The Teachings say it upsets the Seraph."

"He'll do it anyway, or at the very least, have Archippus imprisoned again, but I have a plan. We have to get Lord Ipthsum a text message," said Apphia.

Shear-Jashub looked surprised. "But how? You or I can't scribe, and we can't trust someone else to write it."

"I know something about scribing," said Apphia. "I watched my brother while he was learning from my father."

"Okay, but who will deliver it then?"

Apphia stared at him.

"Me? You're asking me to deliver the message?" asked Shear-Jashub.

Apphia continued to stare.

"But who will watch over you while I am gone?"

"Entimus."

"But what shall I say to Entimus to explain my absence?"

"You both lived in Ai for some time, surely you have reason to go there."

Shear-Jashub was silent for several seconds. "My daughter's grave is there."

Apphia felt awkward for having asked such a question, but she had always wondered when he would tell her of the death of his wife and child.

"I could do it," said Shear-Jashub, "but did your dream indicate how soon this will happen?"

"No."

"Well, Your Eminence, you yourself know how long it takes to make the trek, and if Eri decides to go, he will beat me there by two days."

Apphia furrowed her brow.

Shear-Jashub chuckled.

"What's so funny?"

"I'm sorry, Your Eminence, it's just so difficult to take you seriously with half your head shaved." Shear-Jashub burst into a full-bellied laugh.

Apphia snatched up the hand mirror and eyed both sides of her head. "I think I like it. Perhaps I'll leave it like that."

Shear-Jashub finally stopped laughing. "In all seriousness, I do know someone we can trust to deliver a text message by *air.*"

"An Airborne?"

"Of sorts ..." said Shear-Jashub.

"What do you mean?"

"Well, he is not reptilian, but he is Airborne. In fact, he is the last remaining Airborne known to still make seasonal trips to the Scrimshaw Tower. In short, he is the last remaining Counselor to continue to consult the Seraph."

"How do you know?"

"He plagues the Council of Twenty-four, shows up unannounced all the time, sits through hearings, puts in his two denarius, and states what the Seraph would recommend. All the council members hate him."

"Why do they put up with him?"

"Quite simply," said Shear-Jashub, "because they fear the Seraph."

"How can we find this Airborne?"

"Oh, he'll come," said Shear-Jashub.

"When?"

"When are you to sit for your first council meeting?"

"Tomorrow."

"Then tomorrow you shall meet him. Now, *please,* let me finish your hair."

That night, beneath the oil lamp chandelier, Apphia penned the text. The lettering was primitive and void of any scriber skill, but upon finishing she held it up and it was legible.

Lord Ipthsum: I know of Archippus, the scriber's escape, but do not fear. Tell any inquirers that he died in prison and was buried in a slaves' mass burial and I will spare your life.
~Your Elected High Ruler, Apphia

She folded the top half of the parchment downward, and the bottom half upward, dripping red candle wax on the flaps, and sealing it with the scepter insignia.

↽ ↽ ↽ ↽
↽ ↽ ↽ ↽

The next evening, Apphia donned her armor. She felt very nervous since this was her first council hearing since her inauguration six months ago. She slid the helmet over her head and lowered the metal visor that hid her face. Only her eyes could be seen peering through a slot.

"I'm ready," her voice echoed back into her ears. She turned to face Shear-Jashub.

"Very good, Your Eminence. I am ready to escort you now."

Shear-Jashub was dressed in formal gunner attire—a light brown tunic and skirt, and the Fourth Field sash of gold draped from left shoulder to right hip. He smiled and held his forearm out for Apphia to grasp.

They descended the twenty floors of the tower and turned for the first time to the left, which permitted them to enter the main tunnel thereby leaving the grounds of the sixth tower for the first time in over five long years.

Apphia held Shear-Jashub's arm lightly as they strode through the tunnel. "I don't understand. I would have thought they would have consulted me before now. I was elected High Ruler, and have done nothing since. It's almost as if I'm not needed."

"Of course they need you. They have called for your presence, have they not? I'm sure they wanted you to be under Eri's instruction for some time in order to be ready. It's not an easy thing to lead a Continent." He smiled and glanced sideways at her.

They entered the large starlit courtyard and climbed the stairs to the Iron Hall.

To Apphia's dismay, upon entering the hall, everyone else—all twenty-four of the council members were already present. It was as if she had been invited to a party having been told to show up an hour late. Eri was perched on the hot rock neighboring the heart throne, and twelve thrones with accompanying hot rocks lined the left of the aisle to the heart throne, and twelve thrones and hot rocks lined the right of the aisle.

Shear-Jashub whispered to her, explaining the arrangement. "The two elected council members representing each of the remaining six cities occupy the thrones on the right, and the Council of Twelve for Hieropolis sits to the left."

Apphia felt extremely self-conscious as the room fell silent and all the council members stood, elegant in their long orange robes with ginger-colored sashes. Two thirds were female and a third male and all were brown or black of skin.

The Airbornes on the hot rocks next to each throne seemed to stand also, as near as Apphia could make out. For to her, perching and standing did not make a great deal of difference when a creature has clawed feet.

The walk between the rows of thrones seemed infinite. Her armored feet clanged and echoed with each step. She clung to Shear-Jashub's arm until he released her to climb the three steps to the throne. She ascended, banging her iron toe on one of the steps, almost tripping. She turned and slipped back onto the throne. Her feet were too short to touch the ground. She felt small and uncertain.

Shear-Jashub took his place to stand spear in hand between Apphia and the scepter, facing the front as her posted guard.

A skinny council member with a swath of white hair reaching from ear to ear behind a baldpate stepped forward from the Hieropolis side with scroll in hand. His beady eyes sat close together on either side of a round nose. He dipped a knee and stood again. "Welcome, Your Eminence. We are pleased to have your presence here for the signing into effect of the latest enactments."

Apphia felt suffocated, but wanted to do well. It seemed sensible to her that to be effective at governing she should get know the council members, so despite tightness in her throat and self-doubt in her heart, she asked, "Who are you?"

The council member had begun to unroll the parchment. He lifted his head. "What?"

"Your name. What's your name?" she asked.

"Oh. Reuel, Your Eminence. My name is Reuel."

"Thank you ... uh ... you may proceed."

Several council members chuckled.

"I had every intention of proceeding, Your Eminence."

More council members joined in the laughter. Apphia felt her face flush, and was for once relieved to be clad in armor.

Reuel continued. "We want to obtain your signature for the passage of the following enactments. He began to read from the parchment.

Act LXXvii of the Council of Twenty-four stating, Slave owners will receive a return tithe calculated by a sliding increase proportionate to the number of slaves owned verses coinage earned, and the determined amount will be refunded at the second annual feast each year.

Act LXXviii of the Council of Twenty-four stating—"

A black blur dived through a hot rock roof opening, swooped around the vaulted ceiling continuously cawing until landing on the heart-shaped back of Apphia's throne.

Apphia turned her head and stared at the black breast and under-beak of a raven.

Groans came from the council members, and especially from Reuel who slunk his shoulders in apparent exasperation. "Hello, Aro," he said.

"Continue," said the raven.

"I had every intention of continuing, but you missed that part," retorted Reuel.

Everyone laughed except Apphia, Shear-Jashub, and the raven.

Reuel waited for the laughter to subside and began again. "Act LXXviii of the Council of Twenty-four stating—"

"Wait a minute," interrupted Apphia. She had begun to dislike this Reuel and reminded herself that *she* was, in fact, the High Ruler. What could she possibly have to lose if she spoke out? She didn't even care if they discharged her of her duties, for she'd just as soon walk the Continent in search of her brother. "I have a question."

Reuel looked up again from the scroll. He squinted impatiently as if Apphia's question was an imposition. "What?"

"Well ... if you encourage the ownership of slaves with financial rewards, then won't the nobility and tradesmon try to purchase as many slaves as possible at the risk of not being able to afford or properly feed them?"

"Good question!" shouted Aro from his perch on the back of the throne.

Reuel glared at Aro, and then shifted his eyes to Apphia.

"Your Eminence, all considerations were taken into account when drafting these enactments. As a result, I assure you that the merits of anything I am about to relay to you on this parchment have been thoroughly analyzed to ensure that benefits outweigh detriments. Now, may I proceed?"

"I assumed you had every intention of proceeding," said Apphia.

Many council members laughed again, only this time, to the detriment of Reuel.

Reuel glanced uneasily around the hall. "Thank you. As I was *saying,* Act LXXviii of the Council of Twenty-four. Due to the increasing apothecary costs, scarcity of medicines, and high fatality rates, all eegwuhnuh riders will use the leather safety straps while in transit."

"Question," said Apphia.

"What now?" asked Reuel.

"Who is going to enforce this rule, Reuel?"

Some of the council members chuckled at the play on words.

"You may not be aware," said a seething Reuel, "but recently we approved the lowering in age for gunner recruits and made provisions for an increase in tithes to train them. We will, as a result, have more gunners Continent-wide to not only enforce the laws, but to be available for war. So, I again remind you, that we have taken into account all these silly questions of yours."

"If my questions are silly, then why did you, as you just claimed, take them into account?" asked Apphia.

"Good question!" shouted Aro.

Eri spun, flicked his tail, and knocked Aro from off the back of the throne.

Shocked, Apphia swiveled her upper body to peer behind the throne at the bird on the floor.

The raven ruffled and readjusted his feathers and alighted once more to the back of the throne, seemingly undisturbed by the thwarting blow.

"We must have order!" insisted Eri, his loud voice echoing through the hall.

"But I have another question," persisted Apphia. "What will be the consequence of not wearing a safety strap?"

"I was getting to that," snapped Reuel. "The enactment says that any tradesmon or commoner caught traveling without a safety strap will have their eegwuhnuh confiscated and assigned to use by the gunnership."

"That hardly seems fair!" Apphia exclaimed.

"Any enactment," retorted Reuel, "that protects physical welfare twice over is a suitable enactment as far as I'm concerned. This enactment not only spares initial injury to the Landling, but the eegwuhnuh is put to good use in the service of the protectors of the Continent, and thus the offending Landling is protected twice over."

"It's theft!" cried Apphia. "Why not subject the nobility to the same enactment as the tradesmon and comm—"

"Apphia! Let him finish!" said Eri in a stern voice. "You are here to sign what the trustworthy council members have drafted. Keep in mind, that these enactments were written under advisement of Airborne Council as well, and now is not the time to re-analyze the documents."

"But I wasn't present for the drafting and now I have questions."

"Apphia, you will sign these documents and we will discuss it later," insisted Eri with a dagger-like glance.

"Well … can I be present the next time they draft these things?"

"Good question!" shouted Aro.

"We will discuss this later," said Eri in a hissed whisper.

"Well, fine then. I see no sense in even hearing the rest of it if I am not to have an opinion." Apphia was surprised by her boldness and anger, but this seemed like nonsense—requiring her signature on items with which she may disagree. *The Continent will believe the enactments to have my approval,* she worried.

"Fine," said Eri. "Bring the scroll forward for signature."

Reuel smirked and held the bottom portion of the scroll forward, and another council member brought forth an inkwell and pen.

"Bunch of nonsense!" shouted Aro.

"No one asked your opinion, Aro," snapped Eri.

"Nor the Seraph's," retorted Aro.

Apphia dipped the pen and signed the paper. All the while her hand shook with anger at Eri for undermining her and insisting she sign. She penned the signature.

~Your Elected High Ruler, Apphia

Reuel looked at the signature. "You were taught to sign, *The* Elected High Ruler."

"But *Your* sounds more personal," insisted Apphia.

"Apphia!" snapped Eri.

"Fine!" She crossed off *Your* and wrote *The* above it. "Can I go now?" she demanded.

"*Please,*" said Reuel.

Apphia hopped from the throne and stomped with intentional clanging loudness out of the Iron Hall.

On his way out Shear-Jashub whispered to Aro, "A word outside?" and hurried after Apphia.

The council members had apparently chosen to continue the hearing for none of them followed Apphia, Shear-Jashub, and Aro out of the hall.

"You've become a handful of a High Ruler," said Shear-Jashub. "I don't think they were expecting that. Perhaps you could tone it down a bit."

"Nonsense," said Aro, who had perched on a bush top. "It's precisely what they need."

"Aro," said Apphia, "I'm pleased to meet you. Regrettably, I have a huge favor to ask of you, and Shear-Jashub has attested to your trustworthiness."

"Name the request," said Aro.

"Can you see that this text message is delivered, unopened, to Lord Ipthsum as quickly as possible?" she asked, holding the sealed parchment up.

"To protect your brother?" asked Aro.

Apphia's eyes widened behind her visor, her heartbeat increased. "You know of my brother's escape?"

Aro hunched and extended his wings. "Of course, Your Eminence. I myself gave him the key." He snatched the text in his beak, launched himself, and flew off.

Apphia stared after him. "What did he mean, he 'gave him the key'?"

"I think it meant … well … probably … that he gave him the key." Shear-Jashub also squinted upward. "He's as honest as the day is long."

Eri barreled forth from an archway, swooped toward them, and landed abruptly. "That was an embarassssment!" he hissed.

"For *me!*" snapped Apphia. "You *undermined* me!"

"Apphia, I am your Counselor! You made it look as if you had not received an ounce of counsel in your life, and if you repeat that behavior again, you will not attend any future hearings!"

"But the laws are corrupt! They're making things up for their benefit!" her voice boomed from the helmet.

Eri thrust his leathery head in her face. "They are *governing* for the *good* of the *Continent,* not for the approval of some *pale-skinned commoner of thirteen years!*"

"Then why did they elect me?" A tightening in her throat made her voice high pitched.

"I'm beginning to wonder that myself," said Eri. "Do not overestimate your worth. Until now, now that I am being provoked, I did not inform you that I counseled the *last* High Ruler. She grew arrogant and full of opinions and tried to rule with the Iron Fist that grasps the scepter. And now she is no more."

Apphia tried to assimilate where he was going with this newly revealed assertion.

Eri continued. "She felt she could consult the scepter as often as she liked, and it filled her mind with arrogance. Her opinions grew distant from the councils' and so I strongly urge you to learn from her example."

"But I thought the scepter was to be consulted for wisdom …" Her voice trailed off.

"You are incapable of wisdom without my counsel," snapped Eri.

Apphia thought the words cruel and hurtful. She remained silent.

"And another thing, do not interact with Aro. He is a deviant, a mutation. Feathered songbirds are not to speak. His very existence is an abomination. If I see you speaking with him, it will be his last breath." Eri shot upward with rapid swooshes that made the bushes shudder. In less than five seconds, he was out of sight.

Apphia wondered if the fountain of tears pouring down her cheeks could rust her visor shut. As a precaution, she lifted the metal flap and tried to wipe the wetness, but her chain mail clad fingers were cold and ineffective.

"I hate him!" she blubbered.

Shear-Jashub stepped forward and wiped her tears with his golden shoulder sash. "Let's get you to your chambers," he said kindly.

They did not speak a word on the way up the tower.

Sensing she needed to be alone, Shear-Jashub sat in the curtain-blocked foyer. Apphia cursed as she disrobed, throwing each section of armor across the room to clatter on the polished floor. She then climbed in bed, pulled the covers over her head, and sobbed for a long, long while.

-<   -<   -<   -<
-<   -<   -<   -<

Apphia woke the next morning and opened her swollen eyelids. To her dismay, Eri was perched on the balcony rail.

"Good morning, my dear," he said as if nothing at all had transpired the previous day.

Apphia thought about crawling back under the covers, but knew Eri was there for a reason and would demand her attention. She wrapped the red-gold bedspread around herself and waddled to the balcony. The crisp morning air made her shaved head cold.

"I came to check on you," Eri began. "It is important that you understand your role and the point I was making yesterday. You are important to the Continent as a figurehead. The Landlings need someone to adore, and hence the Feasts of Adoration. It unites them to have a common leader to adulate."

"But I thought the feasts were originally to honor the Sera—"

"Tut, tut, tut! Don't say it!" interrupted Eri. "We are getting along so famously this morning. You don't want to go and ruin things by upsetting me, now do you?"

Apphia shook her head.

"Good. Sometimes the old order of things must pass away as a precursor to progress and evolution. We are evolving into a Continent that can self-govern, and you have the honor of playing an integral role in that process. You are young, and I was merely trying to say that you must trust the counsel of those who know best. Sometimes things seem harsh or unfair, but you—"

"—can't fashion iron with feathers," finished Apphia.

Eri smiled his wrinkly little reptile smile. "That's right! The late High Ruler thought she could govern by herself by merely consulting the scepter, and in ruling with the Iron Fist, she grew weak, overlooking many faults. She became too easy on wrongdoers and rejected tough enactments. In short, she was not firm enough, she grew soft, and as you know, mercy is a weakness. A ruler must command respect."

Apphia pulled a portion of the blanket over her head for warmth.

"So," said Eri, "do we understand each other?"

Apphia nodded. She didn't want to understand Eri in the least, but nodded nonetheless.

"Good," said Eri. "Now, I trust you will behave. There are no more hearings that will require your signature for some time. Focus on your gunner class and look to Shear-Jashub while I'm gone."

"Gone?"

"Yes. I will be gone for a few weeks."

"Where?"

"To rid myself of parasites in Rephidim."

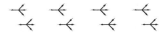

PARCHMENT V

"And many creatures extinct or
believed to be mythological,
actually roamed the earth."

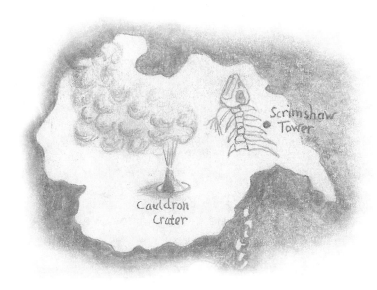

Ezbon-Ishuah came around the boulder.

"Hark! Under the white orb that rules our waking hours, you will never guess!"

Archippus, startled, dropped his shovel. He inhaled deeply, shrugged, and ventured a guess. "You are … increasing my pay?"

Ezbon-Ishuah laughed. "No, *but* I have news that will bring you merriment!" His eyes twinkled.

It dawned on Archippus what it might be. "A rider-sized pterodactyl?"

"Yes!" Ezbon-Ishuah shoved his hands out front for emphasis. "I just saw him land in our lairs. I haven't even been up there yet. I believe it is Pterodactyl Eri of Hieropolis. You can begin his treatment this very evening-morn."

Archippus began to feel nervous. *The creature must be huge.* "Is he ill-tempered?" he asked.

Ezbon-Ishuah drew his head back and furrowed his brow. "What do you mean 'Is he ill-tempered?' What difference does it make? All this time you've been pining to see a full-sized pterodactyl, and now one has come, and you want to know what *mood* it's in? Why don't we wait a harvest season to see if a *congenial* full-sized Airborne arrives?"

Archippus took a deep breath. "You're right. This is what I've wanted. Should I go now?"

"Yes! Yes, go now!" encouraged Ezbon-Ishuah.

Ezbon-Ishuah accompanied Archippus up the trail and opened the gate. He pointed to the second lair on the right and gave a nod and a wink.

Archippus continued up the trail. His stomach churned and his knees felt weak. He rounded the boulder to the lair.

Archippus' imagination had not prepared him for the magnitude of the thirty-foot wingspan that shot outward as the Airborne spun to face him.

"*Who* are you?" demanded Eri.

"I-I-I-I'm Ar-r-r-rchippus, s-s-sir."

"Where's Ezbon?"

"H-h-he's taken ill."

"Do you know the treatment?"

"Yes," Archippus swallowed. "Ezbon-Ishuah taught me everything because of his ill health."

The pterodactyl took two lurching steps toward Archippus, folded his wings, tilted his head, and squinted. "You ... look like ... someone I know," said the reptile.

"I would imagine that would be every pale-faced commoner on the Continent," said Archippus.

The Airborne chuckled. "Quite right, quite right, all pale faces have similar semblances. I can scarce tell them apart, much like rats."

It was not a flattering analysis, but Archippus had no trouble holding his tongue.

"Well stop staring, and get the treatment started," commanded the Airborne.

Archippus' hands shook as he brushed the rows of razor sharp teeth. He was terrified, but knew he would have to speak eventually if his plan to fly to Ai to impress the noble girl were to come about. He thought of Dedan's advice, "Appeal to greed." Perhaps flattery would be a good place to start though.

"I have never seen an Airborne of your stature," said Archippus as he brushed the long sharp teeth. "Of course, I am honored to work with any of the Airbornes, but I suspect the first-borns of nobility don't realize how fortunate they are to receive counselors and council."

A pitch-black eyeball shifted to examine Archippus. He swallowed hard. "I often have wished that I might be assigned an Airborne. I would swear daily to appreciate the honor, for I imagine, many a wingmon takes the privilege for granted." Hodos flashed through his mind.

"That is intuitive of you," said Eri through the thick suds on his teeth, "and you are right. Most wingmon don't appreciate their Counselors, and sad will be the day if airborne counsel were to cease."

Archippus scrubbed away and asked, "But airborne council will never cease. How could it?"

Eri swiped the suds from his jaw by flicking his tongue outward and to the right away from Archippus "You had better hope our counsel never ends, for it will be the destruction of the Continent. However, there is a prophetic possibility alluded to in the book of Ezdra wherein it states that the scepter will be yielded by a fleshed hand. If that were to occur, the time of airborne counsel will be no more."

Archippus thought on his words for a moment. "But hasn't every High Ruler had hands of flesh?" he asked.

"Of course, but, the scepter itself emanates light, the purity of which burns through skin if touched directly. As a result, it is wielded only with the Iron Fist. I believe the High Ruler spoken of in the prophecy is an abomination. Nevertheless, the prophecy says she will advise the Landlings to sense the Seraph through their inner heart thrones, teaching them to consult the scrolls and Seraph on their own. This is an incredibly dangerous idea, because frankly, Landlings don't know how to guard their own heart thrones, let alone the heart thrones of the Continent. Without guidance, the Landlings will become undisciplined, and chaos will overtake the earth, for too much freedom leads to slavery in the end.

"This is why the scepter must be protected at all costs, and why knowledge or discussion of the Seraph must be tempered. We must buffer and protect Landlings from growing arrogant. It is safer that they look to their councils and their beloved High Ruler."

"I'm not sure I believe in a Seraph," said Archippus, shocked that Eri would even say *the name* aloud to him.

"That bodes in your favor," said Eri.

The compliment encouraged Archippus to seek a service that would permit him to manipulate the ride to Ai. He thought quietly for a moment and then again ventured to speak.

"It must be difficult," said Archippus. "There must be many Landlings and even well intentioned nobles, lords and lordess' who grow arrogant. I would think you would continually have to be on guard for threats to the throne."

Eri widened his eyes and nodded. "Oh yes, quite right you are."

"Any problem areas at present?" Archippus prodded.

Eri sighed. "The snock growers of Calidron have been shorting the Council of Twenty-four on their biannual tithes, and so we had to increase the number of law-ers Continent-wide. We may have to resort to imprisonment if the matter does not improve."

"That's terrible. Any other problem areas are the Landlings behaving in, well, say for example, the City of Ai?"

A groan came from Eri. "You would not believe the problems we are now encountering with Ai. Two months back, Lord Ipthsum, very respected in the eyes of the High Council, had the great misfortune of taking a wife."

"Really?"

"Yes, unbelievable is it not? He married the most headstrong female on the Continent. She is arrogant and aspires to have sovereignty in her city with issues other than simply civil matters and petty crimes. There are two parties among the councils, the Automons and the Govnens, and she is most definitely an Automon. The High Council gives all subordinate councils an allotment of funds to run the cities, but she wants an additional portion of the biannual tithes to remain in her city to help fund the local council. I suspect, more specifically, her own purse. And the most treacherous part of it is she circulated a petition among the other cities requesting similar allotments. She has created dissension everywhere."

"What is her name?" asked Archippus.

"Lourdes." Eri spat out the name. "Her name is the epitome of egotism. Her mother, Jemuel, named her *Lourdes* because she always intended on her daughter becoming a *Lordess*. And as you know, it is possible but extremely rare for a pale skin to become a noble much less a Lord or Lordess. Females with exceptional skill and aspiration, on rare occasion have attained such high rank. However I can count the number of times this has occurred on my tail feathers, though she has now attained the rank of Lordess also."

Archippus glanced at Eri's tail and noted three feathers.

Eri continued. "Jemuel was bent on her daughter's career from birth as demonstrated by the name, and as a result, her daughter's title, quite ridiculously, is now *Lordess Lourdes*."

Archippus blinked twice. "That *is* ridiculous."

"Even more ridiculous is the fact that Lourdes was married once before. Lord Ipthsum's first wife died, and so he at first refused Lourdes' affections most likely because he suspected her motives. Everyone wants to be in power and atypical is pure intent when a Landling of lower station marries one of higher station, hence the High Ruler can never wed. But when Lord Ipthsum refused Lourdes, she married Lord Ipthsum's brother, Nadab, approximately fourteen years back. I suspect Nadab was vulnerable for although he was born to a family dark of skin, his skin was very light in tone. As you know, Landlings are naturally insecure about skin color, and when Lourdes pursued Nadab, I'm sure he was flattered, for no dark-skinned female would have him.

"Well, just last year, Nadab died at evening meal. He fell face first in a half shell of porridge. Of course, poisoning was suspected, but no one could surmise by whom.

"And according to Landling marital laws, a brother is to marry his brother's widow just as a sister is to marry her sister's husband if the sister were to die.

"It is a silly law, if you ask me. I suppose it was originally intended for financial security and familial continuity, but whatever the original reason, I believe this power hungry Lourdes woman planned the whole ascension and poisoned her own husband. The pathetic thing is, she and Nadab had a child, and so the entire power-crazed ascent will continue for I'm certain Lourdes will goad her offspring into control, command, and supremacy, causing continual problems for the High Council.

"Yes … the troubles of governing a Continent …" Eri mused.

"Well, I wonder if there is something I could help you with," said Archippus.

Eri tilted his head. "You?"

"Yes. I mean, being a pale commoner, I go unnoticed many places. If, for example, there were any information you wanted ferreted on Lordess Lourdes, I could quite possibly garner it."

Eri chuckled. "I like you, Landling."

Archippus felt encouraged by the comment.

"Hmmm …" Eri looked upward as if in thought. "I suppose it could be useful to know her greatest weakness."

"Of course," said Archippus. "To know an enemy's weakness is a great strength."

"Yes, I *would* like to know what she values above all else. For if we knew that, we could apply some pressure to keep her, well, let's say, seeing things the right way for not only her own good, but the good of the Continent."

"I would be honored to perform a service for the good of the Continent," insisted Archippus.

"Good. Then as soon as I am rid of the parasites, I shall transport you to Ai and you shall see what can be determined."

"Agreed," said Archippus. He felt a rush of joyous empowerment. He lifted the dipping bucket, said his good evening-morn to Eri, bowed and departed.

As Archippus walked the trail toward the main lair, he replayed his manipulative dialogue in his mind and thought he felt the ground tremor beneath his feet. *Perhaps it is from the elated spring in my step,* he thought.

As he entered the main lair, a bloodied slave collapsed on the dirt in front of the fire. He watched Raimi, Emoticas, and Gershom grab up shovels in a panic.

"Grab a shovel!" Raimi yelled at Archippus.

Archippus halted and furrowed his brow. "To bury the slave?" he asked, wondering why such speed was required.

"No! There's been an attack!" yelled Raimi. "The eegwuhnuhs and slaves on the flatlands are being attached by two-legged reptiles!"

"Why the shovels then?" he asked.

"We must fight them off!" She threw a shovel at Archippus. "The gunners are on their way!"

He caught the shovel, but quickly dropped it. "Let the gunners do the gunner work then, I've *seen* a two-legged reptile."

"Uugghh!" shouted Raimi. "You *are* a two-legged reptile!"

The three philanthropists ran from the lair and Archippus was left alone with the bloodied, unmoving slave.

Archippus picked up the shovel and poked the slave with the handle end. The brown-haired slave moved slightly and groaned. His metal neck clamp was firmly fastened, but the chain that led from the clamp appeared to have been broken mid-link. The slave was pale and thin with sunken eye sockets, probably from malnutrition, Archippus surmised.

Archippus peered uneasily at the slave. The sight reminded him of his own semblance and lengthy imprisonment. The slave appeared to be in pain. Archippus backed up a step. He knew nothing of medicine. "Do you want some water?" he asked.

The slave groaned again.

Archippus dropped the shovel and sought out Raimi's water pitcher from among the metal working utensils on her wooden table. He dribbled water on the corner of the slave's mouth. The slave licked it and then his head went limp.

Mortified that the victim may have perished in his presence, Archippus backed away again and slowly picked up the shovel. He stared at the face of the slave inadvertently touching his own eye socket with his free hand.

He took off at a run down the trail. It was no mystery to determine the direction of the flatlands. Two long lines of gunners were trotting up a cart road. Archippus fell in line behind two of them.

"We hurry to save slaves?" asked one gunner of another.

"Right. The two-leggeds are attacking the slaves *but more importantly* the eegwuhnuhs," responded the other. "It's a massacre."

The gunners picked up their pace, and in turn, Archippus sped up to avoid getting trampled from the line of gunners behind. Up ahead, Archippus heard loud roars and to his horror, screaming slaves.

He followed the gunners through a tree line onto a clearing lit by early sunlight and multiple campfires. The chaos brought Archippus to a halt. A gunner shoved him to the left and the line of defenders trotted past him.

Three two-legged reptiles were in the midst of fifty chained eegwuhnuhs who kept the two-leggeds back by lashing the attackers with their tails. In the center of it all, a group of slaves screamed and tugged at their neck chains.

Archippus watched the gunners form a ragged line right in front of him. The panicked eegwuhnuhs strained at their chains and flipped their tails about, accidentally slapping several gunners across the head. The fallen gunners crawled blindly about screaming. A two-legged snatched a neck-chained slave in his mouth, the chain snapped like a blade of grass, and the reptile flipped the slave violently into the air. The gunners let go a round of spears; the two-leggeds roared from the stabbing pain of the sharp tips. The slaves yelled and struggled against their neck chains.

Archippus watched Raimi whack her shovel at the chain that strung the slaves together and tethered them to a heavy iron post. A two-legged whacked her with his tail and knocked her into the center of the fray. Gershom ran to Raimi and got her back on her feet. They both sprinted back to the chain and hacked away in turn on one of the links next to the post. The chain broke. The slaves, still connected together at the neck, fled in all directions at once. In their panic, they kept falling and getting up and running and falling again until they figured out they had to all run in the same direction at once, the direction of the cart path where Archippus stood. Raimi and Gershom fled on the heels of the slaves passing Emoticas, who was whacking at the chain of a captive eegwuhnuh. They hollered at him to follow.

Archippus suddenly felt self-conscious and non-productive. He quickly ran his hand in the dirt, smeared some on his face, rumpled his dreadlocks, and squinted as if fatigued.

The chained together slaves followed by the entourage of Raimi, Gershom, and Emoticas fled past Archippus toward the main lair.

"Come!" Raimi yelled. "The gunners can finish, we freed the slaves!"

For a brief second, Archippus thought he should perhaps stay and help the gunners to make up for his lack of action. But then he heard *the* voice.

"I saw the whole thing, you know," said Hodos from a nearby branch.

"What? The massacre?" asked Archippus.

"Yes. That ... and you feigning to have been in the fray."

"Shut your beak, Bird."

"You are becoming more imprisoned each day."

"Leave off, Bird!" Archippus spun on his heels and ran toward the main lair.

Raimi roamed about the main lair tending the wounds of the ten remaining slaves while Gershom broke apart the chains. The injuries included lashes and welts and sailing spears sliced two slaves. Every one of them had raw skin under the metal neck clamps from straining to break free. The slave that Archippus left for dead had awakened and was sitting by the fire, hugging bent knees to his chest and rocking back in forth.

"They chained them together in the middle of those open flatlands?" Emoticas said as more of an incredulous statement than a question.

"The two-leggeds have never attacked before due to the sheer number of eegwuhnuhs who are safe in herds by day. I saw the Key Master run to try to reach the slaves, but he must have been struck down," said Raimi, pouring water down her bloodied arm.

"Why are the slaves not kept in the pit burrows?" asked Emoticas.

"Space," said Raimi. "But I expect they'll go there now. We can't afford to lose any more slaves. There will be no one to care for the eegwuhnuhs."

Two dark-skinned female council members entered the lair dressed in orange robes with crimson sashes. Their official attire indicated a just completed emergency hearing. Surprised by the unannounced visit, everyone except Archippus bowed their head a moment.

"Will they live?" asked one of the council members referring to the slaves.

"I believe so," said Raimi.

"Good, place them in the bottom burrows," said one council member. "The gunners have killed off the attacking reptiles. Only four of fifty eegwuhnuhs were lost. There will be plenty for the slaves to tend to once they are well. See to it they heal quickly."

The council members surveyed the lair a moment and departed.

"That was awfully heartfelt," said the knee-hugging slave as he continued to rock back and forth in discomfort. The sarcasm in his voice was overt.

"Your name?" asked Raimi.

"Hazo."

"Well, Hazo, you can bunk with Archippus. Archippus, take him now. The light has begun and we must all get inside the pit."

Archippus felt indignant. It was bad enough to have the bottom burrow. *But now I have to share it?*

Hazo lifted a bloody arm. "I'm weak, my friend. Please assist me."

Archippus stared at the bloody arm. He did not want to look at it, much less touch it.

"Please," Hazo repeated.

Archippus tentatively clasped the bloody arm and pulled the slave to his feet. Hazo smiled and draped the wounded arm across Archippus' shoulders and leaned on him.

"Thank you, friend."

Archippus wanted to say, *I'm not your friend, I'm not your kind, I'm not even remotely happy about any of this.* But resentfully he held his tongue and silently hoped Pterodactyl Eri would be quickly rid of his parasites to fly him far away from this disturbing place.

The next morning-eve, Archippus crested the stairs and then gained the ladder top.

"So what did we learn today?" asked Hodos expectantly.

Archippus gave no answer.

"Hello?" said Hodos.

Archippus spun toward him. "I learned you deserve to be spit upon," and then Archippus spit on Hodos.

Hodos blinked. "That really has nothing to do with the stairwell, you realize."

"Aarrgghh! Why can't you leave me be! I'm miserable! I shared my burrow with a slave who was in such pain he screamed periodically and stunk continually! I'm tired and hungry and ready to leave this cursed city, and I will leave soon and you can't stop me!"

"No, *you* can't stop *you*," said Hodos.

"What do you mean, *I* can't stop *me?*" Archippus screamed. "I don't *want* to stop me!"

"Precisely my point," said Hodos.

"Aarrgghh!" Archippus stomped off, his resolve to leave increased with each step away from the bird. He had saved all the coinage he could. Eri would soon be rid of parasites, and then he could leave Rephidim and lay eyes upon the noble girl in Ai. But he was concerned with Ezbon-Ishuah's statement about the Airborne flying so high, the lack of air might make him pass out and fall to an untimely death. But he hated to spend his limited coinage on a 'shrieking seedling' to help him breathe. Consequently, he decided to manipulate Raimi to give him a free plant.

Still immersed in anger, he got in the morning meal line behind his trio of co-workers. They were in the midst of conversation.

"… but if we enter the cliff race and win," said Raimi, "we can request better living accommodations for the slaves. Each winner is granted a request from the council."

"How do you know they'll let us enter?" asked Emoticas.

"Oh, they'll let us enter. Remember? Everyone is afraid to ride the newly trained eegwuhnuhs. Most of the time, they make slaves do it, and then the owner of the slave gets the request granted. And now, they won't want to lose any more slaves. They'll let us enter."

"But what if we don't win?" persisted Emoticas.

"Oh, we'll win," said Raimi. "You can ride Hemi."

"Which one is Hemi?" asked Emoticas.

"He's in Gershom's fourth lair," said Raimi. "He's the fastest eegwuhnuh Ezbon-Ishuah has ever seen. He said that in a test run on the flatland, the lizard beat every other eegwuhnuh by five tail lengths. And he can cross the *hemisphere* faster than any eegwuhnuh alive. That's why Ezbon-Ishuah named him Hemi."

"But I thought speed wasn't as important as skill in the cliff races," said Emoticas. He licked his lips as if the prospect of riding one of the big lizards made him nervous. "What good is fast if the darn thing slips and falls?"

"Like Ezbon-Ishuah always says," responded Raimi, "in competition as in commerce, 'swiftness wins, rapidity reigns, and velocity is victorious.'"

"Oh," said Emoticas. He glanced at Gershom nodding in agreement. "I suppose we should do it then … I mean, I want to help the slaves and all …"

"You'll do fine," said Raimi. "You'll have the safety strap."

"How high up is it?" asked Emoticas.

"Five hundred feet," answered Raimi.

The morning meal was gruel in a hollowed out coconut shell. This meant they would have to eat the gruel in the area and promptly return the shells for recycling.

Archippus joined the others sitting on nearby boulders.

"How's Hazo getting along?" asked Raimi, savoring her bowl of gruel.

Archippus thought to tell her how un-aromatic his cellmate was and how he hated to share the burrow with him, but knew it would not help his cause. "Fine, I think," he answered.

"Did he sleep well?"

"I believe so, the only thing is ..."

"What?"

"Well, you know how the air gets musty down there ..."

"Yes?"

"Well, with two of us sharing the same air ... and you know ... with the dampness and all, I think the musty air may have troubled him some. I wish there was something that could help in a pinch if the air grows overly stale. If he were to have trouble breathing, I'm not saying that he will mind you, but it's just a thought."

"Oh, I know something that could help!" Raimi exclaimed. "A shrieking seedling! If he has any trouble at all, he could just clamp it on his nose and it will help!"

Archippus, impressed by his own manipulative skills, smiled. "That is a terrific idea."

"I'll get one for you right after work," insisted Raimi.

Archippus smiled again, shaking his head left and right. "That is so kind of you, Raimi. Thank you."

Archippus watched Raimi furrow her brow. Perhaps he had overdone the 'so kind of you, thank you' thing. He would keep it in mind next time not to be so overly out of character.

"How's Ezbon-Ishuah today?" asked Archippus, changing the subject.

"He's taking another day off to rest," answered Raimi. "I told him all about the massacre, but prefaced it by telling him that only four eegwuhnuhs were lost and that all will be well. I am so relieved he didn't see it happen. It would have been hard on his heart." She looked down and swallowed hard.

Morning-eve arrived and Raimi presented Archippus with a shrieking seedling planted in a coconut half shell. The plant had a dark green stem with two sturdy leaves at the base, and the stem arched upward with a deep purple flower at the end. In the middle of the flower, long purple petals shot out in a widening cone shape. "Keep in mind," she said, "that the seedlings shriek if air grows scarce, but they also shriek when they grow."

"How will I know the difference?" asked Archippus.

"Oh, you'll know," said Raimi. "Here, take this bowl of gruel for Hazo."

Archippus took the items and descended the stairs carrying the seedling and gruel and harboring a great deal of confidence. *My plan will soon come to fruition.*

⤚ ⤚ ⤚ ⤚
⤚ ⤚ ⤚ ⤚

That night-day, Archippus slept very little. He was awakened repeatedly by screams. Hazo insisted it was not so much the pain as the nightmares. But to make matters worse, the plant was apparently growing. It too shrieked on occasion with a high-pitched screech. Between the two, Archippus received less than an hourglass worth of sleep. He thought to toss the shrieking seedling down the Echoless Pit, but he needed the plant for his flight. *Perhaps Hazo then ...* He wrestled with the thought until he thought the better of it. He decided instead to wake Hazo now and request he stay awake for the daylight hours.

"Hazo," Archippus shook the slave's leg.

Hazo groaned. "Yes?"

"Wake up."

"What? Why?"

"You have been keeping me awake all night-day. I need sleep. You stay awake *now* because *you* can *sleep* while I *work*."

"Huh?" He attempted a half sit up and then groaned again.

"Stay awake so I can sleep!" Archippus snapped. "I may be able to get an eighth of an hourglass if you stay awake and quit screaming!"

"Oh."

Archippus flopped on his left side facing away from Hazo.

"Why do you loathe me?" asked Hazo.

Archippus heaved a heavy sigh and shot to a seated position. "Don't talk to me or I won't be able to sleep!" He flopped back onto the soft earth.

"But I can't help but wonder what makes you think you're so different," said Hazo.

Archippus sat up abruptly again. "Because I'm not *stupid!* If someone said, 'Let me sleep,' I'd let them sleep!"

"But I'm not stupid. I understand what 'Let me sleep' means. It's just that you've upset me so much, I feel I must have an answer to why you loathe me and the rest of the slaves."

"Because I am not a *slave,* you dullard!"

"So?"

"So?"

"Yes. So?" repeated Hazo.

"So I am not the bottom rung, the stench of society, the lowest of Landlings. That's what!"

Archippus flopped back down on his bed of dirt.

"You have the same skin color," said Hazo.

"Aarrgguuhh!" Archippus shot up once more. "Let me repeat, *I'm not stupid!* I know a trade! I am a wordsmith and a scribe and could easily be a pleator!"

"I could be those things too with some training," said Hazo.

"No, you could not!"

"Why not?"

"Because you *are* stupid!"

Hazo, stunned, stared at Archippus.

"You know what? Forget it," continued Archippus. Not sleeping is better for me than trying to sleep with your idiocy hanging in the air about me." He jumped to his feet, bumping his head on a low portion of the burrow's ceiling. He cursed, strode out of the burrow, and stomped up the stairwell.

When he got to the top, he saw Hodos perched on a boulder.

"I hate you!" Archippus yelled, and stomped by.

Two weeks later, Archippus applied the final parasite treatment to Eri's teeth.

"We'll know tomorrow if they are completely gone," he told Eri. The big pterodactyl just nodded.

Archippus hiked the trail toward the main lair. Raimi and the others were eating dinner. Archippus sat on a nearby boulder. Raimi tossed him a papaya. As he peeled the fruit, Raimi continued with a conversation already underway.

"If we win the cliff race and make our request to the council members, how shall we word it?" she asked. "We only get one request."

Gershom was playing softly on the flute. Archippus noticed that even with his missing pinky, he had enough fingers to play the seven-holed instrument. Unfortunately.

Gershom stopped playing, set the flute aside, and made motions with his hands.

Emoticas interpreted for Raimi. "Gershom thinks we should ask for freedom for all the slaves."

Archippus could not help himself. "Why do you care about pale-skinned slaves?" He turned to Gershom. "You don't even have pale skin. If I had your advantage, I certainly wouldn't be here now. I'd have achieved a fortune and be in power. I'd have made myself a leader, and I still will

147

mind you, but these slaves could do likewise, earn their own advancement, and make their own way. *I'm* going to."

Gershom gave Archippus a disproving look.

"They'll never grant freedom to the slaves," said Raimi, ignoring Archippus. "And we only get one request. If they don't grant it, we lose our chance because a second request cannot be considered."

"Food then," said Emoticas. "More food. They are all too skinny."

"But what good is food if they are still chained in a field where they can be massacred? They need shelter," said Raimi sadly.

Archippus sighed with impatience, amazed at the simple minds about him. "Lodging," he said as he took a bite of papaya.

The three of them actually looked at him.

"What?" asked Raimi.

"Lodging." He chomped as he spoke. "Ask for better lodging conditions for the slaves. Lodging encompasses room and board in one word."

"That's brilliant!" Raimi sprang up, ran to Archippus, and hugged him.

He stared at her, mortified. "That was utter invasion of my space."

"Sorry," she smiled and shrugged. "Anyway," she plopped down in her original spot and continued. "We shall ask for lodging then." She turned toward Archippus. "Are you going to watch the cliff race?"

"When is it?"

"Next week, at the appearance of the full moon."

"No."

"Oh."

"I'll be gone."

"Oh."

Gershom made a single, vehement gesture at Archippus.

"What did he say?" asked Archippus.

"Nothing," said Emoticas.

"No, I can see he clearly said something," insisted Archippus.

Emoticas sat very still for a moment.

"What did he say?" Archippus asked, annoyed.

"He said he wishes you Seraph's speed and happiness and success in your journey ... and may you marry the noble girl, buy a nice hut, and ... uh ... find fulfilling employment," said Emoticas.

"All that in one gesture?" asked Archippus, suspicious.

"Yes ... uh ... all that in one motion," Emoticas answered, while trying not to smile.

Gershom stood and stomped away.

Raimi burst out laughing.

"What?" Archippus asked.

"I don't know the silent language yet," said Raimi, "but my guess would be he just said 'to the grave with you.'"

Archippus jumped to his feet. "Good riddance! I'll never see any of you again, and I'll never regret it!" He headed toward the burrows.

On the way down the stairwell, he stopped at the entrance to Ezbon-Ishuah's burrow. Ezbon-Ishuah was the only one he would regret leaving. Archippus had been checking on the old man nightly by ringing the entrance bell. Some nights Ezbon-Ishuah was too tired, but on other occasions, he would invite Archippus to sit with him on the sofa and they would talk of commerce. The art of scribing had fallen to the wayside because Ezbon-Ishuah's hands had weakened.

Archippus rang the silver entrance bell.

"DM is it? Come in."

Archippus sat next to his mentor on the couch.

"Eri's parasites should be gone tomorrow," said Archippus.

Ezbon-Ishuah turned his head to look at Archippus. "You'll be leaving then?"

"Yes."

Ezbon-Ishuah stared at the wall a moment. "You will do well in life," he said.

Neither Archippus nor Ezbon-Ishuah spoke for a few seconds.

Ezbon-Ishuah continued. "I wish you had been born my son."

Archippus' throat felt tight, he did not know what to say. No one had ever wished a connection with him, much less a familial one. *Ezbon-Ishuah, a dark-skinned master tradesmon, wants me to be his son?*

"Apply the principles we have spoken of," continued Ezbon-Ishuah. "And you will do well at whatever you wish to achieve."

"I will."

"Go now."

Archippus stood and abruptly left. He could hardly see his way out of the burrow for his teary eyes.

$$\begin{array}{cccc} \twoheadleftarrow & \twoheadleftarrow & \twoheadleftarrow & \twoheadleftarrow \\ \twoheadleftarrow & \twoheadleftarrow & \twoheadleftarrow & \twoheadleftarrow \end{array}$$

PARCHMENT VI

"Dark complexions were the mark of innate nobility ..."

The young High Ruler donned full armor and clanged her way to gunner instruction class.

Isui met Apphia at the entrance to the fencing courtyard, a private square open to the sun. A hall with arches that opened onto the square enclosed the courtyard on three sides, and an iron wall blocked the fourth side, affording complete privacy. The floor of the hall was brick and the courtyard grass, with small rolling hills, shrubs, a handful of trees, and an occasional boulder. The uneven terrain simulated a battlefield.

Apphia's trainer, Isui, was perhaps the most muscular Landling on the Continent. He trained gunners all day. The eight to twelve hourglasses worth of exercise daily had given him arms and legs like tree trunks. Despite his heft and occupation, he had a sense of humor. This made Apphia's training as pleasant as possible, though grueling. He presented himself this day without his armor revealing huge biceps wrapped in gold bracelets and gold medallions hanging from each ear. His nearly baldpate sprouted narrow crops of hair over each ear trimmed into spear shapes that ended on his cheekbones. Isui claimed the unusual hairstyle distracted opponents.

Isui, as usual, had reserved the courtyard for Apphia's training. Normally, they sparred for an hour or two teaching Apphia the art of fencing.

Today, however, the courtyard contained a second armor-clad figure.

"We have a volunteer," announced Isui.

Apphia stopped in her tracks. During her previous training sessions, she had never interacted with anyone other than Shear-Jashub, Entimus, and Isui.

"Who's inside the armor?" she asked Isui.

"No one of significance."

"Male or female?"

"Male."

Of course, another male, thought Apphia. She'd never had a girlfriend to laugh with, play with, or confide in, and this vacancy in her life had often saddened her.

"What's his name?" asked Apphia.

"You can call him 'Soon to be Dead' because the object is to kill him," said Isui.

Apphia squinted at the figure through her visor and stood silent for several seconds. She turned back toward Isui and ventured to comment. "You're joking, right?"

"I never joke," said Isui.

More silence.

She stared again at the figure. "You *always* joke, and I don't want to kill anyone."

"But you must!" insisted Isui. "If you don't, then should you have to kill in the future, the thought will unsettle you. You could become distracted and be injured."

Now Apphia realized Isui was serious. "I refuse!" she shouted. Her voice sounded tinny inside the heavy armor. She threw down her sword and turned to leave.

Isui stepped in front of her.

"But you must practice, Your Eminence. I've been commissioned to train you the same as all top gunners! If you don't do this, they'll have my head!"

"Yours ... his. What's the difference!" she snapped.

"The difference?" asked Isui shocked. "The difference is I am a gunner of the Fourth Field, and this ... this ... this figure, is a *volunteer,* mind you. He is a mere slave, a pale-skinned plebeian!"

"Oh, so I'm supposed to slaughter a slave? Do it yourself!" Apphia screamed. She was so distraught she saw red spots in front of her eyes.

Isui looked about to ensure no one had heard. "Your Eminence, listen ..."

He grabbed her arm to stay her. "You don't have to kill him *today.* Just at *some* point."

"That's not the point!" she yelled.

"Heh ... hem," exclaimed the armored figure.

Apphia again squinted at the figure.

"Your Lofty High Rulership." The armored man gave an awkward bow. "Do not fear, I have volunteered for the honor of sparring with you."

Apphia backed and stared.

"And do not fear," the figure bowed a second time, "you will never be able to kill me."

"I won't?" she asked relieved.

"No. You won't."

"Why not?"

"Because my fencing skills are superior to yours."

"Really?"

"Really."

Apphia felt irked. "That's awfully arrogant of you."

"Come see," said the figure and he held up a sorry excuse for a sword.

"Why is his sword cylindrical?" asked Apphia of Isui.

"With no sharp edges, and with you clad in armor, he cannot kill you."

"That's not fair," said Apphia.

"I don't need fair, Your Glorious Exaltedness." The figure emphatically waved the pathetic weapon. "You shall still never kill me."

"Oh, you think?" demanded Apphia.

"Think? I don't just *think,* I *know.*" The figure swooshed the semi-sword with fervor.

"Fine." Apphia stepped onto the courtyard grass and assumed the sparring position.

Isui heaved a sigh of relief.

The slave lunged forward, his sword sweeping toward her. Apphia took two sliding steps backward, brought her own sword around, and blocked the blow. The slave lunged and swung at her again, she blocked again, he struck again, she blocked again. The combatants battled across the courtyard, the slave constantly advancing, Apphia always retreating.

Apphia did not want to kill the slave, but tried hard to strike him to indicate she would have won the match if not for the slave's armor. She knew Isui was scoring them, but try as she may, she could not deliver what would be interpreted as a fatal blow.

Twice, the egotistical slave struck her armor in the area of her heart, and this caused Apphia no small amount of consternation.

"Enough!" cried Isui.

The fighting figures halted.

"So you see, Your Eminence, this is much needed practice," said Isui.

"You can say that again," said the slave.

"So you see, Your Eminence, this is much—"

"I heard you the first time!" shouted Apphia. "But it's not my fault!"

"Why is it not your fault, Your Splendid Supremacy?" goaded the slave.

"Because … because you are so clad with conceitedness it distracted me," she snapped.

"Oh," answered the slave. "Well, let's hope you only encounter unconfident opponents on the battlefield."

"Maybe I don't mind killing you after all," countered Apphia.

"Too bad you cannot," badgered the slave.

"Enough!" cried Isui again. "Good job, slave. Not only did you spar well, but you have succeeded in making the High Ruler wish to kill you. I shall see to it that you are well fed until such time as Her Eminence actually gains the courage and ability to slay you."

"That day will never come," said the slave.

Isui chuckled. "We'll see, anyway, enough for today. Your Eminence, I am very proud of your efforts. You must make your way to the bath now. The council members await you."

Apphia felt frustrated, she knew she had failed.

"Till next time, Your Exquisite Exemplariness." The slave attempted a third bow, then straightened and removed his helmet. His yellow hair arched outward from a V- centered hairline and fell shoulder's length over his armor. His eyes were bright and shockingly blue. He removed his glove and extended a pale hand. "Isn't it customary to remove the helmet and shake hands after a match?"

Apphia's face flushed.

"Her Eminence does not remove her helmet," said Isui.

"Pity," said the slave, "but I understand, Your Illustrious Eliteness. Till next time, then." He bowed his head.

"Till next time," Apphia mumbled, bowing her head slightly in return.

"You'd best make haste to the Iron Hall, Your Eminence," said Isui. He placed an iron cuff on the slave's wrist and led him away. The cocky slave waved an enthusiastic good-bye with his free hand.

Shear-Jashub met Apphia at the courtyard entrance and escorted her to the bath inside the Iron Hall. Once a week, the council members met in a heated pool inside the heavily guarded Iron Hall to bathe and informally discuss the Continent or less pressing matters. They wore saris, floral fabrics tied behind the neck and about the waist and used exclusively for bathing.

Apphia emerged from behind the changing curtain wrapped in a sari and dipped her toe into the heated pool. Steam wafted upward from the water. The water was not as hot today as last week. Last week, Apphia had sat on the pool's edge and dipped only her legs in the water. The slaves that oversaw the flaming furnace in the basement had overheated the water and quite possibly paid dearly for the error. But this week, the water temperature was perfect. She stepped in completely; submerging even her head, then surfaced and swiped the water from her baldhead.

It was a relief to Apphia that the council members knew of her pale skin, for the bath was one of two places where she could remove her armor—the other being her chambers. The fact that the council members had elected her despite her pale white skin remained a confusing issue to her. She had wrestled the matter over and over in her mind, and kept coming back to the suspicion that the counselors didn't really need her and simply wanted her around so they could order her about like a child. What mystified her mainly was that most members spoke kindly to her as if they liked her—apart from those dreadful hearings, when they always sided with the Airbornes.

And then there was Reuel. He was *always* abrasive.

A handful of female council members walked to the water's edge and stepped in. Apphia felt envious of their beauty. One of the females, Duma, had dark short curls pressed against a perfectly shaped face. Her lips were full and her ivory teeth gleamed.

Another female, Shelah, had wonderful thick hair pulled upward in various clasps to differing levels. This arrangement allowed her cascading black locks to tumble down the back and sides of her head, and come delicately to rest on the tops of her shoulders.

Shelah had the prettiest smile too. When she laughed, the corners of her heart-shaped top lip pulled upward revealing perfect white teeth, and her cheeks lifted to form slight half circles beneath eyes like tiny bright suns setting on a hilltop. And Shelah had always been the nicest of the females as far as Apphia was concerned.

Apphia inadvertently swiped water from her bare skull again. The blond haired slave boy flashed into her mind. Whether she was supposed to or not, she must never remove her helmet after a match, lest the boy see that she is ugly and bald. She could endure ugly, but not the baldness.

"How was your match today?" asked Duma.

Apphia snapped out of the daydream. "Huh?"

"Your match; it was your first match against someone other than Isui, was it not?"

"Oh. Yes," said Apphia.

"So, did you slay him?" asked Duma.

"What? No. No, I did not. In fact, I'm not all that keen on the whole slaying thing."

"I don't blame you," said Shelah. "It's like hunting. I never could bring myself to spear a deer."

"But you don't mind eating one," said Duma.

"It's one thing to eat one, and entirely another to slay it," said Shelah, languidly splashing water on her long, dark arms.

"No it's not," said Duma. "You can't be considered innocent if you eat the result."

"Yes I can, once it's dead, it's dead. What does the deer care after the fact?"

"Good point," said Duma. She turned to Apphia. "So you see, my dear Apphia, once the slave is dead, he won't care at all."

"That wasn't exactly my point," said Shelah.

"But a good point to be made nonetheless," said Duma.

"Can we talk about something else?" asked Apphia.

"Like what?" asked Duma.

"Like why is Eri a hypocrite? Why can *he* use the name of the Seraph, but I can't?"

"Our Counselors," answered Duma, "encourage us to focus on the here and now, for the Seraph has grown distant and unavailable. I am certain that Eri only invokes the name for clarification, when necessary, to instruct you. The important thing is to rely on those closest to you who have your best interest at heart."

"And another thing," said Apphia, completely unplaced by the answer, "who is Aro, and why doesn't Eri want me speaking with him?"

Duma and Shelah looked at each other. "Aro is a survivor," said Duma.

"A survivor?"

"When the gargoyles waged the sky war, they killed off all the songbirds that had the gift of speech."

Duma looked at Shelah for assistance.

"A songbird with the gift of speech is made in the image of the *Seraph*," said Shelah, lowering her voice when she said *Seraph*. "The *Seraph*, according to legend, is a great white bird with a wingspan of forty feet, crystal blue eyes, and a golden beak. He speaks things into being and can wield words like weapons."

"So they *fear* Aro?" asked Apphia.

"They would fear to harm him for fear of the *Seraph*," answered Shelah.

"If Airbornes fear the Seraph," persisted Apphia, "then why do they try to erase him from society, from speech, from remembrance in the minds of Landlings? And is this why Landlings have very little access to the scrolls?"

"The Airborne Counselors have been given autonomy," said Duma, "to decide, and to lead, not fly about looking indecisively to the sky. If the Seraph were concerned with our governance of the Continent, he would descend from his tower and come to the Continent and do something about it."

"So we must be governing well," insisted Shelah.

"And as for access to the scrolls," continued Duma, "common Landlings are unable to interpret them properly. This is the trouble with the Barbirians. They have selected and focused on the violent verses and thereby miss the entire body of the message in the scrolls."

"It would be like me," added Shelah lifting her pinky out of the water and wiggling it. "Staring at your pinky and insisting it is you. The Barbirians read the stolen verses and see only uprising."

Apphia frowned and thought on this for a moment. "But on two occasions," she ventured, "I had Shear-Jashub escort me to the scrolls. I wanted to see them for myself."

"And?" asked Duma.

"And I think they are not so mysterious. I think the Landlings should have access to them. I mean, I read one of the verses, and it made me feel … good," said Apphia.

"Whatever did you read?" asked Shelah.

"The verse said, 'Blessed are the poor in spirit, for theirs is the After-sky.'"

"Well, there you go," said Duma. "First of all, you have no reason to feel poor in spirit. You are the most prestigious figure on the Continent. Secondly, you cannot trust the validity of a verse based on a feeling. The Barbirians read of violence and it makes them feel good about themselves. They feel they have a purpose if they war with the established government, for the act of war is one of the two most dangerous lies on the Continent. When engaged in war, Landlings feel they have a reason to live and it makes them euphoric. So again, I must counsel you to never rely on a feeling."

Apphia looked down into the water.

"Do you really feel poor in spirit?" asked Shelah.

"I feel I am the poorest of all poor," answered Apphia, her chin quivering.

"That's awfully ungrateful of you," snapped Duma.

Apphia looked abruptly up from the water. Duma's words were like a punch in the gut. "I *do* feel poor," she argued. "Poor in friendship, poor in freedom, and so incredibly poor that I may not give an opinion, especially at the hearings. To not be permitted to voice an opinion is poverty indeed."

"We summoned you out of poverty as a pale-skinned commoner and elected you High Ruler," Duma countered angrily. "You've been given a palatial suite with two full-time guards and the finest of furniture. You eat the choicest foods, train as an elite gunner, and reside in the safest of all possible cities. Shame on you for your ungratefulness!"

Apphia looked back down trying to hide the tears welling in her eyes.

"Duma!" Shelah reprimanded. "Speak kindly to her. She has been given a lot of responsibility. I'm sure her scrutinized life weighs heavy. She cannot help how she feels."

"But not controlling her feelings is exactly the danger I have been trying to warn her of, and if she feels *that* poor, I must caution her to not fall prey to the second lie," said Duma.

"What's the second lie?" Apphia asked softly without looking up for fear she would burst into tears.

"Love," said Duma. "And I don't mean the type of love that one should have for all Landkind, the altruistic caring for others on the Continent, I mean romantic love. For love, like war, makes you feel fully alive, but it is transient. Those that devote themselves to romantic love waste their lives. You'll do well to not waste your life. Follow the counsel of Pterodactyl Eri and you'll do well."

"I don't even think Eri likes me," whispered Apphia. The tightness in her throat made it hard to speak. "He's hard on me."

"You should respect your Airborne Counselor," cautioned Duma.

"But there's something about him I don't trust!" continued Apphia. "He's not always good ... he seems at times ... cruel. Sometimes I believe him to be the very reincarnation of Lord Gargoyle himself."

"Do not say such things, child!" Duma hissed. "Lord Gargoyle was the epitome of all that is base in the Allurian beliefs! He was arrogant and self-centered and power-hungry, but your Eri has only the best interest of the Continent at heart!"

Apphia felt fearful for having spoken, but Shelah reached out, took Apphia's chin in her hand, and looked directly at her with a warm, caring heart-smile. "He's hard on you because he cares and wants to see you grow strong."

"Yes," injected Duma. "You can't fashion iron with feathers."

"So I'm told," said Apphia. She dipped under the water to hide her tears and swam off whishing fervently that Eri's parasites would eat him alive.

↢ ↢ ↢ ↢
↢ ↢ ↢ ↢

Archippus peered between Eri's teeth. "The parasites are gone," he said.

"Good, and you're ready to travel I take it?"

"I'm ready." Archippus placed the shrieking seedling he had carried from the burrow into his travel sack.

"We won't be flying high enough to need that," said Eri.

Archippus looked disappointed.

"But bring it," said Eri. "Perhaps as a treat if you succeed in your information seeking mission."

Archippus brightened.

Eri lowered himself and Archippus swung a leg over the creature's neck and sat on his broad shoulders. Archippus slung the travel sack on his back and buckled a safety strap about Eri's leathery neck for gripping in flight. Eri dropped his body low to the ground, his fifteen-foot wings shot outward. Archippus' teeth jolted together as the big pterodactyl rocketed upward. Each sinking motion between wing thrusts tossed Archippus' stomach about, but in moments, the queasiness vanished and the jostling of flapping wings smoothed to a steady, straight ahead whir. They were far above the ground; trees looked like grass blades, and the many fires and torches below mirrored the far-off gleam from the uncountable overhead candles that lit the evening sky. The constant flow of warm air pushed Archippus' dreadlocks pleasantly back. He clutched the strap tightly for fear of falling, but despite the height, a nervous smile spread across his face. *I'm riding a pterodactyl!* He had achieved the first part of his ambitious plan.

He looked left, right, up, down. He even twisted backward to take it all in. He did a double take—he could have sworn Eri had three tail feathers, but now he counted four!

No matter.

Archippus twisted back to face the front. Eri flew through a moonlit cloud; cool moisture enveloped his skin.

This is unreal ... I can do anything!

Soaring on Eri's back, Archippus wished he could become Eri's permanent wingmon.

But even without Eri, I will become a noble. I was born to lead!

He felt like screaming *Look at me* at the top of his lungs, but kept the feeling to himself to act respectable, though he really felt he was more than deserving of the pleasure of riding high on Eri.

His thoughts sprang forward to his landing in the city of Ai. Hodos had said his mother was dead, and his sister no longer in the city. *But where could she have gone? It is uncommon for a commoner to leave his or her birth city without good reason.* Though he questioned Hodos' accuracy, he felt saddened.

They flew on through the night. After a time the sun crested the mountains to his left. Gold and red rays bathed the terrain below. Archippus spotted landscapes of browns and greens and shimmering rivers winding like snakes. Each mountain seemed like a pinched-up pile of sand found in the bottom of an hourglass. They flew far above a lake. Flocks of birds below resembled hovering gnats. They continued on and on for hours and hours until the sun had passed well overhead and had again begun its descent.

"You should lower me into the quarry," suggested Archippus. He wasn't sure of the location of a pterodactyl's ear so he spoke to the back of Eri's head.

"How so?" asked Eri.

"So everyone will notice me, of course."

"I suppose we never discussed a plan," answered Eri, "but I could lower you there to make my announcement."

"Announcement?"

"Yes. I was thinking I would tell Lordess Lourdes that in honor of her wedding, the council members have sent her a scribe to assist her with her daily texting to friends or relatives, of crafting house rules, of drafting enactments, of whatever it is she may require. As a gift of course."

Archippus thought on this. "I like it."

"Of course you do," answered Eri.

They sailed on in silence. Archippus daydreamed of the noble girl. His arriving on Pterodactyl Eri was sure to impress her. Archippus was amazed that a single night and day flight on this creature could get him to Ai, when it had taken many days to hike the opposite way to Rephidim.

He smelled the scent of trees and soon spotted what seemed from this elevation, a toy city. It appeared the Judgment Hall could easily have been carved from a hand-sized granite stone, and the building that had imprisoned him for so long, looked as though it could be crushed with his foot. He felt powerful and he liked the feeling.

Eri circled the city several times to draw attention. As the Airborne lost altitude, Archippus watched many Landlings running, pointing, and waving. The council members hurried out onto the Judgment Hall steps. Instinctively, they all began to hurry in the direction of the quarry to view the landing. Eri circled the quarry at a low elevation until a sufficient audience had arrived. The council members were easily recognized by their orange robes and crimson sashes, but most importantly, Lordess Lourdes was being transported toward the quarry on a golden carrying lounge with a slave shouldering each of four handles.

Eri was seething. "That can only be her."

Lordess Lourdes reclined on her lounge in front of the very front row of spectators. A slave held up a palm branch to shield her from the setting sun.

Eri dipped a wing, settled into a long smooth glide, and landed directly in the center of the quarry's stage. Archippus dismounted and stood smiling alongside the huge Airborne.

"Greeting, Landlings!" Eri's voice boomed outward from the acoustic rock quarry. "As you know, I, Pterodactyl Eri, am Counselor to the High Ruler of the Iron Hall and as such, I am head advisor on the High Council of Twenty-four. I have come today, to honor the new Lordess of the City of Ai."

Lordess Lourdes sat up quickly. She seemed surprised, but pleased as she thrust out an arm, tacitly demanding that a slave assist her to her feet. As she rose, she reached to straighten her brown pinned-up locks with her free hand.

She curtsied to Eri. "The honor is mine, Pterodactyl Eri."

Eri bowed and continued. "I have come to bestow upon you a gift."

A rumble of approval rippled through the crowd.

Eri pointed a gigantic wingtip in Archippus' direction. "I give to you this master scribe to assist you with all your texting requirements."

Lordess Lourdes curtsied again, beaming, obviously enjoying her position as the center of attention. "A gracious and practical gift, Pterodactyl Eri. I shall use his services with gratitude and hopefully wisdom."

"Yes, hopefully," muttered Pterodactyl Eri to himself. Then aloud he announced, "I bring news that the High Council ..."

Eri droned on extemporaneously about recent laws and enactments under the guise that he had come to present a speech, though actually the gift of the scribe was the important thing. Archippus was extremely impressed by Eri's impromptu deception.

Archippus scanned the audience in hopes of spotting the noble girl, but could not find her in the crowd. Disappointed he thought, *No matter, she will hear of my arrival.*

Archippus was of course worried about being recognized as an escaped slave. He warily avoided eye contact with all of the council members, though he figured they had not laid eyes on him for almost six years, and he had put on weight and gained muscle. *It's not like the council members have ever visited me in prison, and Lord Ipthsum has never laid eyes on me.*

He thought that the only two Landlings who might recognize him were Guard and the noble girl, and he believed the noble girl cared for him, and Guard would never question Pterodactyl Eri. He heaved a sigh of relief and decided he should not worry, but instead, feel confident.

Eri finished his speech, leaned his head toward Archippus, and whispered. "I must check on a matter with Lord Ipthsum, and then I must leave. But I shall return to check on your progress in one week."

Eri lifted off toward the meeting with Lord Ipthsum. His massive wings fanned the hair about on the heads of every Landling. The setting sun cast Eri's shadow across row upon row of seats. In a matter of seconds, he disappeared into the gathering gloom, and the Landlings began to file out of the quarry.

"Oh, scribe!" called Lordess Lourdes waving a hand. "Come, come. I must tell you of all the projects I have in mind. Come fan me with a palm branch as they carry me back to my home." She reclined on her lounge. Archippus thought her face held a sickeningly silly grin, though he took up the palm branch.

Fanning Lordess Lourdes was not exactly how he wanted to be seen entering the city. *What if the noble girl sees me? It's slaves work.* He reluctantly waved the branch over Lordess Lourdes' head and walked alongside the lounge.

"The very first thing I must have you do," said Lordess Lourdes, "is prepare a text message for my cousin. I have not seen her in a century's time, it seems, and she has been residing at the Citadel by the Sea. I shall open a dialogue and ask her how that illustrious singer and actor, Rueben, is doing. I hear he is at some point going to travel to the remaining cities to perform. I would so love to see him in person."

"So you are close to your cousin?" asked Archippus, working hard to fan her and keep up with the lounge.

"No. She's jealous of me, naturally," said Lordess Lourdes.

"Understandably."

"Understandably," repeated Archippus.

"And then, I must have you draft a note for the shawl makers in the sixth city of Shambala. I had a shawl transported there for mending, and I have not seen it in several months. I need to check on the progress."

"So you are fond of your fine clothes, of which I am sure you have many," ventured Archippus.

"Well, clothes are clothes you know. As my mother used to say, it is not so much what is worn, but who is wearing it."

"Yes. Of course," said Archippus. He began to wonder if Lordess Lourdes were so wacky as to only hold herself dear. *Her only weakness may be her love of self,* thought Archippus.

"And then, I need for you to correct a bill I received for the repair of my gemstone necklace. I was charged four hourglasses worth of time, and I have it on experienced authority that the type of repair he performed should only take two hourglasses."

"You must have a lot of gems to complement your beauty," said Archippus. "Do you keep them safely hidden? I am sure you value them greatly."

"You flatter me," said Lordess Lourdes. "Actually, I suppose I deserve to be showered with jewels, but my former husband could only afford the one necklace, and Lord Ipthsum is not a gift giver. No matter. It is not trinkets that give one prestige, it is position. And I have power, you realize, over this entire city."

"I realize that," said Archippus. *Drat! I already knew she valued power, a week's time may not be sufficient to find her weakness.*

They arrived at a large wooden door with iron knockers. Her fifth slave used an iron key to open the door. Archippus tilted his head upward to view the exterior of the small castle as he entered. He noted two large round spirals with several floors of arched windows shooting upward on either side of the arched door. Ivy clung intensely to the towers like veins on an angered neck.

They entered a large round room lit by an oil lamp chandelier. Arches on either side of the room led into dark hallways. Arched windows allowed twilight to fall upon the brownstone floor. Beginning near the entrance he had just come through, Archippus saw that a large iron aviary ran the length of one wall, turned the corner and went halfway along another wall. The big cage held a variety of chirping songbirds, maybe twenty different birds in all, ranging from tiny finches, to pigeons, and parrots, and even a raven.

Across the room, a plush stuffed chair and a footstool of scarlet fabric dotted with yellow leaves, sat at an angle near the window. Next to the chair was a wooden writing desk with a three-legged stool, parchment paper, and an inkwell.

The slaves lowered the lounge onto the brownstone floor and Lordess Lourdes extended her arm for Archippus to hoist her upward. The Lordess took her seat in the scarlet chair. Above and behind the chair was a portrait of none other than the Lordess sitting in the same scarlet chair. The resemblance was uncanny, and Archippus found himself staring at it, and having to endure two Lordess Lourdesses: the real Lordess Lourdes and the painted Lordess Lourdes. The redundancy seemed arrogant and irritated him greatly.

"We shall begin with the letter to my cousin." Lordess Lourdes motioned him to sit at the desk to the left of her shoulder.

A slave took the sack containing the shrieking seedling and Archippus reluctantly took a seat. He was miffed that she had not even offered him any refreshment—he had not eaten for a night and day. A washbasin might also be nice. He seethed at how self- centered she was, but picked up the pen, and dipped it into the ink. As Lordess Lourdes spoke, Archippus scribed the dictation. She faced away from him affirming his insignificance. He thought to flick some ink on the back of her head, but stayed his hand due to an abrupt interruption from a sixth slave dressed in green garb with a yellow waist belt.

"Lordess Lourdes," said the slave as he bowed. "Your daughter asks to picnic in the field outside the quarry." He bowed again.

A huge sigh came from the seated sovereign. "I worry when she is away," said Lordess Lourdes. "I don't know why she can't entertain herself inside these walls. A young noble girl risks danger to be out of doors, especially when she is the envy of every other daughter of nobility."

"Yes, Lordess." The slave bowed again. "I only asked at her behest."

"Well, go to her and tell her *no*," said Lordess Lourdes.

"You are wise to protect your daughter," said Archippus. "She must be the pride of your heart throne."

Lordess Lourdes abruptly swiveled in her scarlet chair and looked at him. "She is the future. What good is it to light the world, if not for someone to receive and carry your torch forward?"

The sincerity with which she spoke the words struck Archippus as out of character for the self-centered Lordess. And then he realized, this very first day, *I have discovered her weakness!* He puffed his chest forward feeling pleased with himself, but all the air was sucked from his chest the very next second as the daughter of Lordess Lourdes walked into the room from one of the hallways. Her reddish-brown hair flowed back from her ivory forehead crowning two emerald green eyes. Archippus could not breathe. *The noble girl!*

"Mother! I will not be kept a prisoner in these walls! I shall suffocate!" She marched directly to a footstool and placed her sandaled foot upon it. For added emphasis she leaned forward and glared at her mother with hands on hips.

Lordess Lourdes leaned forward also and an argument ensued. Archippus did not hear what was said for his brain had ceased functioning. He was suffering from shock. He guessed that in the end, the Queen of Mean had won, for the noble girl spun and strode angrily back into the hall.

"Wait!" yelled Lordess Lourdes.

The noble girl stopped, but did not turn.

"Your manners," said her mother.

The noble girl turned slowly, stiff with reluctance.

"This scribe was presented to me from none other than Pterodactyl Eri as a wedding present. Not *everyone* is resentful of our union," said Lordess Lourdes.

"Scribe, this is my daughter, Jazelle. Jazelle, this is my new scribe who is a master scribe, which means he is very adept at the nuances of language and unparalleled in his usage of vocabulary."

"Pleased to meet you, scribe," said Jazelle with a flat tone through reluctant lips. "Do you have a name?"

Archippus stared. His throat was tight and there was no saliva in his mouth.

Jazelle waited with an impatient stare. She raised a single red brow.

"A-a-a ..."

"Fantastic, Mother. You've been given a scribe with a speech impediment. It's like having a cracked water pitcher. I'd trade him in for another." She spun and left.

Lordess Lourdes swiveled toward him. "You don't have a speech impediment, do you?"

Archippus mustered a dry swallow. "No," he said hoarsely.

"Good. Now let's continue."

Somehow, the words that came out of Lordess Lourdes made their way to the parchment, though all Archippus could do was replay the horrifying scene over and over in his mind.

My name—I couldn't even say my name!

He wished upon wish that he could re-do the introduction and at least utter his own blasted name.

Finally, the droning for the senseless message ceased, and Lordess Lourdes snatched up the parchment, read it, fanned it dry, and rolled it up. She then went to the aviary, swung open the full size, crisscrossed iron door, stepped inside, and snatched up an Olive Warbler. Archippus thought the bird looked eerily like Hodos. The warbler however, didn't speak, only chirped. Archippus squinted at the bird as if remembering something far away and long ago. *I'm finally rid of Hodos,* he realized. He watched Lordess Lourdes tie the small, rolled parchment to a string around the warbler's foot.

"What are you doing with the bird?" asked Archippus.

Lordess Lourdes twisted her head toward him over her left shoulder. "For a scribe, you know nothing of delivering a text message? The perfect bird to deliver a text to the Citadel by the Sea is, of course, an Olive Warbler. That is where they come from, and that is where the bird will return. The peasants there will gather the texts from beneath the famed olive trees, check the recipient's name, and deliver them. They are given a loaf of bread for every seven delivered."

"Oh," was all Archippus could think to say. He wondered if Hodos had ever been to the olive groves.

Lordess Lourdes tossed the bird out the window. It disappeared downward a moment, but then scooped itself upward, and flew southwest as predicted.

"It's quicker than eegwuhnuh transport," the Lordess affirmed.

"Well, the kitchen is that way." She pointed through the arch where Jazelle had came and left. "And your room is through this opposite arch, the third room up the spiral staircase in the east tower. Eat, for I have more for you to scribe later." And with that revelation, Lordess Lourdes turned and walked out the entry door.

Archippus wandered into the kitchen. There was a square wooden waist high table in the center of the room. Cupboards lined the far wall on either side of a window. To the right was a cauldron suspended from chains over a fire pit, though no fire burned. Thankfully, a fruit bowl graced the center of the table. Archippus grabbed an apple and bit into it ravenously. He took several bites in a row before swallowing in order to stuff as much of the sumptuous fruit into his mouth as quickly as possible.

"Hey, A-a-a, can you toss me an a-a-a-apple?" Archippus spun around. Jazelle had approached him from behind.

For a second time today, he found he could not speak. His cheeks were stuffed too full of apple bites. He tossed Jazelle an apple.

"Th-th-th-thanks," giggled Jazelle who quickly departed, her brown-red curls flouncing like bats hanging from a windblown branch.

Archippus was again furious at his failure.

"That went well," said a familiar voice.

Archippus spun back toward the kitchen window and laid eyes on none other than Hodos. Archippus gulped down the remaining apple. "How *did you get here?*"

"I held on to Eri's tail all the way," said Hodos.

That explains the fourth feather, thought Archippus. "I thought I was rid of you."

"Never," said Hodos.

Archippus shook his head and sighed. The day was not going well.

"She's not very nice, is she?" said Hodos.

"Who? Lordess Lourdes? No."

"No. I mean the noble girl."

Archippus stiffened. "I'm sure she is very nice. She's upset today, understandably. Her every move is monitored, and strangely, I know what that's like!" He glared at Hodos. "The mother is the one who's unbearable. She's arrogant and power hungry."

Hodos blinked at Archippus. "And that bothers *you?*"

"Of course, it's very irritating."

"Really?"

"Yes. Really," said Archippus, failing to fathom the ironic implication as to his own character.

"You do realize you have not been obeying me," said Hodos.

Archippus just stared at the bird.

"You are going to make yourself miserable," said Hodos.

"No. I am going to make myself happy, look. This is me making myself happy." Archippus turned and left the kitchen.

When he entered the scribing room, he immediately spotted Jazelle slipping a piece of apple to a parrot inside the aviary.

"I've seen you before," said Jazelle, hearing Archippus' footsteps. She continued to face the cage.

"Have you?" questioned Archippus. He weighed revealing that he had been the prisoner she sought each year to free, for *what if she reports me to her stepfather.*

"Yes. Somewhere I have seen you. I'll think of it, I'm sure." She continued to stare into the cage, her back to Archippus.

"Well, I'm Archippus, forgive me for stuttering earlier. I was overwrought by your beauty." He felt euphoric that he had strung together two complete sentences and been bold enough to compliment her. He stared at the back of her head.

She turned around. "That is kind of you to say."

Archippus felt his face flush. "Perhaps if you need any scribner work done, I can assist you. Sometime. Maybe."

"That would be nice."

Archippus eyes were immobilized by her bright green gaze. He could only stare.

"If you'll excuse me, I must go practice my harp. I play for the evening meal tonight."

Archippus snapped out of his stupor and stepped aside. "Of course." He bowed his head as she passed.

Archippus' head was spinning and his heart was thumping. He inadvertently clasped the pouch scroll about his neck. *I spoke to her!* "I think she likes me!" he said in a whisper.

"I don't think so," said Hodos, fluttering into the room and landing on the back of the carrying lounge. "She's a flirt."

"Bird, take it back!"

"I cannot take back a truth," said Hodos. "A truth is a truth whether spoken or not. If I were to un-speak it, it would still be true though left unspoken."

"Well, try this truth." Archippus snatched up Hodos; flung open the aviary door, tossed him inside, and shut the door tight.

"What are you doing?"

"What does it look like? I am shutting you up. Literally."

"Well, I'm freer in here than you are out there," said Hodos. "I warned you of prison if you disobeyed me."

"What's that suppose to mean?"

"Exactly what I said."

"Well, I think I'm very free. Look. This is me being free."

Hodos watched Archippus walk to the inkwell. He uncurled the parchment from his pouch scroll, dipped the pen into the ink, and crossed off some words on the scroll.

"I hope you are modifying your quest," said Hodos. "I noticed you left behind the scroll I entrusted you to write back in Rephidim."

"This is the only scroll I need," said Archippus, waving the parchment to dry it. "I have modified my quest to now say *I will marry Jazelle.*"

Hodos sighed.

"And look, Bird, this is me being free to leave the room." Archippus made exaggerated strides into the arched hallway. He walked through a dining area containing a highly polished long, dark wood table and twelve chairs, and then ascended a spiral staircase to the third floor where he found a bed with a *real* mattress!

He flopped backward onto the mattress and stared up at the ceiling some ten feet above him. The ceiling was lined with thick wooden beams beneath wooden slats, which provided a floor for the room above him. The wood had dark circular knots. He stared at the ceiling imagining one of the knots to be heart shaped, and he daydreamed of Jazelle. After a long while of replaying the three sentences he had successively delivered to her, he remembered that she had said he would scribe for her. He wondered what she might reveal of her interests, and he dreamed of how impressed she would be with his scribing. Archippus lie on the bed and daydreamed for quite some time.

Finally, he sat up. He noticed a washbasin on a stand. He washed his face and then walked onto a small balcony with a wooden railing covered by ivy. He heard music and glanced around for the source. He saw Jazelle on the balcony of the opposite tower, one floor above him, her reddish brown locks swaying gently while she leaned forward playing a golden harp. He stepped quickly back inside his room hoping to go unnoticed so as not to disturb her playing. He stood by the balcony door listening intently, fascinated by her beautiful playing, and wholly caught up in the music.

Suddenly a terse voice hollered from behind him. "Time to scribe!"

The almost forgotten call reminded Archippus of the prison and the guard calling him to work. He snapped to attention. Lordess Lourdes stood in the doorway. "Time to scribe," she repeated. Her verbiage disturbed him greatly, but he followed her down the spiral stairs with reluctant obedience.

"I have decided to get directly to the most important matter," said Lordess Lourdes. She glided across the dining room floor on into the entrance room and lighted upon her gaudy chair. "I want you to scribe a request to the High Council of Twenty-four to ask for more funding, and for a right to sit in as a substitution on the council."

Archippus sat and took up the pen. All of a sudden, it dawned on him that Hodos was still in the cage. This made Archippus nervous. The bird could not be trusted. He had made threats of prison. *What if he were to pipe up and reveal that I am an escapee?*

Archippus jumped up, flung open the cage, snatched Hodos, and pinched the bird's beak shut.

"What are you doing?" demanded Lordess Lourdes.

"Uh …" Archippus cleared his throat. "Uh … I thought you could drop a second quick note to your cousin … use the bird as a messenger."

"Don't be ridiculous, I just dictated a note to my cousin. Why are you pinching that bird's beak? You'll suffocate it!"

Archippus had a moment of delirium. *To suffocate Hodos would fix everything.* He looked down a moment to confirm he had covered the beak's breathing holes. Suddenly Archippus felt a violent blow to his ear.

"Ouch!" He dropped Hodos and looked up. Lordess Lourdes stood glaring indignantly at him. "What was *that* for?" he asked rubbing his ear.

"You could have killed my warbler!" she yelled. Then in a softer voice, as if to herself, "I didn't know I had *two* warblers …"

Hodos flitted from the floor up to the top of the aviary. "You don't," he said.

"Excuse me?" said Lordess Lourdes to the bird. "Did you *say* something?"

"Yes. I said you don't have a second warbler. I belong to the boy. He shut me in there."

Lordess Lourdes, apparently at a loss for words, just stared at the bird.

"Allow me to introduce myself," said Hodos with a slight bow forward. "I am Hodos. I am the Airborne Counselor for this boy."

Lordess Lourdes arched a brow. "Really … I didn't know songbirds could speak." She squinted upward and to the left, as if trying to recollect ever hearing of such a thing.

"We are few in number, but we exist," added Hodos.

"How remarkable," said Lordess Lourdes. She turned to Archippus. "Well, I suppose that bodes in your favor, Scribe, for if you qualify for an Airborne Counselor, I shall perhaps overlook the startling act of attempted suffocation you nearly performed in front of my sensitive presence. Especially since the bird belongs to you as opposed to being one of my own."

"Oh. Don't spare him any consequence," said Hodos. "The boy is unruly, irreverent, and arrogant. He needs discipline."

"Well … I could arrange a punishment for his rudeness …" Lordess Lourdes mused.

Archippus shot a hateful glance at Hodos. "My Lady, don't you have an *important* message you wish scribed, and wouldn't you want me to be in the *best* of moods to ensure the most *eloquent* calligraphy to impress your most *prestigious* audience?"

"Oh, yes, yes, you do have a point. Now where were we?" She slid back onto the scarlet chair. "I should perhaps have my own Airborne present for this, but she has gone to Rephidim for parasite eradication. I wonder if I should consult Jazelle's Airborne ..." She seemed to think these options through for a moment. "Well, no matter. I know what I wish to say. Let's proceed."

Archippus sat again, still very nervous about the bird.

"Dear Members of the High Council of Twenty-four," began Lordess Lourdes. "As you must know, I have many concerns about our city and the lack of funding received—"

"That is very good of you, Lordess," interrupted Hodos. "A ruler with a conscience. I do believe it is a fantastic idea to ask for more funding."

She stared at Hodos. "You do?"

"Most definitely."

"Why thank you, now what was I saying?" She glanced at Archippus.

"Funding received," he muttered.

"Oh yes." She continued with the letter. "And the lack of funding received for my labor—"

"Heh, hem," interrupted Hodos again.

She looked at the bird. "What now?"

"I don't know that I would go directly at the matter of compensation," said Hodos.

"You don't?"

"No. I don't."

"Well ... what should I say, then?"

"You are more likely to gain what you desire if you go about it in a philanthropic manner."

"Define *philanthropic,* please."

"Charitable, benevolent, humanitarian, generous, goodhearted, giving, and altruistic." Hodos look at Archippus. "Was that seven?"

"Yes," snapped Archippus.

"Well, I'm not sure I follow you," said Lordess Lourdes.

"Ask for funding, but apply it to the greater good of the people and any prestige, fame, or worship that you may be seeking is more likely to be gained, not merely for the duration of your lifetime, but long after," said Hodos.

"Explain further," said Lordess Lourdes.

"Ask for funding for the elderly and orphans, for example. Then the council members are more likely to respond with open purse strings, and you can create assistance centers. You could call them the 'Lordess Lourdes Life Centers,' designed for assisting the less fortunate. If you help the needy, the Landlings will love you, and your name lives on and on through posterity, et cetera, et cetera."

"Do you think?" asked Lordess Lourdes.

"Madam. I don't merely *think*. I *know*. I am, after all, an Airborne Counselor."

"Quite right. You did mention that, all right then," she motioned a hand at Archippus, "write what he said."

"Which part?" Archippus squinted distastefully at the back of Lordess Lourdes' locks.

"Repeat the important part," commanded the Lordess to Hodos.

"Funding received for assistance to the elderly and orphans, is all you really need," said Hodos. "You can name the centers later. The less you emphasize yourself, the more appealing the request."

Archippus reluctantly scribed the sentence. **As you know, I have many concerns about our city and the lack of funding received for assistance to the elderly and orphans.**

"It's so nice to have you scribing for me again," said Hodos to Archippus.

Archippus restrained himself from throwing the inkwell at Hodos.

"Now. I do want to add something else," said Lordess Lourdes.

"By all means," encouraged Hodos.

"Put this down," she said, flailing her arms arrogantly in the direction of Archippus. "As you also know, it is appropriate though rare for a Lordess to substitute in for one of our two elected officials. But given the need for my input—"

"No," said Hodos.

"No?"

"No. They won't want to read that they *need your input,*" said Hodos.

"What shall I say, then?"

"Say, 'But given I care so deeply about my subjects,'" encouraged Hodos.

"I do?"

"Yes."

"Oh. Well, put that down then." She motioned her arm again at Archippus and then addressed the bird. "Why don't you just finish it?"

"All right," said Hodos. "Write, 'But given I care so deeply about my subjects, it would pain me greatly to not be involved in discussions regarding funding for our less fortunate, as a result, I humbly beg that you consider my substitution.'"

"I never *humbly beg* for anything!" insisted Lordess Lourdes.

"*Humility* is endearing," explained Hodos. "And *beg* is simply a figure of speech for heartfelt imploring."

"It is?" asked Lordess Lourdes.

"It is, and to *humbly beg* is an act that would look very good on you, I might add."

"It would?" asked Lordess Lourdes, pushing her brown locks upward.

"It most definitely would," Hodos asserted.

"Why, thank you." Lordess Lourdes rose and took her raven from the cage. She nodded at Hodos. "A sturdy bird to cross the middle mountains to your homeland." She took the scribed note from Archippus, tied the message to the leg of the raven, and tossed the bird out the window. She turned to Hodos. "Thank you, Counselor, for your assistance."

"The pleasure was all mine," said Hodos giving a slight bow.

Lordess Lourdes left the room. Archippus waited until her footsteps had receded down the hall, and then launched the inkwell at Hodos. The bird flittered upward and fluttered downward landing perfectly pristine. The ink, however, splattered everywhere, even giving the birds in the aviary dark speckles. Archippus, mortified by what he had done, quickly retreated to his bedroom.

↤ ↤ ↤ ↤
↤ ↤ ↤ ↤

Archippus lay on his back wondering how he would explain the speckles on the birds. *The wind. I will insist that a huge gust came through the window. I'll say I told the servants, but they neglected to do anything about it.* He felt better having concocted an excuse for the ink splatter, but remained nervous about attending the evening meal, and perhaps having to defend himself from foolishness in front of Jazelle. He had only barely earned her graces thus far.

A bell rang for evening meal.

Archippus descended and sat on the long wooden bench on the far side of the highly polished dark wood table. In the center of the table on a large wooden tray were bread, boiled chicken, and grapes. A tall glass bottle of what he surmised to be snock sat within arm's reach of the high-backed chair to his right. *The wealthy always have snock with evening meal,* he thought.

Servants stood by at each corner of the table. One of them produced a water pitcher to fill Archippus' clay goblet. Archippus would have savored being waited upon except for his dread over having splattered ink on all the birds in the aviary. In a moment, a scream emerged from the entrance hall.

"My birds! My flock! My messengers!" Lordess Lourdes shrieked. "Whatever happened to my messengers?"

Archippus gulped his water.

Lordess Lourdes flew into the dining room like a puffed up rooster, her evening cape flailing outward from her elbows, her hands clasped to her hips. She glared at Archippus. "What happened to my birds?"

Archippus removed the water goblet from his lips. "The wind, My Lady, I told your servants!"

Lordess Lourdes turned to the nearest servant. "Go clean up my birds!" she yelled.

Archippus heard the servant behind him spit, and produce the water pitcher to refill Archippus' goblet. *No more water for me tonight …*

The ruffled Lordess plopped on the end chair to his right and Lord Ipthsum entered from his left. Archippus stood quickly to his feet and bowed.

Lord Ipthsum motioned him to sit.

Archippus glanced left. He had never laid eyes on Lord Ipthsum, the man who refused his father work and oversaw a corrupt council. A mixture of anger and fear rose inside him as he examined the man. He was average of stature, but had a rounded mound of frizzy hair, thick brows, and a black moustache. The moustache hid his mouth, making his expression difficult to read, but his eyes looked impatient and indifferent. He grabbed the plate of food, plopping portions of bread, grapes, and chicken onto the plate in front of him.

"You don't even wait for your daughter?" asked Lordess Lourdes.

"*Step,*" said Lord Ipthsum through a mouthful of food.

"You don't even wait for your step-daughter? She *is* also your niece, and she *is* performing tonight."

Lord Ipthsum rolled his eyes briefly upward, then to the right, then down. He kept eating.

Lordess Lourdes grabbed the snock container, filled her cup, drained it, and poured another.

Archippus sat frozen, uncertain whether to eat, or speak, or even breathe, but certain he was not going to drink from the saliva-contaminated water goblet next to his plate.

Suddenly a servant entered with the harp. Jazelle followed. She curtsied, sat in a chair along the wall, and began to play.

Archippus stared hard at the pearl-skinned performer. Her hands seemed as swans plucking the strings. The reverberating notes made his heart dance. Archippus thought she probably played for several minutes, but it seemed mere seconds. Everyone in the room clapped except for Lord Ipthsum, who merely lifted a chicken leg high in acknowledgement and then lowered the leg and took a bite.

Jazelle curtsied and took a seat at the table across from Archippus.

Lord Ipthsum grabbed a second handful of grapes and shoved the food tray toward mid-table. Lordess Lourdes downed and then refilled a third glass of snock. Archippus stared at Jazelle. A period of awkward silence ensued. Archippus thought Lordess Lourdes looked a little tipsy from the snock.

"Ipthsssum," said Lordess Lourdes, taking another sip.

Lord Ipthsum looked up and grunted.

"You won't believe this," Lordess Lourdes continued. "Thiss sscribe, here, hasss an Airborne Counssselor."

Lord Ipthsum and Jazelle looked at Lordess Lourdes and then at Archippus.

Lordess Lourdes continued. "He hasss a teeny, tiny, feathered friend."

They looked back at Lordess Lourdes.

"He has a chirping, cheeping, chatty little Counssselor," Lordess Lourdes insisted.

"She's had too much snock. Remove it," said Lord Ipthsum to a servant.

"No, I'm ssserious!" Lordess Lourdes snatched up the snock container, refusing its removal. "He hasss a sssilly, wwwilly, wwweeney little wwwarbler." She giggled. She poured more snock, and then spoke to Archippus. "Where isss your wwwarbler?" she asked.

"Mother!" cried Jazelle.

"I-I-I don't know," said Archippus.

"I'm right here!" said Hodos, flittering into the room and landing on Archippus' right shoulder.

"*There* he isss!" Lordess Lourdes yelled, delighted. "There'sss my itty, bitty, bird!"

"At your service," said Hodos with a bow.

"Tell them of the Lourdesss Lordesss Life Centersss," she commanded him.

"A noble cause," said Hodos. "Lodging for the less fortunate. She is going to the High Council of Twenty-four to request funding to build centers for orphans and the elderly."

Lord Ipthsum raised a single shocked eyebrow.

"We sssent a raven off today," affirmed Lordess Lourdes. "Ssspeaking of raven—did you sssee what happened to my aviary?" she asked Hodos.

"Oh yes," said Hodos.

Archippus tensed.

"The boy did it."

Archippus turned red.

Lordess Lourdes swayed forward in her seat and swung her head toward Archippus. "I thought you sssaid it wasss the wwwind?"

"Of course he did," said Hodos. "He was trying to be humble."

"Humble?" asked Lordess Lourdes.

"Yes. *Humble*. That word I explained earlier that looks charming on you," said Hodos.

"Oh." Hiccup. "Yes." She straightened her curls. "That one."

"The boy knew that if he were to speckle your flock, then everyone would be able to identify a text message arriving from Lordess Lourdes," answered Hodos. "They would see a speckled bird approaching and say, 'Look! A letter from Lordess Lourdes!' So you see, he has in fact, performed a great service to you. It is cutting edge advertisement if you ask me."

Lordess Lourdes swayed forward and back. "That'sss fanatassstic." She turned her head and yelled over her right shoulder, "Ssslave! Ssstop cleaning the cage!"

A slave emerged from the entrance hall with speckled feathers in his hair. He looked as relieved as Archippus, whom having been betrayed, now felt delivered by the bird.

"Yes. The boy is quite humble," continued Hodos.

Archippus wished vehemently to shove the grape he was placing in his own mouth, right down Hodos' throat.

"I'm sure he has not told you of his humble past," said Hodos.

Archippus panicked, nearly choking on the grape. *Don't tell them of my imprisonment!*

"What passst isss that?" asked Lordess Lourdes.

"He was a mole before coming here," said Hodos.

"Mole?" asked the swaying Lordess. "Isss that sssome underground top sssecret thing?"

178

Hodos chuckled. "Hardly. No, a mole is not a position of intrigue. A mole works with the eegwuhnuhs in Rephidim."

"Really?" asked Jazelle. "That sounds important. Did you cliff race?"

Archippus shifted on the bench not wanting to answer.

"Gracious, no," said Hodos. "His position was, however, very important as a dung shoveler."

"Dung shoveler?" asked Jazelle. Her wide-eyed interest switched to a disgusted squint.

"Yes. Shoveling dung is very important in Rephidim," insisted Hodos.

Archippus wanted to slide beneath the table.

"Oh," said Jazelle, and then, *"Eew."* She looked distastefully down at her plate, and then back up at Archippus. "Have you washed your hands since you arrived?" Archippus opened his mouth, but nothing came out.

"Well, I've lost my appetite," said Lord Ipthsum. He stood, gave an obligatory nod at Lordess Lourdes, and left the room.

Jazelle giggled, Lordess Lourdes downed snock, and Archippus envisioned himself choking Hodos.

"Well, good evening to all of you," said Hodos who bowed and flew out of the room.

Jazelle stood. "Yes. Good evening, Mr. Dung Shoveler." She giggled, performed a mock curtsy, and flounced out of the room leaving Archippus with the drunken Lordess.

"Doesss the dung sssmell?" asked Lordess Lourdes.

Archippus wanted to die, but only after annihilating the bird. "Excuse me, My Lady." He stood, nodded, and returned to his room where he found Bird waiting on the water basin.

"How could you do that to me? *I hate you!*" he yelled.

"I'm trying to save you from an insufferable obsession," said Hodos.

"Well suffer this!" Archippus launched a bed pillow at Hodos who flittered upward and fluttered downward landing entirely un-grazed. The water pitcher, however, fell to the floor and shattered.

"Aaarrrggghhh! You ruin everything! Why can't you leave me alone?" Archippus grasped his dreadlocks and pulled hard.

"If I don't counsel you correctly, I'm not doing my job," answered Hodos.

"But I don't want your help! If you left me alone, she would like me. But as it is, she thinks I'm disgusting!"

Hodos took a deep sigh inward and an equally long sigh outward. "All right," he said.

Archippus felt shocked. He looked intently at Hodos. "All right?"

"Yes. All right. I shall not intervene for the remainder of the week. I suspect you'll have your hands full with Eri. If you decide you want my advice, you know where to find me." Hodos flew from the room.

Archippus could not believe it. If Hodos would leave him alone, he was certain he could gain Jazelle's affection. He felt relieved, and yet felt anxious; anxious to find something other than Jazelle to reveal to Eri as Lordess Lourdes' weakness.

And one other matter made him anxious. He needed to return to his family's old hut to see for himself if his sister no longer lived there.

The following morning, Archippus slipped from his room before the sun rose. The moon was almost full, and he hurried through the streets recollecting the way. As he passed the prison that kept him a captive for so many years, he felt frightened. The hideous images of hunched knee-clutching gargoyles appeared to sneer at him from the rooftop.

At last he came upon the dilapidated hut. It appeared someone was inside because smoke came from an opening in the roof indicating a fire.

Archippus knocked on slats nailed together to form a makeshift door. He heard a faint male voice. "Come in."

Slowly, Archippus pushed inward on the door and stuck his head inside. The odor made him gag. He saw an old man lying on shredded feed sacks. The open wounds on his body told Archippus the man had contracted the 'skin disease of death.' The man turned his head to look at Archippus. "Did you come to visit me?" he asked, a tiny glimmer in his eye.

"Uh … no." Archippus watched in horror as what appeared to be hope, disappear from the dying man's demeanor to be replaced by a tear that slid down from the corner of the man's eye. "Sorry," said Archippus. He backed away and let the door fall shut.

≼ ≼ ≼ ≼
≼ ≼ ≼ ≼

It was sad not to have found his sister, but the image of the dying man now haunted Archippus' dreams as well. Oddly, he caught himself wondering between sleepless tossing if the Lordess Lourdes Life Centers would come to fruition. Such an institution would have possibly assisted not only the old man, but also Archippus' orphaned sister. He half thought to venture out again to look for Apphia, but inwardly he wrestled with the sinking suspicion that Hodos had been telling the truth.

Archippus did not venture out again for the remainder of the week. Each day he scribed for Lordess Lourdes during which time he would probe her for a weakness. At each evening meal Lord Ipthsum remained sullen, Lordess Lourdes got snockered, Jazelle looked angelic, and Archippus sat smitten.

Occasionally, Jazelle would say something and her emerald eyes would land on Archippus. He interpreted the look as a sign of affection. Her green gaze made him feel elated, euphoric, overjoyed, delighted, thrilled, blissful, and rapturous.

But panic had set in by day seven. Archippus had failed to procure a second weakness from Lordess Lourdes. He paced his bedroom floor debating what to say to Pterodactyl Eri.

Swoosh!

Archippus jumped.

Pterodactyl Eri landed on the balcony. The Airborne squatted, folded his wings, and ducked his head through the arch. "Well?" he demanded.

No hello, or how are you? Or anything, thought Archippus.

"Pterodactyl Eri! How are you? It's good to see you," said Archippus, stalling.

"I'll know how I'm doing when I hear your report," said Eri.

"Oh, yes." Archippus cleared his throat. "Would you like some water?"

"No."

"Oh," said Archippus. "Yes." He cleared his throat again. "Well, I was thinking—"

"Stop avoiding the question. What did you discover?" demanded Eri.

Archippus sighed. "I think she only values herself," he lied.

Eri thrust his head forward until it was inches from Archippus' face. He peered intently into Archippus' eyeballs. "You're lying," he said.

"I am?"

"Yes. You won't look directly at me. You're lying."

Archippus shifted his weight from one leg to the other. "I don't look directly at you because you're ugly," was all he could think to say.

Eri actually chuckled, but then continued. "Do you know the consequence of lying to a Counselor?"

Archippus shook his head and Eri snapped his beak and razor sharp teeth together. "I snap off your neck."

Archippus inadvertently placed protective hands about his neck.

"Now. Isn't there something of value you discovered during your weeklong stay?"

Archippus sighed. He wondered if the beheading would hurt.

181

"What about the daughter?" asked Eri.

Archippus' eyes bulged.

"Ah-hah!" said Eri with delight. "That's it! I suspected as much, but I needed a confirmation. Landlings are so unpredictable. Sometimes Landlings don't value their own offspring. They see them as a hindrance to achievements and even value them less than addictions at times, if you can imagine, and I didn't want to remove the daughter if it would have no ill-effect on Lordess Lourdes. She's so self-centered I half feared she would thrive on the drama and not care for her daughter's return, which would have defeated the whole purpose of the manipulation."

Archippus, now sick to his stomach, stared at Eri.

"Well," said Eri," hop on."

Archippus took a step back.

"Hop on," repeated Eri. "I can't very well leave you here now. You appear infatuated with the girl, and I don't trust you'll remain silent."

Archippus shook his head.

"Get on, or I'll snap your neck and then hers!" hissed Eri.

Archippus thought a moment. It was true. If Eri snapped his neck, he would not be able to prevent any harm to Jazelle. He felt he had no options and stepped forward.

"And bring the shrieking seedling. You've earned a flight to see the curvature of the Continent!" Eri spoke happily as if no discord at all had transpired.

Archippus did not care to see the curve of the Continent, but he obediently picked up the seedling. For some unknown reason, he glanced about the room hoping to see Hodos. Dismayed and disturbed by the bird's absence, Archippus climbed onto Eri's back, and the big reptile launched from the balcony.

As they lurched upward, Archippus looked down for any sign of Jazelle. *Perhaps I can scream out a warning.*

The ascent was rapid, and Archippus felt dread with each swoosh of wings and the City of Ai grew tiny and distant. "Where are you taking me?" he finally asked.

"Back to Rephidim."

"Are you going to harm her?"

"Gracious grave, no. I've arranged for the desert Cyclops to kidnap her and keep her in a cage. I'm sure they'll feed her. If she dies, I'll have no collateral with which to negotiate."

"You already knew then?"

"As I said, I suspected but some self-centered Landlings wouldn't care to have their offspring gone. I wasn't a hundred percent certain."

"So why not simply try it? Why involve me?"

"It is taboo for Airbornes to tamper with Landlings. I only tamper with Landlings if absolutely necessary, but Lordess Lourdes leaves me no options. If one city goes south, there could be an uprising everywhere. It's bad enough that we have to confront the Barbirians and their ruler, King Katalaomer. I cannot overemphasize that in these treacherous times, it is of the utmost importance that all the cities of the kingdom unite against the enemy, for as it says in the Book of Wisdom, 'A kingdom divided against itself, cannot stand.'[5] I operate for the good of the Continent."

Archippus could not see the sense in one harmless girl suffering for the good of the Continent, and it pained him to have been instrumental in the horrific plan. His mind raced to save her, and oddly, the only people on the Continent he could think of to help him, were Emoticas, Gershom, and Raimi. His mind haunted him the entire trip back.

"We are almost to Rephidim," announced Eri who began to ascend instead of descend.

Archippus clung tighter to the safety strap.

"I'm going to show you something that few Landlings have seen before," continued Eri, while making powerful wing strokes upward.

The air began to get cooler. They passed through clouds. The white orb that lights the night sky shone on clouds that were now below them looking like snow-covered ground. Higher. Higher. Swoosh. Swoosh. The seedling that Archippus had transported back and forth began to shriek. The shriek turned to a full-fledged scream.

Archippus gasped for air and clamped the seedling to his nose. *I can breathe!* Notwithstanding his relief at the flower's gift of oxygen, he had a fearful thought that he might suffocate if Eri stayed Airborne this high for too long. They continued to go upward while Archippus only wanted to go downward. He cursed the day he decided to fly atop a pterodactyl and longed to set his feet on solid ground, but the Airborne flew higher.

The Continent increasingly sank as they soared.

Eri finally leveled off.

Archippus looked down. *It does curve!* He could see the top of the Continent dangling from a snow-capped landmass, which he assumed to be the legendary location of the Seraph. The lower Continent was swirls of green, whites, and blues, but what struck him most was that it hung from the upper pure white peninsula by what must have been the Trail of Tears—as a blackened solitary teardrop.

Abruptly, Eri shot downward, spiraling, spiraling, and Archippus felt to vomit. The circular motion suctioned him to Eri's back making it seem impossible to fall, but he felt horrified and sickened. He closed his eyes and didn't open them again until Eri slowed, and straightened over the center of the main lair of the Dells. Archippus could see his co-workers seated around a fire.

Swoosh, swoosh, thud! Dust billowed. Eri landed in front of Raimi, Gershom, and Emoticas. The trio jumped from the rocks and backed against the lair's rock wall.

"I am returning something," announced Eri, folding his wings.

Archippus fell from Eri's shoulders, dropping the shriveled shrieking seedling. The plant rolled from its protective shell, spilling soil and baring roots. Archippus dropped on all fours and vomited.

"No need to spend time thanking me, Landling. Your reeking regurgitation forces my quick departure," said Eri.

Swoosh! The large reptile shot out his wings and lifted into the air.

The three figures stared at Archippus. He sat upright on the dirt, wiped his mouth with the back of his hand, and rubbed his aching temples.

"What are you doing back here?" demanded Raimi.

"Huh?" Archippus squinted. He felt awful and exhausted.

"Why are you back? I thought you never wanted to see any of us again?" she repeated, impatient.

Archippus bent forward and vomited again.

"And what of the seedling?" Raimi persisted.

Archippus wiped his mouth and squinted. "Huh?"

"The seedling! It *was* a gift and it *was* alive! Will you stop at nothing to achieve your ambitions?"

"It's a *plant,*" Archippus managed weakly. He pushed himself to a standing position. His legs felt extremely weak. "I have to rest." He staggered from the lair. Amazingly, he somehow made it down the stairs to the very bottom burrow without falling into the echoless pit. He entered, stumbled over Hazo and passed out.

PARCHMENT VII

**"While white skin was a sign of weakness,
the color of commonness and captivity."**

Far from Rephidim, the young High Ruler sparred with the blond haired slave boy.

Clash! Clang! They bounded about the courtyard swinging fervently at each other.

"Take a break!" yelled Isui. An assistant ran to carry goblets of water to the combatants. Isui turned to speak with Shear-Jashub standing nearby.

Out on the courtyard, Apphia lifted her visor, gulped the offered water, lowered her visor, and faced her opponent again.

"Why did you agree to spar with me, knowing the objective is your own death?" she asked the slave boy.

The boy handed his empty goblet to the assistant, who hurried out of the battle area. He lowered his visor.

"It is not so much the quantity of life as the quality," answered the boy. "I'd rather live several months well fed in prison than a lifetime hungry."

"That makes no sense."

"Sure it does, Your Superb Sovereignty, if you believe in the After-sky."

"Stop calling me *silly titles!* And if you are so certain of an After-sky, why not kill yourself now?" demanded Apphia.

"They are not silly titles, Your Affluent Anointedness. I mean them in all sincerity. By the way, my name is Esek."

Apphia thrust her sword at him. "No you don't, you make fun of me."

Esek blocked her maneuver.

"So, answer the question, why not kill yourself now?"

"To take one's own life is arrogant and unthinking. If I took my life prematurely, I might miss the purpose for which I was born."

"What purpose could possibly be served by being slaughtered during sparring practice?"

"Perhaps my purpose is to make you actually adept at sparring."

"You mock me again! I'm serious. A life is worth more than to teach fencing skills!"

Esek shrugged. "I don't have the answers to such questions, Your Magnificent Monarchship. But I do believe there is no task too small. It is not so much what you do, but how much care you put into it."

Apphia felt frustrated. "Don't you want to *live?*"

"Of course I do."

"Then you should try to escape!"

"That would be my death for certain."

"No, not if well planned! I can help you!"

"I don't think so."

"Yes, you must!"

"No, thank you."

"Why not?"

He lifted his visor, his blue eyes crinkling at the corners. "Are you trying to trick me?"

"No! I just ... don't want to see you killed."

"You haven't come close to killing me yet," he laughed. "Take off your helmet."

"No!"

"Why not?"

"Because." Apphia dreaded the thought of allowing Esek see her ugly baldness. She shrugged her armored shoulders. "I'm not supposed to."

"If *I* win this match, promise me you'll remove your helmet."

"No!"

"If *you* win, I will agree to try to escape ... *if* you can come up with a viable plan."

Apphia's mind raced for several seconds. "All right. But I decide when I will remove my helmet."

"Of course, and I decide when I am ready to escape."

"Of course."

"Shall we continue then?" asked Esek.

✦ ✦ ✦ ✦
✦ ✦ ✦ ✦

Apphia threw her helmet to the floor of her palatial suite. The steel head covering clanged loudly, rolling over several times, and striking a carved leg of her bed. Isui had scored Esek a single point higher than herself. Dread settled over her.

I cannot show him my face and bald skull, and I must still convince him to escape, she worried.

Behind her, Shear-Jashub had just come into the room. He stared at the battered helmet. "What was that for?"

"I'm tired of being ugly!"

Shear-Jashub looked intently at her. "What does it matter how you look? No one sees you."

Apphia plopped on a chair, crossed her arms, and sulked.

Shear-Jashub continued to stare at her. "You're not sweet on someone, are you?"

"No!" She shifted under the scrutiny of his gaze.

"Who is it?"

"Nobody."

"It's the slave boy, isn't it?"

"No."

"I think it is," Shear-Jashub teased.

"No." Apphia tried to suppress a smile.

Shear-Jashub sighed. "What are we going to do about this? You're supposed to slay him."

"I can't!"

"Yes, I can see that now," Shear-Jashub said slowly. His eyes trailed off her in unblinking thought.

"You have to help me find a way to free him." Her lips trembled and her eyes watered.

His gaze shifted back to her. "Yes. I can see that now."

"And you have to let me grow my hair!"

Shear-Jashub sighed a second time exhaling so heavily it puffed the front of his cheeks outward. "Yes. I can see that now."

Apphia jumped up and hugged Shear-Jashub so hard her armor left indents on his upper arms. "Thank you," she whispered.

Tiny tears of gratitude slid down her cheeks. "The sad thing is, as Ruler of the Continent, I don't feel I have the power to free a single slave. The minute Eri knows of my intention, he'll come up with a reason against it, and Esek would be immediately in danger."

Shear-Jashub nodded slightly.

The sound of a key entering the outer door indicated Entimus had arrived for the night guard shift. They heard him enter and take a seat in the foyer. Shear-Jashub winked at Apphia, squeezed her arm, and then went into the foyer. She heard him mutter something to Entimus and leave.

She paced the room a few minutes, realizing she had far too many thoughts to consider sleeping. She stood on the balcony looking up at the candle vigil lighting the night sky and tried to think of a way to free Esek.

She watched the far off flicker of the candles. The tiny flames seemed to dance in harmony with her heart.

For the first time since she had come to Hieropolis, High City of the Iron Hall, she felt herself to be the richest Landling on the Continent for she realized, *I'm in love!*

↞ ↞ ↞ ↞
↞ ↞ ↞ ↞

Archippus woke to find Hazo's feet square in his face. "Uugghh!" He shoved them out of the way and sat up.

Hazo rubbed his eyes and raised himself. "What?"

Archippus was sore, hungry, and unhappy to see the young slave. "Why are you still here? Aren't they going to re-chain you in the field or something?"

"A better question," said Hazo, "is what are *you* doing here? I heard you were off in search of the love of your life or something." Hazo lay back placing his ear on his outstretched arm.

"And I'll have you know I found her," snapped Archippus.

"Yippee for you." Hazo closed his eyes, and then reopened them. "So where is she?"

Where is she indeed, Archippus wondered, worried for her safety.

Hodos fluttered down and landed at the burrow's entrance. "She is already in the custody of the desert Cyclops."

"Hodos!" exclaimed Archippus. "Where have you been, what took you so long? I looked for you the entire trip!"

Hodos looked over his shoulder to see if another Hodos were standing behind him. Seeing that was not the case, he faced Archippus again. "Are you talking to *me*?"

"Yes! Yes! Of *course* I'm talking to you, where have you *been*?"

"But … you *never* look for me." Hodos squinted one eye in puzzlement.

"Well, I looked for you *yesterday,* what took you so long!" demanded Archippus.

"Have you any idea how many warbler wing strokes there are per single wing stroke of a pterodactyl with a thirty-foot wingspan?" asked Hodos defensively.

"Well, uh, I, uh. I don't know … *twenty?*"

"Try forty-seven and a half," corrected Hodos. "If there's a tail wind."

"It doesn't *matter,*" said Archippus impatiently. "You're here now, are you sure they have her? Is she all right?"

"Yes, I'm quite sure they have her, and yes, she looked all right. I flew low over the desert and spotted her in a cage. She had the same sea spray skin, leaf hair, and everything."

Hazo shot up. "You let the *desert Cyclops* capture the love of your life?"

Archippus threw a disgusted look at Hazo. "Not on purpose!"

"Oh, well, I'm sure she'll be relieved to know it wasn't *on purpose*," said Hazo sarcastically.

"Leave off!" snapped Archippus. "Hodos, you have to help me. I have to save her!"

"Yes ...well, I am rather *tiny*."

"But you yourself said, it's not the size of one's stature, but the size of one's intent!" pleaded Archippus.

The same confused squint as earlier came to Hodos' left eye. "I thought you never *listened* to me."

"Well, I'm listening to you *now*. So what can we do? I've no one else. No one will help me."

"If you weren't such a two-legged reptile," interjected Hazo. "Others might want to help you."

Archippus shot an indignant glance at Hazo.

"He has a point," said Hodos.

"But it's too late! I've already *been* a two-legged reptile! They won't forgive me."

Hodos sighed. "Well ... you're right, but fortunately you somehow managed to end up surrounded by three incredibly benevolent Landlings. I highly recommend you speak with them."

"You go talk to them for me," pleaded Archippus.

"No," said Hodos, "but I will go with you."

"Thank you!" Archippus snatched up Hodo and planted him on his left shoulder. He ran all the way to the top of the staircase, up the ladder, and outside. Completely out of breath, he spotted Raimi, Gershom, and Emoticas in line for morning meal.

"Hey!" he called, propping his hands on his knees to catch his breath.

"Hey what?" asked Raimi, resentment noticeable in her voice.

"I was hoping to speak with the three of you." Still panting, Archippus walked over to the group.

"Speak," said Raimi.

"I ... uh ... I can't."

"Then don't," said Raimi.

"I mean, I can't speak to you *here*," he said, scanning the onlookers in the two adjacent food lines.

"Oh." Raimi looked at Emoticas and Gershom who each shrugged, seeming to say, Why not speak with him?

"Okay, let us get our food, and we'll meet you at the main lair," said Raimi.

Archippus felt relief flood over him. "Great, thanks." He ran ahead to the lair and waited, nervously clasping and unclasping his hands until the three of them arrived. Raimi had brought Archippus gruel on the half shell.

"Thanks." Archippus took the gruel and began eating. He felt guilty. Raimi had been kind enough to bring him breakfast, and he knew the only reason he was here was that he wanted something.

He stopped eating and stared at the mush. "I need your help."

Silence settled over the group, then Emoticas said, "How can we help you?"

"The noble girl," said Archippus. "Jazelle."

"Oh. *Jazelle* is it?" asked Raimi.

"Yes."

"What's wrong with her?" asked Emoticas.

"She's been captured by the desert Cyclops," said Archippus. "Because of me," he added. And then he looked at the ground and blurted, "Eri wanted to find something out about Lordess Lourdes because she's being uncooperative with the High Council of Twenty-four, so he said he'd return me to Ai if I would agree to spy on Lordess Lourdes and discover a weakness, which I did. But I tried to hide it from him and it was all to no avail, because he could tell from my face that the only weakness the woman has is apparently her love of her daughter who happens to be, although I did not know it ahead of time, Jazelle. So now Eri's ordered the Cyclops to kidnap her and put her in a cage, and he's pretending he didn't have a hand in the capture because he wants to offer to help free Jazelle if Lordess Lourdes agrees to become more compliant." Archippus halted, drew a deep breath, and looked up. Everyone was staring at him.

"How old is she?" asked Emoticas.

"Our age."

"Is she alone with the Cyclops?" asked Raimi.

"I believe so."

Archippus watched Gershom motion to Raimi and Emoticas. Raimi apparently understood the signals because she signaled something back, and the three of them turned once again to Archippus.

"All right," said Raimi, her voice flat. "We'll help you, but the cliff races have been going on all week and our race is tonight. We have to compete for the good of the slaves. After that we can help you."

Archippus was shocked. He was not certain he would have done the same for them. In fact, he was certain he would not. "Thank you," he said. He grabbed up a shovel. "I'll shovel today. How is Ezbon-Ishuah?"

Raimi shot him a pained glance. "Not good." The trio all grabbed their shovels and left for the lairs, leaving Archippus by himself.

"Well, they weren't overly warm and fuzzy," Archippus said to Hodos, perched on his left shoulder.

"But they did agree to help."

"Yes," affirmed Archippus feeling relieved. "They did agree to help."

After work, Raimi, Gershom, and Emoticas led Hemi the lizard down the pathway of the Dells onto the main road. By the light of the full moon, Emoticas climbed onto the back of the large lizard and slipped the safety strap around the spike on the lizard's back and then around his own waist. Raimi handed Emoticas the reins and then she and Gershom walked alongside the giant, shuffling lizard. Archippus followed, watching Raimi give instructions to Emoticas, who looked more pale than usual.

Up ahead, a cheer came from a crowd in the quarry. Archippus surmised it was for the preceding race. Suddenly, the cheering stopped, the crowd gasped, and then was silent.

They arrived at the quarry and Archippus climbed the steps toward the upper rows reserved for pale skins and commoners, while the others went on down into the quarry to join the other racers. Archippus noticed a great deal of murmuring and whispers. As he passed the middle rows for tradesmon only, he saw Ezbon-Ishuah motioned him over. Nervously, he made his way past the jutting knees of spectators to get to Ezbon-Ishuah. He worried someone seeing he was a pale skin would tell him to leave or throw food at him, or worst of all, spear him, for sitting in the middle-section.

He felt fortunate to have made it without injury and sat next to Ezbon-Ishuah. He noticed the tradesmon looked significantly thinner, and that a walking cane leaned on the stone quarry seat.

Ezbon-Ishuah smiled. "You're back." His voice was weak and raspy.

"Yes. Yes, I'm back. How are things with the reptiles? Are the Airbornes being properly cared for?" asked Archippus.

Ezbon-Ishuah nodded.

"Have you been working on your scribing?" asked Archippus.

Ezbon-Ishuah smiled again, but shook his head. "No, no. I'm afraid I won't be around long enough to truly learn a second trade."

Archippus felt uncomfortable and changed the subject. "What is all the murmuring about?"

"A rider fell."

Archippus stood and tried to peer over the rows of spectators to the base of the cliff wall. A figure had been placed on a mat and was in the process of being carried from the quarry. "Is he dead?"

Ezbon-Ishuah rolled his lips inward, considering. "It's possible, he fell from about there," he said, pointing to mid-cliff.

Suddenly Archippus was apprehensive about the upcoming race. If Emoticas were to fall to his death, it could delay Jazelle's rescue. "Excuse me," he said to Ezbon-Ishuah. "I'll be back."

Archippus again made his way past all the kneecaps and hurried down the steps. He found his three co-workers staring up at the moonlit cliff. The vertical raceway up the cliffside was lit on either side by torches wedged periodically in crags. At the summit, two victory torches awaited. The winner of each race would waive the torch atop his side of the raceway to signify victory.

Archippus watched Emoticas nervously lick his lips. "I can't do it," he said to Raimi.

Raimi's eyes went wide. "What do you mean, you can't do it?"

"I can't do it. I'm afraid of heights."

"You're joking," said Raimi.

"No."

"Why didn't you tell us?"

"I thought I could do it."

Raimi panicked. "Well, what now? We only have a few minutes!"

Emoticas slid from the lizard.

"You're afraid of *heights?*" asked Archippus. "What on the way to the grave did you think cliff racing *was?*"

"Leave off!" snapped Emoticas, removing his spurs. "I don't see you volunteering."

"That's because I don't care about the slaves."

Raimi started to climb onto Hemi's back, but Gershom held her back, motioning a sentence.

"But you've never ridden before!" argued Raimi.

Gershom motioned again.

Raimi frowned and looked to Emoticas for interpretation.

"He says he had his own eegwuhnuh once," said Emoticas.

Raimi's brows shot up, eegwuhnuhs were incredibly costly. Gershom motioned again.

"And, he says if something were to happen to you, who would look after Ezbon-Ishuah," explained Emoticas, handing the spurs to Gershom.

Raimi released her grip on the reins. Gershom tied on the spurs. He climbed onto Hemi's back and fastened the safety belt.

A horn blew to signal it was time to line up, and Gershom goaded the lizard forward.

Raimi covered her eyes with both hands. "I can't watch."

Emoticas' face paled even more.

Hemi was now side-by-side with another eegwuhnuh ridden by a gunner. The two contestants turned the lizards to face the cliff.

"Oh no," said Raimi.

"What?" Archippus asked, still worried about rescue delays.

"He was supposed to compete with a commoner," she said.

"So what's the problem?" asked Archippus.

"Gunners are able to use lances to try to unseat the opponent."

Now Archippus was very worried. Gershom would be useful against the Cyclopes. "That's *wrong*," he said. "Unfair even. Can't we halt all this and move on to *my* problem?"

Raimi ignored him. "Gershom! Beware of the lance!" she yelled.

Gershom lifted his hand in acknowledgement. The horn blew once, twice, and a third time to start the race.

Both riders spurred their lizards to jump onto the wall. The strategy was to go fast on the lower portion where slipping could be safely tolerated. Hemi slithered quickly ahead of the competition. Upon reaching the steeper midsection of the raceway, Gershom slowed the lizard and carefully reined toward crevices where the eegwuhnuh could get a secure grip on the cliff wall. The second eegwuhnuh, not being so careful, soon caught up and both lizards were side by side.

The gunner on the other lizard leaned out and thrust the lance directly into Gershom's ribs. Gershom slid sideways but managed to hang on and pulled himself back into the saddle.

"He has no armor!" yelled Raimi, as if her comment would make a difference to the gunner.

Gershom steered Hemi left to get away from another lance thrust, but too late! The gunner got in a lucky smack across Gershom's back.

"Stop! It's an unfair match!" Raimi screamed to the race officials at the cliff base.

Gershom slowly straightened, in obvious pain. The crowd screamed and cheered.

The gunner swung the lance again, but Gershom, prepared this time, caught hold of the long steel pole, wrenching it away and unseating the gunner. The gunner, now hanging from the safety strap, legs dangling, released the lance.

A deafening roar rose from the crowd. The lance fell straight down, colliding with the stone quarry stage and shattering to pieces. The crowd stood, raised hands, clapped, went wild. Gershom was a length ahead now, and Hemi, picking up speed, continued to find secure niches for his leathery fingers.

The gunner scrambled back into the saddle and goaded his lizard to run without thought of finding proper crevices. Suddenly the gunner's eegwuhnuh made a long upward leap, catching a secure hold, and the two lizards were even again.

Fists jammed the air at the daring move. Cheers echoed from the cliff wall.

Though the din, Raimi thought she heard the distant scrape of metal on metal. She narrowed her eyes and saw in the torchlight that the gunner had drawn his sword and was flinging the sharp blade high overhead.

"No!" she screamed.

The blade flashed down reflecting orange torchlight, and Gershom's safety strap parted. The gunner raised the blade again, pointed the blade deliberately, and stabbed Hemi in the right shoulder. The lizard slipped a full length before catching hold. His safety belt gone, Gershom hung by his right hand from one of the lizard's spiked plates. As Hemi slid back even farther, he swung out desperately, and found a grip on the rocky cliff with his free hand. Hemi suddenly slipped away entirely, leaving him hanging alone by both hands on the sheer rock wall.

The crowd gasped in unison and grew suddenly quiet watching the big lizard slide farther and farther down the cliff, like a broken egg thrown against a wall.

All eyes rose to Gershom. He began to climb.

The gunner having assumed his opponent had fallen, slowed his mount's pace to almost nothing, allowing the reptile to carefully search out finger and toe holds on the last and steepest leg of the raceway.

Unnoticed by the gunner, but not by the whispering, muttering crowd, Gershom had climbed quickly upward until he was alongside the gunner's eegwuhnuh. He reached up and caught one of the gunner's legs. With a single abrupt motion, he jerked the gunner from his saddle. The gunner, dangling from his safety belt, struggled to draw his sword. Gershom snatched the weapon away and slashed the safety strap. The gunner nearly fell from the cliff, but Gershom caught a wad of the gunner's tunic with his free hand and swung him toward the cliff where he found purchase.

The loose eegwuhnuh veered off the raceway, and without a rider for guidance, began picking his way back down the cliff. The two competitors were left to climb on foot to the top of the cliff. Gershom took a quick lead. The gunner grabbed his heel, but Gershom shook him loose and continued quickly upward.

Every single spectator leapt from the stone seats shouting and chanting for the opponent of their choice. Naturally, the front rows favored the gunner while the back rows cheered fervently for Gershom.

The gunner reached out a second time, jerking on Gershom's heel, causing him to slip backward. Abruptly, the two were side-by-side, climbing, pushing, shoving one another. A heavy blow from Gershom sent the gunner dangling one handed. Gershom went ahead. Faster, faster, he climbed. He grabbed the last handhold and pulled himself to the top of the cliff, stood, leapt for the torch, held it high and waved the flaming symbol of victory at the crowd below.

The front rows fell silent.

The back rows roared.

Raimi excited, happy, and clapping, heard the reduction in the cheering of the crowd. She turned and watched as the front rows launched food, rocks and even a few spears at the back rows. It appeared a full-blown brawl had broken out.

She ran to the base of the cliff followed by Emoticas and Archippus. Hemi was still, his snakelike eyes at half lid revealing he was either tired or in pain. Raimi examined the lizard's right shoulder. The wound was a clean, straight in thrust, just above the shoulder. She grabbed Hemi's reins and made him move forward, watching him closely. "He can walk," she affirmed.

The three of them looked upward. The gunner and Gershom were repelling downward via pre-established exit ropes. The gunner dropped first to the ground, cursed, yelled something at the race officials, and stomped off in the direction of the Judgment Hall.

Gershom landed next. His back had a thick welt across it and an ugly bruise was forming on his side.

"Are you badly hurt?" asked Raimi.

Gershom shook his head, but Archippus worried that if Gershom's ribs were broken, it might be difficult to fight a Cyclops.

Raimi poked at the spreading purple bruise.

"Are his ribs broken?" asked Archippus.

"Doesn't look like it," said Raimi.

"Gershom, Raimi … I'm sorry I failed you both," said Emoticas.

"You didn't fail us," said Raimi. "That gunner fought unfairly. It would have been difficult for you to fend him off. Things happen for a reason."

"Well, there's a lesson for you," said Archippus.

"What lesson?" asked Raimi.

"Action is better than preparation and execution is better than theory. You can plan all you want, but if you can't implement the idea, it's useless. If I were under attack, I'd pick Gershom over Emoticas."

"You two-legged reptile!" exclaimed Emoticas. "I can't help it I'm afraid of heights!"

"Whiny, whiny, what a wailer," mocked Archippus.

Emoticas bunched a fist and swung, but Archippus jumped back in time. Gershom grabbed Emoticas to restrain him.

"Stop it!" yelled Raimi. "I'm sure that gunner has gone to protest the race. We should leave before the brawlers start throwing spears in *our* direction." She led the large lizard toward the Dells. Archippus walked on Hemi's right side as a barrier to the hollering unruly crowd.

Raimi led Hemi into the main lair to examine the wound by the light of the campfire. She prepared a poultice and rubbed it on his wound. "I think he'll be all right." She turned the lizard around and led him down the trail to his lair.

"We won!" she announced with her fist in the air as she returned.

"Here, here!" shouted Emoticas.

Gershom raised his fist and shook it.

To celebrate, Raimi jammed meat on a stick and set it in the fire.

"Now we can make our formal request at the hearing," said Raimi.

Ezbon-Ishuah came into the firelight with his cane. "The gunner protested to the council members. The race is forfeited to the gunner."

"On what grounds?" demanded Raimi indignantly.

"For Gershom unseating the gunner."

"Were they not watching the race?" asked Raimi with disbelief. "The gunner stabbed Hemi and nearly killed Gershom!"

"Gershom is a commoner," said Ezbon-Ishuah, reminding her of the obvious.

"Yes! A commoner!" Raimi yelled. She threw her unfinished meal onto the fire. "If it's not skin we must fight for, it's now class!"

"Have we lost the right for a request before the council?" asked Emoticas.

Raimi paced, her face reddened with rage.

"Is there no way to appeal?" asked Emoticas.

"You could enter the stage competitions," suggested Ezbon-Ishuah. "Your music is coming along nicely."

"No, it's not!" exclaimed Raimi. "We can only play a couple familiar songs. We need a new song to stir the hearts and minds ..."

All of them looked at Archippus.

"What?" he asked.

"You claim to be a wordsmith, you could craft us one," said Raimi.

"One what?" asked Archippus.

"A song. Haven't you been listening?"

"A song about what?"

"*About what?* About freedom and fairness and oppression!"

"Well, won't that take some time, and didn't all three of you promise to help me free Jazelle after the race?" asked Archippus.

"We expected to win the race, now things have changed," said Raimi.

"Raimi," said Emoticas, "you wrote a song, tell Archippus."

Raimi rolled her eyes. "I'm not a wordsmith, or a writer, or even a poet."

"I think it's pretty good, go on tell him," encouraged Emoticas.

Raimi sighed. "Okay. It goes like this. First I sing, *They breathe,* and then Emoticas sings, *They breathe*, and then I sing, *Like us,* and then Emoticas sings, *Like us,* and then I sing, *They feel,* and then Emoticas sings *They feel,* and then I sing, *Like us,* and then Emoticas sings, *Like us,* and then I sing, *They fear,* and then Emoticas sings, *They fea—*"

"I get it, I get it!" interrupted Archippus. "Every time you sing Emoticas *repeats it.* So what's the rest of it?"

"Well, actually, after that we sing the chorus together and it goes, *So treat well ee-gwuh-nuhs*—you know with the emphasis on the 'wuh' drawing it out, and then we sing the beginning again and change eegwuhnuhs to *white*

199

skins in the chorus." She finished looking pleased with herself.

Archippus stared.

"What do you think?" asked Emoticas.

"I think, that under the candle vigil canopy that lights the night sky, your song is the worst poetry ever concocted on the Continent."

"Well then write something for us," pleaded Raimi.

"Why should I?"

"Because you want something from us, and we want something from you. Aren't you asking a lot of us to face the desert Cyclops? I feel we should change our minds," threatened Raimi.

"Face what?" asked Ezbon-Ishuah.

"Nothing," said Raimi.

Archippus thought of Jazelle in the Cyclops cage. "All right. I'll write something."

"And you have to hurry, because the competitions are tomorrow and we'll have to put it to music," said Raimi.

"All right. I'll hurry," he mumbled, and headed for his burrow.

"Why are you still here?" demanded Archippus of Hazo as he entered the burrow. "Aren't you well enough by now to go somewhere else?"

Hazo sat up. "Why do you hate me? You're no better than I. We both are pale of skin."

"Because I'm a tradesmon!" snapped Archippus.

"Didn't we have this same argument before you went on your gallivant about the Continent?"

"Yes, and you've obviously forgotten why I am superior. *This ...*" Archippus held up parchment paper, "... makes me superior!"

"What are you going to do with that?" asked Hazo.

"I'm going to scribe words to a song, if you must know," answered Archippus. He sat down and dipped his pen in the inkwell.

"What's the song about?" asked Hazo.

"About idiots like you," snapped Archippus.

"Oh, well, why are you doing *that?*"

"I can't do anything if you don't shut up!"

Hazo lay back down. "You remind me of my first slave master."

Archippus tried to write, but Hazo's comment interfered. "What's that suppose to mean?"

"He spoke impatiently to me, called me names, and acted superior. But that wasn't the worst of it." Hazo adjusted his head on his arm as if getting ready to go to sleep.

Archippus sat silent for a few moments. He tried to write but couldn't think. "So what was the worst of it?"

"Well, the worst of it was that he sold my parents, and I don't know where or how they are. He whipped them to force them into a cage, but they refused to leave me. So he beat them unconscious and dragged them in."

Archippus stared at Hazo, pen in hand. A drop of ink splattered on the dirt floor.

"How old were you?" asked Archippus.

"Eight."

Archippus' mind flashed to the Judgment Hall in the city of Ai on the day he was dragged away from his mother and sister. "Eight," he repeated. The remembrance was painful, and despite his reluctance, a small flicker of empathy prodded him to speak. "We do have something in common then."

Hazo smiled. "I told you. You and I are just alike."

Archippus grunted and went to work writing the song. It only took a few moments to come up with a stanza that could be repeated several times. He carried the finished parchment to Gershom and Emoticas' burrow where Raimi was also waiting.

Archippus cleared his throat. "Okay," he started. "It goes like this,

> *Intellect and wit and strength, combine to earn, manipulate,*
> *Achieve where epidermis fails, gutting bias' stenched entrails.*
> *Look to cunning, seek mislead, it matters not what be your breed,*
> *For honor comes to those deserved whom overcome,*
> *not come unnerved."*

Archippus looked up from the parchment to find three blank stares.

Gershom gestured vehemently at Archippus.

"What's he saying?" asked Archippus.

"He asked, 'What on the way to the grave does it mean?'" interpreted Emoticas.

"It means exactly what I said," said Archippus defensively.

"Gershom says it's confusing," insisted Emoticas.

"What does he know?" asked Archippus. "He doesn't even use words."

"They'll never understand it," said Raimi. "It's too complicated."

"Well there it is," said Archippus tossing the parchment to the dirt floor in front of them. "Use it, don't use it, but I held up my end of the bargain. And if I were you, I wouldn't sing Raimi's song. They'll throw spears for certain." Archippus stomped from the burrow.

≺ ≺ ≺ ≺
≺ ≺ ≺ ≺

The next night-day, Archippus made his way slowly up the stairway lost in extreme worry over Jazelle. He caught up with Ezbon-Ishuah who was relying heavily on his cane to climb the long stairway. Archippus took his arm to assist him.

As they climbed, Ezbon-Ishuah squeezed Archippus' arm. "I do not believe I will walk the Continent much longer," he said.

Archippus glanced sideways at him. "Don't say that."

"I must say it. And I want to say it to *you*."

"Well, I don't want to hear it," countered Archippus. "You're looking better. You'll be fine."

Ezbon-Ishuah chuckled. "No. I have something I want to say to *you*. They are words of wisdom that I wanted to pass on to my son."

Archippus waited wondering what Ezbon-Ishuah meant.

Ezbon-Ishuah continued. "Before the High Council began to limit our access to the scrolls, I would often make my way to the Judgment Hall to read them. And as you know, the sixth scroll is the Book of Wisdom. But what many Landlings do not realize is the book was given to us by the Seraph who travels time, and the writings come from the final millennia."

"Final millennia?" repeated Archippus. His mind tried to grasp the indication that this could mean thousands of years into the future. He was uncertain of a Seraph, much less time travel, or the concept that the Continent could continue for that duration.

"Yes," continued Ezbon-Ishuah. "The sixth scroll is said to come to us from the future. Conversely, there is also a prophecy that a seventh scroll will be written for Landkind in the final millennia as penned by the Airborne Monarch. But the verses I memorized, I share with you now."

Ezbon-Ishuah cleared his throat. "With regard to the wealth you seek—you and I are alike. You love commerce. But, in the verses from the Book of Wisdom, a father speaks to his son, and I memorized one stanza.

> *If you can make one heap of all your winnings*
> *And risk it on one turn of pitch-and-toss,*
> *And lose, and start again at your beginnings*
> *And never breathe a word about your loss:*

202

If you can force your heart and nerve and sinew
To serve your turn long after they are gone,
And so hold on when there is nothing in you
Except the Will which says to them: "Hold on!" [6]

The point being that it is difficult to separate your worth from your wealth, but if you can do that, then you'll be a man, my son."

The words *my son,* perhaps more than all the other words, brought a wave of emotion and water to Archippus' eyes.

Ezbon-Ishuah tightened his hold on Archippus' arm. "It is my wisdom gift to you." Then he chuckled. "And I had to borrow it because I have none of my own to offer."

Archippus' stomach churned. It would anger him to lose this man. "I've learned much wisdom from you," he countered.

"I am pleased you think so," said Ezbon-Ishuah. "For recently, nothing I have gained seems to matter except if part of me continues in the living."

"It will continue," assured Archippus.

Ezbon-Ishuah took a deep breath inward and released it slowly. "Good. Now let's make our way upward to watch the stage competition."

The two took their seats in the mid-row trades section.

The first competitor took the stage.

"Our first contestant," announced the crier, "is gunner Phicol performing the Art of Dancing Daggers."

Loud cheers came from the front rows.

Gunner Phicol walked mid-stage. He drew a dagger from sheaths on each hip and held them up crisscross.

The crowd fell silent.

Gunner Phicol then leaped forward and threw the daggers spinning upward. They came back down, and he caught each by the handle.

Cheers came from the crowd.

He then tossed one up and then the next catching each in turn.

More loud cheers.

The dance continued and a third dagger was tossed to him from side stage. He caught it amid tosses of the others, and inserted the third dagger into the rotation.

An upsurge of cheers ensued.

Gunner Phicol completed his act by spearing all three daggers into the trunk of a nearby tree, one atop the other, in perfect alignment.

The crowd jumped to its feet.

"Well, that will be tough to beat," said Archippus to Ezbon-Ishuah.

The next performer was announced: "The Belle of Bells."

A set of tiny bells strung from wooden poles was carried onto the stage, and a noblemon took center stage behind the poles. She used an iron rod to tap on the bells in turn, producing a beautiful melody. The music continued for several minutes, until she finished by running the bar against each bell quickly to produce a sweeping crescendo that hung in the air as a finale.

The crowd applauded, and the noblemon curtsied.

Next, a long white fabric was held in front of the stage by rope, concealing what was going on behind; though it was obvious, the next act used fire, as flames shone through the fabric.

"And now for our Shadow Show being performed by our very own MSC students," said the crier.

The shadows of children were visible behind the white curtain. A handful of the children ran to the center revealing outlines of what must have been neck chains. A large figure then burst forth from one side costumed to depict a two-legged reptile. To Archippus' surprise, the entire mishap of the eegwuhnuh attack was re-enacted.

Archippus couldn't help but wonder if the slaves behind him weren't somewhat disturbed by the performance, as small children in the audience screamed and started crying.

Well, that was loads of wholesome entertainment, thought Archippus sarcastically, as the sheet slid to one side and the young performers bowed.

"Our next contestants," announced the crier, "are performing for the very first time. Please welcome ..." He looked to stage right for coaching, unsure of how to announce the act.

A whisper came from the side stage.

"Please welcome ..." continued the crier, "... the Moles."

Clang, clang, clang.

Three figures clad in armor traipsed to the center of the stage. Laughter ensued for the armor was oversized.

Archippus recognized the flute, tambourine, and dulcimer. He felt grateful he was not part of this embarrassment. "Why are they dressed in armor?" he asked Ezbon-Ishuah.

"Raimi rented it from Gunner Phicol and two of his comrades. That way, they won't get injured," explained Ezbon-Ishuah.

The town crier waved both hands overhead to shush the crowd.

Emoticas strummed his instrument, and Gershom lifted his visor to play his flute. Raimi banged her tambourine in rhythm and began to sing.

"Intellect and wit and strength—" sang Raimi.

Archippus was mortified—they were singing his verse.

Several spectators booed.

"Combine to earn, manipulate—"

"Learn a real song!" heckled a front row gunner.

"Achieve where epidermis fails," Raimi sang sweetly.

The first spear sizzled across the stage. Clang! It bounced off Gershom's breastplate.

"Gutting bias' stenched entrails—"

Clang! Clang! Two more spears bounced off the armor suits.

"They're butchering my song," said Archippus.

The performers continued among a barrage of tossed projectiles, including pieces of fruit.

Raimi stepped sideways to avoid a spear. Her heavy armored foot slipped on the fruit littered stones, and she fell face forward onto the stage. Her heavy armor would not permit her to get back up, so she sang the final line, "not come unneeerved," face down in the helmet.

This unusual ending made the crowd burst into laughter. More spears were tossed. Gershom and Emoticas lifted Raimi under each arm and pulled her back up into a standing position. The three whispered among themselves as several additional weapons clattered about their feet.

Completely unabashed, they clanged themselves back to center stage. To Archippus' dismay they began to sing Raimi's song.

The crowd was still laughing, but soon caught onto the rhythm and repetition of "They feel/they feel; Like us/like us; They breathe/they breathe; Like us/like us; They fear/they fear; Like us/like us; So treat well ee-*gwuh*-nuhs."

Despite Archippus' predictions, the more the stanza repeated, the more the crowd sang the echo along with Emoticas. During the second stanza, the crowd stood, and clapped, and swayed left and right with the rhythm. Ezbon-Ishuah also struggled up and swayed to the extent that he could. Archippus remained seated.

The song continued with much merriment and the three performers were able to transition to the substitution of "white skins" for "ee-gwuh-nuhs."

Much to Archippus' surprise, the crowd went along, for he felt this affront would have drawn spears.

The song was successfully completed and the competitors bowed clumsily and clamored off stage with hoots, hollers, and cheers from an appreciative audience.

"Unbelievable," muttered Archippus.

"Yes, it was quite impressive," said Ezbon-Ishuah. "The second song, anyway. Where on earth did they come up with that first one?"

Unseen by Ezbon-Ishuah, Archippus squinted his left eye defensively, then he assisted Ezbon-Ishuah down the steps to enable him to congratulate the performers.

As Archippus and Ezbon-Ishuah walked up to the three glowing contestants, they were removing their helmets.

"The armor saved us," said Emoticas. "We have completed our first heavy metal performance. Perhaps we should call ourselves 'The Moles in Heavy Metal.'"

Raimi laughed. "I'm hoping to abandon the metal at some point."

"We won't need it if you don't sing Archippus' song again," said Emoticas.

"It wasn't my *lyrics*," insisted Archippus defensively. "It was the manner in which Raimi sang them. She strung out the notes on 'unnerved' for so long that the audience thought she was suffering." He turned to Raimi. "In fact, I'm quite certain the spear throwing was a merciful attempt to put you out of your misery."

"Very funny," said Raimi. "You try singing face down on a stone stage."

"I have no intention of ever singing anywhere."

Ezbon-Ishuah cleared his throat. "No reason to be tense, now Archippus. They have every reason to celebrate." He turned to Raimi. "When will you get to place your request for winning the stage contest before the council?"

"On the Night of No Orb," answered Raimi. "The requests are formally considered on the Night of No Orb—meaning no moon—along with the regular civil hearings."

Ezbon-Ishuah nodded. "Well, congratulations. I'm very proud of you. And very tired. The suspense nearly killed me." He smiled. "I'm off to my burrow now."

"I'll help you back," said Raimi.

"No. Stay for the feast. All of you. They're serving quite a meal, and I hear they've imported juice of lemons from the Citadel by the Sea."

"I'll bring you some," said Raimi.

"I look forward to it," said Ezbon-Ishuah. He smiled and hobbled toward the burrows.

"Can we focus on *my* problem now?" asked Archippus.

"Which one?" asked Raimi. "You have so many."

Archippus shifted his weight and crossed his arms. "Look, I know you don't like me, but you agreed to help. In your efforts to save the *entire* Continent from corruption, why not start by seeing if you can save even *one* solitary Landling." He swung his arms wide.

Gershom motioned a couple sentences.

Emoticas sighed and looked at Raimi. "Gershom agrees we should help Archippus. He says the sacred scrolls state, 'A single Landling saved serves all.'"

Raimi crossed her arms and squinted at Archippus. After a few seconds, she uncrossed her arms. "All right. I guess I'm ready. We'll need weapons and an eegwuhnuh."

"And perhaps a bite to eat first?" asked Emoticas, eyeing the tables spread with food and drink.

"Grab me an avocado," said Raimi. "I'll go negotiate with Gunner Phicol to add five spears to our armor rental."

As she left, a snocked-up gunner raised his clay goblet to her. "Treat well the white skins—Hear, hear!"

A few of his dark-skinned cohorts raised their goblets high in turn. "Hear, hear!" They shouted in agreement.

Archippus rolled his eyes.

Emoticas, Gershom, and Raimi left their armor behind after Emoticas made the point that any encounter with the Cyclops should be stealthy, and the armor clanged. But Raimi had managed to negotiate four spears from Gunner Phicol despite his insistences that only nobility had the right to bear arms. Her successful negotiation resulted in all four travelers climbing onto eegwuhnuh Tandy, with spears in hand.

Raimi sat in front to rein, Gershom behind the next spiked plate, then Emoticas, and Archippus last. Raimi cautioned Archippus to hold tight for the swaying motion is strongest near the tail.

Hodos landed on Archippus' left shoulder. Since the bird had been relatively quiet, as of late, Archippus did not grumble, but he quickly regretted the bird's intrusion.

"So we're off to save Ocean Eyes," stated Hodos.

"Why do you do that?" asked Archippus angrily.

"What?"

"Speak ill of Jazelle!"

"They're *your* words."

"But you say them with *disrespect.*"

"It is not the girl I disrespect, but rather your displaced adoration."

"What do you mean by that?"

"Each day, the Seraph sets fire and water before you. Stretch out your hand for whichever you wish."

"What's that supposed to mean?"

"Your displaced adoration will burn you."

"What in your infinite wisdom, *Bird,* do you suggest I adore then?"

"Seek the Seraph. Find your quest."

"There is no Seraph to be found. No one has ever seen him."

"He reveals himself through nature. The unseen through the seen."

"You speak mysteries! Tell me plainly. What is my quest?"

"Stop choosing fire and you might find out."

"I choose love!"

"Love does not demand, but gives freely from a position of strength. You do not love, Archippus, for you are desperate for affection in return. Your heart throne is vacant."

"I *do* love! Jazelle is on my heart throne!"

"Hunger and thirst for your quest and you will be filled. Otherwise, your thirst will slay you."

"Aarrgghh!" Archippus shoved Hodos from his shoulder.

Hodos flittered alongside the eegwuhnuh.

"You can ride with me, Hodos," said Emoticas. "I understand your point perfectly."

Hodos landed on Emoticas' shoulder and Raimi spurred Tandy into a run.

Archippus fell off.

Raimi reined Tandy around, and Archippus climbed on a second time. He was angry but held his tongue. He required this pathetic entourage to assist him. He even withheld screaming, "I hate you" at Hodos, because he needed the blasted bird too.

Tandy covered the ground with amazing speed. The jungle foliage turned small and stunted, the land grew dry, and the desert arrived.

Archippus realized that it was on this trail that the Cyclops based their camp. He recognized the rock formation some distance ahead and Raimi reined Tandy to a halt.

"So what's your plan?" Raimi asked Archippus as she and the others dismounted.

"Plan?"

"You do have a plan, don't you?" Raimi demanded.

"Uh …" Archippus' voice trailed off.

Gershom made gestures to interrupt and Emoticas interpreted. "Gershom says that we should have Hodos scout the key to the cage, wait for the Cyclops to fall asleep, then steal the key, free Jazelle, and run like lizards with our tails on fire."

Raimi and Archippus were silent for several seconds.

"Okay," said Raimi. "Sounds good to me."

"Me too," said Archippus, relieved that someone had at least come up with something.

They stealthily crept to the rocks and climbed to peer at the enemy— twelve in all—lounging and snorting, gesturing and chortling around the fire.

Archippus squinted. The cage was some twenty feet behind the seated Cyclopes. He could see an outline of a figure inside the cage and huddled under a cape. His heart leapt, but then he felt sick with sadness and fear for Jazelle.

The rescuers waited and waited and waited.

Finally, each Cyclops reclined, but each one also, to Archippus' dismay, left their eye open.

Gershom motioned to Hodos. The bird flew off to scout the key.

"What are you doing?" whispered Archippus. "They're not yet asleep!"

Gershom signaled to Emoticas.

"He says that the desert Cyclops has no eyelid, and so they sleep with their eye open," said Emoticas.

"How can he tell they're asleep?"

More gestures from Gershom.

"Their pupils grow tiny when they sleep and large when awake," answered Emoticas.

"How would he know this?" asked Archippus.

Emoticas gave a wide-eyed shrug and Archippus eyeballed the eyeballs. It was very unnerving. All the wide-open eyes and they were really too far away to see the pupils.

Hodos fluttered in out of the darkness. "Naturally, against any facilitative luck, the key is with the Cyclops farthest from the cage. So one of you will have to make your way quietly through the bodies, secure the key, and throw it to whomever is waiting by the cage."

The four rescuers looked blankly at each other.

Gershom outlined a plan and Emoticas interpreted. "Gershom says he will get the key. Archippus is to wait by the cage, and I am to stay up here with spears ready to launch if need be, while Raimi waits on Tandy for our escape."

Everyone nodded agreement. Archippus felt a fleeting moment of gratitude for Gershom's courage and assistance. Simultaneously, all four set themselves into motion.

Archippus made his way toward the cage glancing at each single open eye he passed. It did appear they had no pupil.

He slipped over to the cage and reached in his hand to touch the hunched caped figure. Startled, the figure threw back the hood of the cape.

A pair of green eyes switched from fear to surprise.

"It's you!" she whispered.

Archippus made a 'shush' sign and glanced over at Gershom who was untying the key from the key-bearer's leather hip strap. The Cyclops snorted, shifted. Gershom tried again. He fumbled with the leather string a moment, freed the key, and tossed it gently to Archippus. Archippus fumbled it, the key clanged the cage, and dropped to the ground.

All the Cyclopes startled awake and jumped to their feet. Archippus dropped to his knees franticly searching for the key in the loose dirt. Jazelle screamed. He glanced up to see Gershom thrown against a boulder. His fingers closed around the key. He shoved it in the lock, twisted it. A Cyclops howled behind him. He turned quickly and watched the creature fall forward—a spear stuck in his back. The lock turned. He pulled open the door, grabbed Jazelle by the hand, and jerked her from the cage. All the Cyclopes roared like lions.

Archippus held Jazelle tight and glanced hurriedly about for the safest way to get to the lizard. Angered Cyclopes' were climbing the boulders to get at the spear throwing Emoticas, and Gershom was wrestling the key-bearer. Emoticas let go another spear and the Cyclops wrestling Gershom roared and collapsed.

Archippus saw that none of the engaged Cyclopes were paying attention to him. He took the opportunity, and he and Jazelle leapt over the fallen Cyclops by the cage, ran around the campfire, and zigzagged through the rocks to Tandy.

Emoticas threw a third spear, and a fourth. Both hit their marks and two Cyclops fell from the boulders. Gershom, clearly weakened by his struggle with the key-bearer, limped unseen beneath several furious Cyclops climbing the rocks toward Emoticas. Emoticas scurried down the backside of his high position, intercepted Gershom, and helped the injured Landling hobble to the lizard. The Cyclopes crested the boulders howling and screaming, spotted the lizard and the escapees, and charged down off the boulders throwing rocks and roaring.

Emoticas pushed Gershom up onto Tandy. Archippus, already in his saddle with Jazelle, pulled from above and got the exhausted Gershom settled in a saddle. Emoticas grabbed a hold of one of Tandy's spikes just as Raimi spun the big lizard around and put the spurs in her. Tandy shot off with Emoticas still dangling.

Temples and heart pounding, Archippus clutched Jazelle. Her hair flew in his face. He realized, to his astonishment and relief, the rescue, against all odds, had been a success!

Emoticas skipped along on his sandals a few times and then jumped into his saddle. Tandy ran for many miles in the direction of Ai until finally, with enough desert behind them, Raimi reined up. She jumped quickly from the saddle. Archippus released his grip on Jazelle and she slid to the ground, pale and quiet. Archippus got off behind her, took her by a trembling arm, and helped her to a nearby log. Hodos landed next to her.

Gershom limped about gathering wood for a fire. Raimi drove a stake and chained Tandy's leg. Emoticas tossed sacks to Archippus. He dug around inside and gave Jazelle a handful of sweet, dried fruit.

"Thank you," she said softly. As she chewed the fruit, Archippus noticed that her eyes drifted about, seeming to lack focus. Archippus surmised she was overwhelmed.

Raimi walked over to him and Jazelle. "We'll camp here tonight and should make Ai by tomorrow evening." She reached into the sack Archippus was holding and picked out a piece of fruit. Gershom and Emoticas also came to secure food.

"You missed the key," said Emoticas. "How on the way to the grave could you miss the key?"

"It was dark," said Archippus defensively.

"Well, no matter, we did it," said Raimi. "No sense arguing now. I am amazed, however, that the Cyclopes missed you guys with all those rocks they threw."

Gershom motioned something.

"Oh …" said Emoticas. "Gershom says that the reason the Cyclopes missed us with the rocks, is the same reason they don't use weapons, just brute strength."

"Why is that?" asked Raimi.

"Having only one eye, they've no depth perception," said Emoticas.

"Well," said Raimi, "if that's the case, then Archippus catches keys like a Cyclops."

The group burst into laughter, even Jazelle, and although the joke was at his expense, it pleased Archippus to see her laugh.

⤎ ⤎ ⤎ ⤎
⤎ ⤎ ⤎ ⤎

Eegwuhnuh riding is not conducive to conversation, so the next morning's windy trip went predominantly in silence. Jazelle sat in the second position behind Raimi in order to have a smoother ride. This meant Archippus could only stare at her windblown locks from his seat near the tail. He held the last remaining spear in the event that the Cyclopes still pursued them.

But they arrived without incident at Ai. Raimi reined in Tandy in front of Jazelle's castle and they all dismounted.

"We don't dare come inside," explained Archippus.

"I know," said Jazelle. "I recognized you to be the prison scribe when I saw you through those bars at the Cyclopes camp. And I remember Gershom and Emoticas to be cellmates as well."

"If anyone in this city were to recognize them ..." Archippus began.

"I know," she said. "I can't thank you enough." She looked directly at each of them in turn, and then headed for her door.

Archippus jogged after her. "Jazelle ... wait!"

She halted and turned.

"When you reach the age to be betrothed—"

"I can't," she said, "my mother would never permit it."

Archippus felt punched in the gut.

"I'm sorry, but you are poor," she said softly.

"Then I'll spend the next four years making a fortune. And then I shall come for you," he pleaded.

She smiled, took the spear from his hand, and used the spearhead to cut one of her red-brown locks. She handed it to him, then spun quickly, pushed the door open and was gone.

Archippus stared at the lock of hair.

"Archippus!" yelled Raimi. "Come on! We must hurry!"

He tucked the treasure in the leather scroll pouch and dazedly returned to the others. Overcome with euphoria, he climbed back onto Tandy with a happy heart and took his seat behind the others, and the rescuers headed back to Rephidim.

The first day of the ride back, Archippus planned how to achieve riches. But when they stopped for camp, worry took over. He knew he owed thanks to his cohorts, but thanking was an awkward thing for him. He reasoned he didn't owe them thanks anyway, for they would have done this type of thing regardless, and the rescue was good practice, since they seemed bent on saving the Continent.

Then he reasoned that Gershom and Emoticas owed him something for freeing them from prison. But this wouldn't explain why he shouldn't thank Raimi, who owed him nothing.

Then he reasoned the rescue had been the trio's opportunity to stick it to the corruption seeping into the councils by undermining Eri.

Then he gave up reasoning all together and simply dreaded the moment. When it came, seated around the campfire that night, with all the eloquence he could gather as a wordsmith and a master scribe, he finally mustered his resolve. He cleared his throat and said, "Uh …" cleared his throat again and mumbled, "Thanks, you guys."

PARCHMENT VIII

"And the Continent was matriarchal,
for females are the womb bearers,
the gatekeepers of the future."

They reached Rephidim the following day, and Raimi invited the three of them to join her in telling Ezbon-Ishuah of the rescue. She had not mentioned the rescue effort to Ezbon-Ishuah before their departure for fear of worrying him. Instead, she had feigned a trip to Calidron for metal working supplies.

They descended the stairs and entered Ezbon-Ishuah's burrow. He lay dead on his sofa. Raimi fell to her knees and sobbed on his cold, still chest. Archippus stood frozen with shock and sadness. All was silent except Raimi's sobbing.

"I was gone!" she cried. "I was gone when he died! Curse you Archippus! You robbed me of his final hour! You and your stupid obsession!"

The words hurt Archippus. "But I cared for him also!"

"You care about *you!*" she sobbed again. "And I forgot to bring back his juice of the lemon!" She spun and threw the inkwell at Archippus. "Get out!"

Quick of reflex, Archippus caught the inkwell. He carried it to the ledge outside the burrow. He and Ezbon-Ishuah had spent hours with this inkwell, and now it was completely dry and empty like he felt. It was wrong of Raimi to be angry with him when he himself was suffering. He could not return to his own burrow for he could not endure Hazo. As an alternative, Archippus went up the stairs and made his way to the Dells.

The embers from the fire crackled in the center of the main lair. He sat and stared and poked the cinders with one of the metal working tools.

Swoosh!

The embers flamed and ignited.

Pterodactyl Eri dropped to the ground in front of him.

Archippus jumped up and backed away.

"Well," said Eri, "I see you've become interested in the affairs of the Continent and taken it upon yourself to decide the proper action for inner-city relations."

"Uh ..."

"Have you any idea the length I went to, to arrange that capture?"

"Uh ..."

"And did I not stress to you the importance of applying influence in order to maintain order in these treacherous times?"

"Uh ..."

"I half think your deed so treasonous that I should snap your neck in half this moment." Eri snapped his jaws and they made a loud clack that echoed through the Dells.

"Uh ..."

"But, seeing as I have used your misdeed to my advantage and taken credit for the rescue and implemented a cautionary warning to Lordess Lourdes, I *may* spare you your immediate death. That, and for the additional fact that slaying Landlings, for who knows what possible rationale, upsets the Seraph.

"Additional terms for the sparing of your life, are that if asked, you will credit the rescue as being under my direction, and you must bring me information of value from the Barbirians regarding their uprising over the course of the next year. And do not bring me something that I already know, or something that I could have suspected. Discover something that would surprise me, something of their strategic plans for an uprising, something that would *shock* me.

"If you do not manage to infiltrate their camp and garner information of *great use* to the High Council, I may completely forget the sentiments of the Seraph by implementing your deserved punishment. Am I making myself clear?" Eri lowered his head to glare into Archippus' face.

"Y-y-yes."

"And do not breathe a word of this essential assignment to anyone, for a spy can only be successful if his identity is a complete and utter secret, and if you were to squeal, the appropriate penalty might very well be a swift beheading. Am I making myself clear?"

"Y-y-yes."

"Good. Yes, you had no thought for the good of the Continent in your reckless actions, but thanks to me, and you *can* thank me now you realize ..." Eri eyeballed him.

"Th-th-thanks."

"Yes, thanks to me I have rectified the situation. I told Lordess Lourdes that this was a terrible misfortune, but that I would appoint two Fourth Field Gunners to watch over her daughter. Such security is a privilege provided to only the High Ruler herself. I explained that she should try to do her best to cooperate with the High Council in all matters concerning the Continent. I told her it would be a terrible shame if the council members voted to withdraw the protection to her daughter due to any perceived dissension.

"Well, the Lordess blubbered and groveled and thanked me. I think she may have a predilection for dipping a bit heavily into her snock selection, but no matter, I do believe I have earned her undying gratitude.

"So ... I think we have an understanding, and I look forward to our reunion next year." Eri lifted off and was gone.

Archippus crept back toward the fire and sat. He looked up occasionally out of nervousness, but soon fell to staring at the embers once again. His mind raced. Yesterday had been the happiest day of his life and today the worst. *Where is the sense in that?* he wondered.

Hodos landed on a rock to his right. "I see you've been entertaining company," said the songbird.

Archippus shook his head. "And I've finished, thank you, so you may leave."

"Why so sour? We saved Breezy Locks."

"Leave off, Bird. Ezbon-Ishuah is dead."

Hodos took a deep breath in and out. "I know. I'm sorry."

Archippus could not contain himself any longer. "Curse your Seraph! He takes everything! Everyone I've ever cared about is gone!"

The Landling and the songbird stared into the fire.

"You are learning of life and death," said Hodos. "Why do you think the shrieking seedling shrieks when it grows?"

"Because the Seraph is merciless!"

"No," said Hodos. "The Seraph is above all the most merciful. The seedling shrieks for the simple reason that it hurts when it grows."

"I hurt when you speak!" snapped Archippus.

"Well," said Hodos. "What of your 'winding-staircase-corruptible-containers-a deadline-gives-life-meaning' theory?"

"I don't believe a word of it!"

"I see."

"Especially if there's no After-sky!"

"I would agree."

"And I hate you!"

"Of course."

Archippus lowered his forehead onto his palms.

"You realize," said Hodos, "that Landlings should live in such a manner, that once they are gone it will have mattered that they lived."

"What do you mean?" Archippus tilted his furrowed brow to glance down at the bird.

"Ezbon-Ishuah did that," said Hodos. "He mattered for you and Raimi."

Archippus placed his forehead back into his palms.

"If you need me—" began Hodos.

"I never *need* you," snapped Archippus.

"Of course." And Hodos flew off.

⫞ ⫞ ⫞ ⫞
⫞ ⫞ ⫞ ⫞

The following night-day, Emoticas, Gershom, Archippus, and acquaintances of Ezbon-Ishuah, all carrying torches, silently followed Raimi to the burial grounds. Being female, it was Raimi's honor to dig the Sheole. In solemnity and rain, she dug. The dark and the downpour made it difficult to ascertain if her mud-caked cheeks were of tears or rain, but Archippus knew his own to be tears.

Raimi refused to speak to him before, during, or after the ceremony. And as a result, Archippus had Emoticas convince Raimi to permit him to work and receive pay until the Night of No Orb conveying there was something important to attend to at the hearings, and that after that, Raimi would be free of him.

⫞ ⫞ ⫞ ⫞
⫞ ⫞ ⫞ ⫞

Apphia heard a significant *swoosh,* and Eri landed on her balcony.

"Did you miss me, wingmon?" he asked her.

"I dreaded every second."

"Of course you did," said Eri with a smile.

"Of your return," said Apphia.

Eri laughed, reconfirming Apphia's suspicion that the reptile had absolutely no inkling that she loathed him.

"Are you *growing* your *hair?*" asked Eri.

Apphia placed her hands on her prickly skull. "Yes," she said tentatively, fearful that he would object.

"Good," said Eri. "In a few months then, I will be able to commission the renowned artist Malchiel Merari to come and paint your portrait. There has been grumbling among your subjects to *see* their High Ruler so they may know what she looks like."

"Oh," said Apphia. It puzzled her that he would permit a portrait given they had gone to such lengths to conceal her skin color, but she did not question him for she was relieved to have his consent on the re-growth of her hair.

"I have terrible news," Eri stated.

Apphia's heart leapt.

Eri continued. "I spoke with Lord Ipthsum."

Her heart was now pounding. She feared Lord Ipthsum might have ignored her request not to speak of her brother's escape, and ...

"Your brother is dead. He was buried in a commoner's mass grave."

Apphia was relieved. She tried to look sad. "Oh," was all she could muster.

Eri eyed her. "Very good. You are taking this well. I sense a maturity in you."

"Well ..." Apphia tried to select her words carefully, all the while trying to appear saddened. "You had indicated his heart had grown dim in the darkness of his cell and that he could pose a threat."

"Yes. Yes, I did. I am proud of you for your ability to place the needs of the Continent before your own concerns."

"Thank you."

"And now I can tell you," continued Eri, "in the Prophetic Book of Ezdra, there is reference to a twin destined to lead the Continent in conjunction with the Airborne Monarch. Also predicted was a defining struggle that has now been prevented. The prophecy states, *Two images of flesh atop the tower carved from bone/Will fight until the meek is cast and Justice reigns upon the throne.*"

Apphia's mind raced with confusion.

"I know this is a lot for you to take in," said Eri. "But I think it best that you know the entire truth for this will reconfirm the importance of your brother's passing."

Apphia squinted intently at Eri as he continued. "Your brother's passing has prevented a potentially devastating conflict. It is the end of a very real threat to the throne. Speaking of which, have you had any dreams of the scepter?"

Apphia tried to process the question. "No. No, Pterodactyl Eri, I have not." She bowed her head at him in deceptive adulation. "But if I do, you will be the first to know."

Eri leaned low to examine her face. "Yes. I actually believe I will be. Well, it is good to be back. I am pleased at your progress in my absence."

Eri spread his wings and lifted off from the balcony.

Apphia felt weak in the knees. She came in from the balcony and sat on the bed. What does it all mean? If what Eri revealed were true, then her reign was prophetic. *Does Eri believe himself to be the Airborne Monarch?* The thought revolted her. *And if my brother continues to live—are we to be enemies, brother against sister?* She feared such a thought.

Eri's revelation unsettled her greatly. Her heart had been happy as of late, but the reptile could ruin anything. She walked to the balcony and stared in the direction of the sparring courtyard. She feared he could even ruin her plans to help Esek. She would have to convince him to escape as soon as possible.

⤙ ⤙ ⤙ ⤙
⤙ ⤙ ⤙ ⤙

The Night of No Orb arrived. A long line had formed outside the Judgment Hall entrance. Raimi and her co-musicians arrived. Archippus trailed behind and got in line behind Raimi. Emoticas nodded to him, but Raimi completely ignored him. Archippus overheard her speak.

"They handle affairs on the Night of No Orb because it is the least productive night-day in Rephidim. The utter darkness hinders productivity, or so they say," she explained. "I hope their judgment doesn't prove to be as dark as the night. They are going to also be reading Ezbon-Ishuah's testament in public for the first time. They will read and interpret his Last Will and Testament and I hope they are fair by it."

Archippus thought Raimi looked sad, worried, and tired. He felt all those things too, but had no one to be his friend.

The next instant, Hodos landed on his shoulder, startling him. Archippus glanced at the bird, feeling a mixture of disdain and comfort at the company.

"So, what are we doing this evening?" asked Hodos.

"*We* aren't doing anything," answered Archippus. "*I* am going to represent myself as pleator for growing snock crops, so that I can remove myself from this place in pursuit of wealth."

"I see," said Hodos, "and is that to be your quest?"

"Yes," snapped Archippus. "I believe it to be my *quest* if you want to call it that."

"I see," said Hodos, "well, it's not."

"Yes it is! *You* said Ezbon-Ishuah mattered to *two* people, and so *I'm* going to matter to *two* people, myself and Jazelle, so stay out of it!"

"Different Landlings are called to different quests, and Ezbon-Ishuah fulfilled his quest. But you must matter to the entire Continent."

"Why? What for? I don't *care* about the Continent. Find someone else! Why *me?*"

"The better question is, why *not* you?"

"No, the better question is why not anybody *but* me!"

"Hmmm ..."

"Hmmm *what?*"

"I may be able to work your pursuit of wealth to your advantage in the long run," said Hodos.

Archippus squinted. "Who *are* you? What do you mean 'work it to my advantage?' I'll find my own advantage, thank you! *You* have no control over me or my plans or my life or my interests or my love! Go torment someone else!" He brushed the bird from his shoulder. Anger rose within him, red spots swam before his eyes. "I want to be *free,* and *yooou* are *overbeeearing!*" he yelled.

Raimi was a patron in line in front of him. She leaned out, turned, frowned, and stared at him. Archippus ignored her, though with the bird gone, he now felt truly alone. He noticed the line had hardly moved since he arrived. Some of the entrants and petitioners had resorted to sitting on the ground, and nobility with Airbornes on their arm straps, sent the reptiles off to wait in the trees.

Off to the side of the line, Archippus noticed a carrying lounge with gold drapery concealing the occupant, if in fact an occupant were inside. He pondered who it could be.

The line moved in fits and starts and finally Raimi, Gershom, and Emoticas entered into the hall through the arches.

Archippus, with only one Landling in front of him, could now see and hear all that went on inside. He felt sick, because in a similar hall in Ai, the row of twelve thrones had condemned him for life. He reassured himself that no one here knew his history or who he was, save for the three petitioners in front of him. Even if Raimi were angry with him, he knew she would not betray him. This realization bothered him; it seemed that the three misfits ahead of him were all he had. He could trust them, but they *hated* him. He didn't understand why.

He watched them standing before the council. It did not matter that they came as celebrities having won the talent competition with music, the members appeared intimidating. Eight females and four males stared out coldly from the looming thrones, and the Airbornes on the hot rocks glared, flicking their uncaring tails, and shifting here and there for warmth.

Archippus worried that the trio would be thrown in jail as dissenters for merely caring about the slaves, but Raimi stepped forward confidently. Her arms appeared strong, her posture straight, and her voice steady.

"We would like to humbly request as our reward for winning, better lodging for the slaves. This would include their continued residence in the burrows and three meals a day."

The council members murmured, some turning to consult their Airborne Counselors. The proconsul glanced the length of the thrones to read a yea or nay nod from other members.

"Agreed," she announced, and one by one the gavels fell in approval. Only two gavels did not fall, which meant the request had passed with a 10-2 vote.

This surprised Archippus, but he surmised the slave shortage had something to do with the decision. He believed that councils looked to their own interest. He knew this firsthand.

Raimi looked delighted. She smiled at Gershom and Emoticas, excited about what they had all achieved. They turned to leave.

"Wait!" cried the Proconsul. "Since you are here, we should take care of the matter of Ezbon-Ishuah's testament." She waved a hand at a guard. "Fetch Rueben from his lounge."

Archippus saw Raimi's eyes widen. It was not a happy sign. Archippus turned to watch Rueben fling back the gold drapery on the carrying lounge and saunter toward the hall. Those in line murmured. Onlookers tried to shake his hand or get his attention. They cheered as he passed. One desperado yelled, "Rueben! I saw you perform at the Citadel by the Sea! Can you carve your mark on this coconut for my daughter?"

Rueben lifted a hand in refusal and the celebrity entered the hall. His hair was shaved save for a cropping like a shark fin at the top of his skull. Gold jewelry hung from his ears, gold rings draped his neck, and a narrow bone pierced the center flap of his nose. Dark purple garbs draped his heavyset body and complemented his black skin. Encircling his biceps were gold rings, and on his feet, golden sandals.

There actually is someone more ostentatious than Lordess Lourdes, thought Archippus. He was thoroughly disgusted to watch the council members twitter, smile, and wave at Rueben as if the council was truly in the presence of greatness.

The Proconsul unrolled the scroll, smiled, cleared her throat, and glanced adoringly at Rueben. "I must just say, before reading this, that it is such an honor to have you here. I am such a fan of yours."

Rueben nodded in her direction, his voice was deep. "The pleasure is mine."

The Proconsul batted her eyelashes. "Yes, well, here we go." She cleared her throat again.

"The Testament of Ezbon-Ishuah: I hereby bequeath all my wealth, all stored coinage, my entire business, all working instruments, furniture, clothing, jewelry, and livestock along with my burrow, to my estranged son, Rueben." The Proconsul smiled quickly at Rueben and back to the scroll. Rueben smiled and nodded. The Proconsul continued, "...with the exception of Hemi, my fastest eegwuhnuh, whom I leave to Raimi."

The Proconsul rolled up the scroll.

Raimi spun toward her friends for support. "That's it?" she whispered to Emoticas and Gershom. She appeared panicked. "That's it?"

Emoticas took her arm. "Come on, Raimi," he muttered, "we got our request. Let's not make a scene." He led her out of the hall.

Archippus saw Gershom glare at Rueben as they passed the thrones. Archippus realized the only remaining person in front of him was the gunner who had cheated Gershom out of the race. The gunner stepped forward to present his request to the council. "I request a higher burrow, the closest available to the top of the pit."

The council nodded unanimous approval. The gavels all fell together. Archippus realized that, oddly, the request did not resonate well with him. It seemed slightly self-centered. The gunner turned and left, and it was Archippus' turn.

"Raimi," Archippus called to Raimi being consoled on the steps by Gershom.

"Next!" yelled the Proconsul.

"Raimi," Archippus called again.

She darted a look at him. *"What?"*

"Come here," he motioned to her.

Raimi heaved an exasperated sigh and walked slowly over to Archippus.

"Who is next?" yelled the Proconsul.

Archippus grabbed the person behind him and shoved him forward. "You can go ahead of me."

"Look, you have no future here now," Archippus explained to Raimi who was staring at him with her arms crossed. He glanced in the direction of Emoticas and Gershom watching from a distance. "I am going to act as pleator for snock growing funds. But my problem is they will surely object due to the fact that male commoners cannot own land. But, if I plead the funding on *your* behalf, *you* can own land. We can venture into a new business as partners and leave this place."

Raimi's glare softened. She drummed her fingers on her elbows, then she un-crossed her arms. "You're right," she said. "I have no future here. I can't believe Ezbon-Ishuah—"

"We don't have time for that now, are you with me?" He waited, holding his breath.

"Yes," said Raimi. "Go ahead. I'm with you."

"Next!" screamed the Proconsul, having dispensed with the last petitioner.

Archippus and Raimi stepped forward.

"What is your case?" demanded the Proconsul.

Archippus had planned what he would say. He moved slightly ahead of Raimi.

"My esteemed Council Members and Airborne Counselors. I come before you as pleator on behalf of Raimi of Rephidim, head trainer for the late Ezbon-Ishuah's eegwuhnuh trade.

"Her experience in nurturing and training the reptiles was instrumental in increasing the desirability of said deceased's livestock, and thereby also increasing the incoming coinage to such profit margins that Ezbon-Ishuah became one of the top ten tithers in the city. This benefited the local occupants due to local coinage spent, increasing hiring, and word of mouth reputation that drew interest to this city. The profits, I am certain, were also noteworthy to the High City and their council, which can only have reflected positively on your governance.

"In short, I believe her to have proven herself to be a successful commoner of commerce who would responsibly handle snock crop funding in such a manner as to return optimum profits."

Archippus searched the faces of the council. They shifted and squinted and murmured and scratched their heads. Some got up to walk down to co-counsel and whisper, others conferred with their Airbornes. It seemed to Archippus that this issue of relinquishment of funding was a far bigger issue than any former matter that night-day. The only thing that he felt would bode well in his favor was the Proconsul was seated in a throne all the way to the right, which meant she was an Automon under an airborne of right wing counsel. The Automons supported entrepreneurial commerce and power to small businessmon.

Archippus looked at Raimi and shrugged. She returned the shrug.

Finally, the council members returned to their seats.

The Proconsul spoke. "Pleator …"

"Archippus."

"Pleator Archippus, we find that within your very argument is a persuasion to reject your petition. You state that Raimi has benefited our city greatly with her skills increasing local coinage and making a reputation for our city. That being the case, why would we want to encourage her departure? What would make you think we don't value her presence in Rephidim?"

Archippus thought to scream, *because you just gave her entire livelihood to Rueben, you idiots!* But then he thought better of it. Instead, he decided to respond with a contrived calm. "With all due respect, Proconsul, all that was entrusted to Raimi has been bestowed upon Rueben as of this evening ..."

"Oh." The Proconsul squinted upward as if she had forgotten that.

"And unfortunately, Raimi cannot continue her employment since the relations between Rueben and herself are tenuous."

"Oh. I see. That would make sense. Well, perhaps she can seek employment with one of the other eegwuhnuh traders."

Archippus felt he had reached an impasse. All he could think of was Pterodactyl Dedan's advice: *appeal to greed.*

Archippus inhaled deeply. "But Proconsul, I do believe there could be a mutually beneficial resolution."

"Yes?"

"When Raimi succeeds in Calidron in the snock farming business, she can send an additional two percent tithe directly here, to Rephidim, for use as seen fit by yourselves to benefit your city as a token of her undying alliance and gratitude."

"Hmmm." The Proconsul got up as did some of the other members, and they spoke among themselves a second time.

Once again, the Proconsul returned to her seat. "Agreed," she stated and dropped her gavel. All eleven remaining gavels dropped in succession.

Archippus was impressed with himself for pleading a unanimous decision, albeit by appealing to greed, but unanimous nonetheless.

"Now, you must be advised on the process," said Proconsul. "You have the potential to receive two years of funding. This is the same as for all the trades that are funded by the High Council, such as horticultural-ists, astrolog-ists, econom-ists, art-ists, and pharmic-ists. You will be an agricultural-ist. All first year coinage you receive is directly imprinted on the coin itself with an 'ist' right in the middle with a lower numeral 'i ' representing your first year in business.

"When you go to purchase your property and obtain your initial start up inventory, the Calidronians with whom you transact business will know that this is your first year as a crop grower, which can work to your favor or to your detriment. Part of the challenge is to know which suppliers will look favorably upon you and hope for your success versus those who want to suppress you.

"If you prosper your first year, you can apply for a second single year of funding, and will receive coinage with the upper numeral imprint of '*Ist*' with a capital 'I,' which will represent one additional year.

"Keep in mind, this is the final year of funding, for if you can build a good foundation in two years, you will succeed and no additional coinage will be needed. On the other hand, if you fail your second year, you obviously are not to be entrusted with more.

"The goal, of course, is to complete your first year with a profit in order to receive more funding and become a Capital-Ist."

"Of course," said Archippus. "Raimi will not disappoint you. We thank you." He bowed his head in respect and Raimi did likewise.

"You are dismissed. Gunner Phicol will escort you to receive the coinage."

Raimi and Archippus stepped out onto the Judgment Hall steps.

"What was that all about?" asked Emoticas.

"Archippus obtained the snock funding," said Raimi.

"Are we leaving then?" asked Emoticas.

"*We?*" said Archippus. "The money belongs to me and Raimi."

"But what about the Moles in Heavy Metal?" cried Emoticas.

"Of course you can come," said Raimi. "The music means as much to me as it does to you and Gershom."

"Well, I don't know what they'll do," said Archippus. "There is only so much funding to go around."

"We'll need hired hands, won't we?" asked Raimi. "Or can we farm the land ourselves?"

Archippus knew nothing of snock crop growing, but did *not* want to act as if he knew nothing. "We can discuss it later," he said. "Whatever the case, they could seek other employment in Calidron."

"We're all going then?" asked Emoticas.

Archippus eyed the silent Gershom.

"Of course!" said Raimi. She looked at Gershom who nodded approval.

"This really surprises me," Archippus sneered. He felt smug to have an upper hand with everyone wanting to follow *him*. He then added sardonically, "I thought Gershom *hated* me."

Gershom motioned something that appeared almost humble. Archippus was again surprised in light of the verbal scorn he had just dealt him. He looked to Emoticas for interpretation.

"Gershom says he will follow along not only for our musical cause, but he said he believes you to be a leader." Emoticas swept three fingers across his forehead to signify leader.

Archippus' jaw dropped, his eyes jumped wide.

More gestures from Gershom and Emoticas continued the interpretation. "He says he read in the Prophetic Book of Ezdra that '... a leader will arise under songbird council.'"

Archippus laughed the kind of laugh that bursts forth first from shock, and then continues because of amusement. The laughter caught on and Raimi and Emoticas joined in. All thought the concept of Archippus as a prophetic figure was ludicrous given his implied self-centeredness. Even Archippus saw the absurdity, but Gershom remained serious.

The laughing tittered to a halt.

"You're serious," said Archippus to Gershom. "I think you've been overexposed to fecal fumes."

Gershom did not even smile.

"Well, I will lead us, Gershom," said Archippus. "I was born to lead, and I will lead us into wealth. But don't look to anything loftier than that."

← ← ← ←
← ← ← ←

Archippus and Raimi went with Gunner Phicol. He guided them to the back of the Judgment Hall and down a stairwell that took them underground, and used a key to open a thick wooden door. They entered a large musty smelling room. Gunner Phicol held his torch up.

Archippus sucked in his breath. Piles of coinage lay all about! He imagined what he could do with this much coinage. The thought staggered his mind.

Gunner Phicol sifted through coins here and there, brushing coins, moving a few different sacks, peeking and prying until, "Aha. Here you go."

He picked up a sack. It was heavy enough to flex his biceps. He handed the sack to Raimi. The weight of it caused a sudden sag in her shoulders.

"Thank you."

Archippus stared at the bag.

"Good job," said Gunner Phicol. "On negotiating for the snock funding, and good luck to you."

"Thank you," Raimi said again. "I will miss working with you. Look after Tandy, won't you?"

"My pleasure."

They stepped outside and Archippus asked her to open the bag. Raimi set it on the ground and they peeked inside. There were hundreds of round gold coins with an 'ist' imprinted in the middle. Archippus stuck his hand inside and lifted a handful letting the slick, newly minted coins slide through his fingers.

He and Raimi laughed. He pulled a coin out and stared at it.

"I'm worried," said Raimi.

"Why?"

"Won't it be difficult for us to succeed having to give not only our ten percent tithe, but an additional two percent to the council?"

"Raimi, a difficult chance is better than no chance."

"Huh?" Raimi exhaled and then gave a short burst of laughter. "I suppose you're right."

Archippus put the coin back and hoisted the sack over his shoulder. "Let's get our stuff and leave this place."

They headed for the Dells, gathering Gershom and Emoticas on the way. They arrived to find Rueben standing in their fire circle.

"Well," said Rueben, "I see you've done marginally in my absence."

Raimi seethed. Gershom tensed. Emoticas looked nervously from Rueben to Raimi.

"Rueben," said Archippus, "Raimi made this business a success, and the council has acknowledged her prowess with *this*." He dropped the heavy sack on the ground and the coinage clanged and shifted.

"Oh," said Rueben in a mocking tone. "Well. I'm *very* impressed. They've paid to get rid of her."

"Weave your lips, Rueben!" yelled Raimi. "You abandoned your father! You don't deserve any of this. She flailed her arms emphatically. You don't even care about this!"

"You're right, I don't care about it. In fact, I'm selling everything. Too bad your paltry amount of coinage is woefully short."

Raimi stomped over and shoved her face in his. "I wouldn't give you a single coin if my life depended on it!"

Rueben shoved her back to arm's length. "Be careful what you predict."

Archippus stepped sharply toward Rueben. "What do you mean by that?"

"I simply mean it would be a shame should she ever find herself in that situation."

"Sounds like a threat."

"Well, aren't *you* perceptive."

Gershom picked up a shovel.

Rueben glanced at Gershom. "Well, I have things to attend to. Don't take anything that doesn't belong to you or you'll regret it."

"I'm taking Hemi and four saddles," Raimi spat.

Rueben stopped and turned. "The testament read by the council said you just get Hemi."

"I'm taking the saddles, I *made* them myself," she countered.

Gershom smacked the shovelhead on his palm.

"Very well," said Rueben. "You are pathetic." He turned and left.

⤙ ⤙ ⤙ ⤙
⤙ ⤙ ⤙ ⤙

The young High Ruler woke with a start in the middle of the night. She swallowed hard, she had dreamt of the scepter.

She climbed out of bed, pulled on a robe and paced. She wished Shear-Jashub were here so she could tell him of the dream, but it was Entimus standing guard in the foyer. Her mind raced. She knew she must tell Eri, but she did not trust him. Yet she reasoned she must continue to cultivate *his* trust, then he might not scrutinize her every move. Then she might have a chance to free Esek. The sooner she reported the dream to Eri, the more he would believe she shared his urgency.

"Entimus."

The foyer curtain slid aside.

"Yes, Your Eminence?"

"You must take me to Eri. Do you know where he sleeps?"

"Yes, Your Eminence."

She draped herself in a cloak and followed him down the stairway through the iron tunnel and up the Judgment Hall steps.

"He sleeps in *here?*"

Entimus nodded, stepped aside, and then followed Apphia into the hall.

Eri was perched on *her* throne. It seemed arrogant and … eerie, but she decided not to dwell on it and continued with her plan.

She hurried toward the throne. Eri opened his eyes wide in surprise.

"Apphia, what is it, child?"

Apphia bowed as a sign of respect. She raised her head. "I dreamt of the scepter."

Eri straightened.

"I saw the Iron Fist slide from the scepter and clatter to the floor. And I saw wings, a giant wingspan."

"What color?"

"Dark."

"Like black?"

"I don't know, just dark."

"Were they feathered or leathery?"

"I don't know. I'm not sure. All I remember is the wings were some twenty or thirty feet in width and dark in color."

"Twenty *or* thirty?" Eri sounded impatient. "Which is it?"

"I ... I ... don't know. I have told you all I remember!" She felt annoyed by his seeming ingratitude. She had done her part to report her dream instantly and he appeared angry with her.

"*Details*, child! I need *details!* This is of the utmost importance!"

"I know! Why do you think I'm *here?*" she yelled.

Eri eased back on the throne. "Forgive me. I realize you believe it to be important. But is there anything else you remember?"

Apphia shook her head.

"Very well. I am sorry for my impatience. I am only concerned for the well-being of the Continent and the protection of the throne. I appreciate your having come to me instantly with your dream. I trust you will tell me if you have another or if you remember any further details."

"Yes," said Apphia. Eri's softened tone eased her indignation. "Of course."

"Entimus, see her Highness safely back to her quarters."

Entimus bowed his head and guided Apphia back to her room.

⤙ ⤙ ⤙ ⤙
⤙ ⤙ ⤙ ⤙

The next morning, Apphia strode to the sparring court. In whispers, she told Shear-Jashub of last night's events.

"You have to distract Isui. I have to convince Esek to escape *now,* while I'm on Eri's good side."

Shear-Jashub agreed, and Apphia donned her armor and began her scheduled sparring match with Esek.

To implement the distraction, Shear-Jashub sought out Isui to discuss defensive maneuvers. He demonstrated several jabs, making up moves that

Isui strained to observe or understand.

Apphia, sparring and watching Shear-Jashub from a distance, called out from behind her visor.

"Esek."

"Yes, Your Utmost Omniscience."

"Stop it."

"Stop what?"

"You have to escape now!"

"Right now?"

"Well ... no ... I guess I don't have a plan right now, but we need to make one right away."

"Why?"

"Just trust me."

"I won't leave until I see your face."

Apphia sighed. Her hair was only a stubbly quarter inch long. *So what.* Her vanity seemed suddenly silly. She lifted off her helmet.

Esek stared.

"I know. I shave it because I'm in armor all the time. It gets hot."

Esek continued to stare.

"And I'm pale. Nobody is supposed to know that."

Esek was still staring.

"And I'm ugly, but so what, stop staring."

"You are more beautiful than I imagined."

Apphia took a step back, surprised.

"Hey!" Isui noticed the helmet-less High Ruler. "Hey!" He ran over. "Your Eminence, what are you doing?" He stopped in his tracks to stare at Apphia.

"You should not have done this, he's seen you! I'll have to kill him!"

"No!" she yelled. "You cannot deprive me of the slaughter!"

Isui gaped. "But Your Eminence, it is taking a long time—"

"Don't call me 'Your Eminence' and then question me! You treat me as a child! Am I your High Ruler or not!"

Isui dropped to one knee. "Yes, Your Eminence."

"Then see to it that no harm befalls him or I'll have your head!"

"Yes, Your Eminence." He looked up nervously. "If I may ... since he has seen you ... should we perhaps place him in isolation?"

"No!"

"Very well." Isui nodded and stood. He took hold of Esek and began to chain his hands. "You must not speak a word of this to anyone," he cautioned.

As Isui pulled Esek away, Apphia mouthed, "I'll come up with a plan." Esek nodded.

It saddened her to see Esek pulled forcibly away in chains. But she had no choice. *I must free him. Though it kills me to see him go, I must free him.*

⤙ ⤙ ⤙ ⤙
⤙ ⤙ ⤙ ⤙

Archippus stepped over Hazo. "This is your burrow now, the council has approved food and safe lodging for all slaves."

Hazo lifted himself onto his right elbow. "Are you leaving?"

Archippus picked up the Hodos scroll. He wasn't even sure why, but he'd come to retrieve the bothersome parchment. "We're going to Rephidim. I negotiated the snock funding."

Archippus headed for the landing.

Hazo called out, "If you ever happen upon my parents …"

Archippus halted. His back was to Hazo, but he turned his head slightly to listen.

"Tell them I love them."

Archippus turned to face Hazo. "If I ever encounter your parents, you will know of it."

Hazo cupped his free elbow over his eyes and whispered, "Thank you."

⤙ ⤙ ⤙ ⤙
⤙ ⤙ ⤙ ⤙

The four riders climbed onto Hemi. The wound was healing nicely and Raimi had pronounced the big lizard fit.

This Night of No Orb was ending and they wanted to go to the quarry for the closing statement from the crier. They rode to the edge of the quarry, dismounted, and looked down at the stage. The town crier climbed to the stage wearing his long brown robe with hem bells. He rang the bells on his belt to silence the audience, lifted his megafone, and faced an assistant holding an un-rolled scroll.

"In this first month of our two non-agricultural months, we face an additional month of no growth until the first month of planting arrives."

Archippus realized it was his birthday.

"It was just made known to me that snock funding has been awarded to a local commercemon. In light of the cooling of the Continent, let us acknowledge her accomplishment and wish her success for the good of all Landkind."

234

Clapping and whistling rippled through the crowd, though Archippus thought few even knew who the recipient was.

"Next, I bring you news this quarterly writ DLVIi, delivered by Airborne directly to Rephidim's Council of Twelve from Hieropolis, the city of the High Ruler of the Iron Hall, as drafted by the Council of Twenty-four:

"Lordess Lourdes of Ai has been approved by the High Council as substitute for one of Ai's two elected officials on the Council of Twenty-four."

Archippus snapped to attention. His heart leapt and he wondered about Jazelle.

"Also, the Biannual Trek is approaching, and a reminder is being issued to use only the High-Way for transport and pay accurate tithes as overseen by the newly appointed law-ers. Any inaccuracies will be penalized with additional tithes.

"And most importantly, Barbarian Ruler, King Katalaomer, was discovered to have erected a fortress on the Island of Glacier Lake, and it has been reported that a rudimentary Fire Propulsion System has been designed. However, they have not mastered the weapon's ability to launch long distances or the fireball itself.

"The rebel king is referring to the contraption as the Kata-pull-it, in honor of himself."

Murmurs came from the audience.

Archippus turned to his travel companions. "Let's be rid of Rephidim."

Raimi heaved a sigh and nodded her agreement.

The four riders climbed into their saddles and Raimi spurred Hemi to a fast walk, the ever-present Hodos flitting alongside.

Archippus thought back on the year. He had gone from slavery to freedom, gained employment, sought Jazelle, freed her, and possibly won her consent. He had gained and lost a surrogate father, and come no closer to knowing his sister's whereabouts, but he had negotiated a unanimous verdict for the snock funding, and was well on his way to wealth.

He worried about Eri's request to infiltrate the Barbirians to discover something shocking of their strategies. He would have to work out a plan. Perhaps with the wealth he was hoping to acquire, he could pay someone to infiltrate on his behalf. He breathed easier, this sounded like a good plan.

Then his thoughts turned back to Jazelle. He would gain this wealth for her. He knew in his heart that this was his quest no matter what Hodos had said.

"Oh, Boy!"

Archippus glanced at the bird. "What?"

"Happy birthday."

Archippus wondered if that were it. No lecture, no questioning, no ridicule. "Is that it?"

"No."

"I didn't think so."

"Because I'll be happy to help direct you on your quest when you're ready."

"I'll never be ready."

"Oh, yes you will."

Archippus sighed and thought for a moment about this tiny creature that had come to him, refusing to forsake him despite Archippus' repeated attempts to reject him. It made him wonder *why*. This Airborne annoyance who often angered him had been ever at his side. *Albeit to relentlessly pester me over some stupid quest, but beside me nonetheless.*

"Bird?"

"Yes?"

"I brought your silly scroll."

"I know."

"But it doesn't change anything because you realize I don't like you," Archippus said in a matter-of-fact tone void of any anger.

The olive warbler eyed him up and down with a twinkle in his tiny orbs. "So we've progressed from you hating me to merely disliking me. But either way, it's good for you."

Archippus smiled, Hodos flew up ahead, and Raimi reined Hemi onto the High-Way to seek their fortunes among the snock crops of Calidron.

End of Book One

WORKS CITED

KJV   King James Version

NIV   New International Version.
      Grand Rapids: Zondervan (1983)

Kipling, Rudyard   If. Rewards and Fairies. (1909)

NOTES

[1] John 4:32 (NIV)

[2] Matthew 13:13 (NIV)

[3] Job 11:12 (NIV)

[4] I Corinthians 6:12 (KJV)

[5] Matthew 12:25, Mark 3:24, Luke 11:17 (NIV)

[6] Kipling, Rudyard, "If" (1909)